D3

Rushing
Waters

Also by Danielle Steel

* Published outside the UK under the title PASSION'S PROMISE

For more information on Danielle Steel and her books, see her website at
www.daniellesteel.com

Rushing Waters

Danielle Steel

BANTAM PRESS

LONDON • TORONTO • SYDNEY • AUCKLAND • JOHANNESBURG

TRANSWORLD PUBLISHERS
61–63 Uxbridge Road, London W5 5SA
www.penguin.co.uk

Transworld is part of the Penguin Random House group of companies
whose addresses can be found at global.penguinrandomhouse.com

Penguin
Random House
UK

First published in Great Britain in 2016 by Bantam Press
an imprint of Transworld Publishers

Book design by Virginia Norey

A CIP catalogue record for this book
is available from the British Library.

ISBN 9780593069141 (cased)
9780593069158 (tpb)

Typeset in 10.5/18.5pt Charter ITC
Printed and bound by Clays Ltd, Bungay, Suffolk

Penguin Random House is committed to a sustainable
future for our business, our readers and our planet. This book
is made from Forest Stewardship Council® certified paper.

MIX
Paper from
responsible sources
FSC® C018179

1 3 5 7 9 10 8 6 4 2

To my darling Toto,

for being so brave,

for all you went through,

for living through what others

        can only imagine,

may the memory of it dim,

and may you be forever blessed,

       I love you, Mama.

And to all my beloved children,

Beatie, Trevor, Todd, Nick, Sam,

Vanessa, Maxx, and Zara,

with endless gratitude for all that you are,

and all my love and heart always,

             Mom/ds

Sorrow has its reward.
It never leaves us where it found us.

—MARY BAKER EDDY

Rushing Waters

Chapter 1

Ellen Wharton was pensive as she studied the clothes she had hung on a rolling rack, and the folded items she had laid out on the bed for her trip to New York. Organized, impeccable, meticulous, she was a woman who planned everything and left nothing to chance—her business, her menus, her wardrobe, her social life. She was consummately careful and precise about everything she did. It made for a smooth, orderly life, with few surprises, but also very little opportunity for things to go awry. She had been planning this trip to New York since June, as she did every year, to see her mother. She also went on Thanksgiving every other year, and she usually went once in spring. She intended to do some shopping for two of her clients, and she had an additional purpose to her trip this time.

Ellen ran a successful interior design business, with three assistants, a color specialist, and clients in several cities in Europe who loved her work. She created beautiful environments for them, which they couldn't have put together themselves, with the best fabrics, handsome furniture that suited their lifestyles and needs, and unusual and inviting color schemes. She wasn't shy about her fees, but she didn't need to be—she was well known in the business, had won several awards for her work, and had been published in the most important decorating magazines. She had learned at the feet of the master, she liked to say. Her mother was a greatly respected architect in New York, who had studied at Yale, begun her career working for I. M. Pei, and gone out on her own years before, designing houses mostly in New York, Connecticut, Palm Beach, Houston, Dallas, and anywhere her clients wanted to build a remarkable home.

At thirty-eight, Ellen still loved spending time with her mother and gave her credit for most of what she knew about interior design. She learned something from her mother every time she saw her, and occasionally her mother sent her a client—in Europe or, like the current one whose home Ellen was working on, in Palm Beach. She had decorated the client's yacht the year before. Her jobs always came in right on budget and on time, which was remarkable in her field and had helped to make her as successful as she was. She had a good solid business and had done well.

Ellen and her mother were very different but respected each other, and Ellen liked working on jobs with her. She loved her mother's open, airy, clean lines and style of architecture. It was a pleasure doing the interiors of a house her mother had designed, and she often sought her advice about other clients too. They had solved more than one knotty problem together, and at seventy-four, her mother was still full of great and innovative ideas. Grace Madison frequently said that the right answer was always the simplest one. She didn't like complicated things or cluttering up the houses she designed with gimmicky tricks, a concept Ellen espoused too.

Ellen tried to foresee potential problems and ran a tight ship. Her mother was more spontaneous and open to new ideas, to the point of being thought eccentric at times, but Ellen loved that about her too. Grace was a talented, strong woman, who had survived breast cancer ten years before and hardly missed a day of work while undergoing chemo and radiation. She had been cancer-free ever since, but Ellen worried about her anyway. Her mother didn't look or act her age, but nonetheless she was gathering years, despite her seemingly limitless energy and youthful looks. Ellen was sorry they didn't live in the same city, but she had lived in London for nearly eleven years, ten of them since she had married George Wharton, a barrister, and British to his core in every possible way. He had gone to Oxford, and Eton before that. His family was in Burke's Peerage and typically British in all their history, habits, and traditions. She had made every effort to fit into his life, and learn his very English ways, although she was American, and originally had her own ideas about how to do things. But she respected his, although it wasn't easy at first.

Ellen ran their home precisely the way George liked it and expected her to. She had enjoyed learning about British customs from him and had adopted many of them herself. But she missed the ease of New York at times, and the familiar ways she had grown up with. She had given up her world for his, and had been young enough to want to do so to please him when they married. And in the ten years since, his preferences had become comfortable for her too.

Her parents had seemed to get along but startled her by getting divorced as soon as she left for college, which her mother said they had been planning quietly for several years. They didn't hate each other, they just had nothing in common anymore. Her mother described it by saying they had "run out of gas." Her father had worked for a Wall Street investment banking firm and had been ten years older than her mother and died shortly after Ellen married George. Neither of her parents had ever remarried, and they had stayed close and on good terms, but they both seemed satisfied with the divorce, said they had no regrets, and seemed happier on their own. Ellen was grateful that, whatever their differences, they had remained married while she was growing up. They were the kind of people who did things nicely, never spoke ill of each other, and kept their disagreements to themselves, which was what had made the divorce such a surprise. But the fallout from it for Ellen had been minimal, and they had both been happy for her when she married George, although her mother had asked Ellen pointedly before the wedding if she found him a little rigid and set in his ways. He was so emphatically English, but Ellen said she found it charming, and in some ways he reminded her of her father. George was a quiet, competent, responsible man, all virtues she felt sure would make him a good husband even if not an exciting one. George was the kind of man you could count on. He was solid, which Ellen found reassuring. She wanted a well-ordered life without surprises.

The only disappointment in their marriage, one that Ellen hadn't expected or been able to control, had been Ellen's inability to have a baby, despite considerable efforts to make it happen, with full cooperation from George. He had undergone all the necessary tests to determine the problem, and they had discovered very quickly that it wasn't due to him. Ellen had a battery of exams as well, and they had attempted in vitro fertilization ten times in four years, with heartbreaking results. They had changed specialists four times, each time they heard of a new and supposedly better one. She had been pregnant six times, but each time it ended rapidly in miscarriage, no matter how careful she was in the weeks after IVF, during the first trimester. Their current doctor's conclusion was that her eggs were prematurely old. They had started the process when she was thirty-four. She had been too busy building her business before that, and they thought they had time, but apparently they didn't. Neither of them wanted to consider adoption. George was adamant about it, and they agreed on that. Ellen didn't want to use a donor egg instead of her own, and they liked the idea of surrogacy even less, since they would have no control over how responsible a surrogate might be about carrying their baby, and what unhealthy behaviors she might indulge in and conceal from them. They were determined to have their own baby or none at all, which was looking more and more likely with every passing month.

Ellen couldn't imagine what their future would be like with no children to surround them in their old age, and they were determined to try again. And between IVF attempts and the hormone shots George had to give her, Ellen had put them on an ardent schedule of "natural attempts," which required George rushing home from his office at a moment's notice, and Ellen leaving hers, when her home kit told her she was ovulating. She had gotten pregnant a few times that way, and lost the baby just as quickly as she did with IVF. They had taken a break for the past few months—it had become too stressful, and something of an obsession for her. Some of the romance had gone out of their marriage with their scheduled attempts to get pregnant, but Ellen was sure their efforts would bear fruit in the end and be worth four years of stress.

She had an appointment in New York with a fertility expert she'd heard of, and wanted to get another opinion about new procedures they might try. She wasn't ready to accept defeat yet, although her hormone levels hadn't been good for the past year, which supported their London doctor's theory that it wasn't going to work. Ellen couldn't accept that, and George had been a good sport about going along with their dogged efforts to try again, no matter how depressing the results were. It wasn't fun, but if they got a baby, Ellen thought it would be worth it, and George agreed with her. He didn't want to break her heart by giving up, although he wasn't optimistic about their chances for success anymore. He was trying to accept it with grace, and hoped she would do the same in time. Their determined efforts and repeated defeats were so hard on her, and not easy for him either, although he never complained.

Despite more than ten years in England, Ellen still looked totally American—tall, thin, with well-cut blond shoulder-length hair, and something about her had the look of an all-American girl. She was casually well dressed in cashmere sweaters, slim skirts, and high heels, and jeans on the weekend, when they visited friends' country houses, or went to shooting weekends, which were an important part of George's traditions. They hadn't bought a country home of their own yet. They had promised themselves they would when they had children, and that hadn't happened.

George was forty-four years old, as tall and lanky and fair as she was, though he looked European, and he was a very handsome man. People always said they would have beautiful children, with no idea what they had gone through for four years to have them. The only people Ellen had confided their efforts to were her mother and her closest friend in London, Mireille, a French woman, also married to a Brit, who had four children, and agonized with Ellen over every failed attempt. Mireille was a talented artist, although with four young children, she no longer had time to paint. Her husband was a barrister like George, and the Whartons often visited them at their country home on weekends, along with all of George's longtime friends, who invited them almost every weekend.

Ellen squinted intently at the clothes on the rack, made a final selection, and put them in her suitcase, with some summer clothes as well. In mid-September, it was liable to still be hot in New York. She had just zipped up her suitcase and set it on the floor when George walked in.

"Have you heard about the hurricane?" he asked, worried, and then he smiled and kissed the top of her head. He wasn't passionate, but loving, and even if not demonstrative, she knew he'd always be there for her. He was the kind of person you could count on.

"Vaguely. They always have hurricanes in the East this time of year." She looked unconcerned as she said it, and set her briefcase down next to her suitcase. She had notes and floor plans, color samples, and fabric swatches with her, for her clients.

"That's a little cavalier, after Sandy, don't you think?" he said seriously, remembering the monster hurricane that had hit New York five years before.

"That's a once-in-a-lifetime occurrence." She smiled, looking relaxed and happy to see him. "The year before Hurricane Sandy, they had one called Irene," she reminded him, "which all the forecasters said would level New York, and it turned into an ordinary storm when it hit land. You can't panic every time they announce a hurricane this time of year. It's not a big deal," she assured him. "Sandy was just a convergence of unusual events. It probably won't ever happen again," she said confidently. Hurricanes were not something she worried about. She had enough other things to think about that seemed far more real, like when they would do IVF again, and how her mother's next mammogram would turn out, although she had just had a clean one two weeks before. Hurricanes were not on Ellen's radar screen.

"Well, it better not, while you're there at least," he said, with a warm look in his eyes as he put his arms around her and held her for a moment. "I'm going to miss you," he said, noticing her suitcase. "I'd better pack too. I'm going to the Turnbridges' for the weekend. They're having quite a big house party, and a shoot." It was the kind of very British weekend he loved, an English tradition that hadn't changed in centuries, and she was sorry to miss it. The weekend parties they went to were an important part of their social life, with old friends and new ones, and people George had grown up with and gone to school with. Even ten years later, Ellen was considered the newcomer in the group, but they were nice to her.

"You won't even miss me," she teased him. "You'll be having too much fun." He smiled sheepishly—they both knew it was somewhat true. He spent his time talking to the men about business, while the women talked about their children, who were all at boarding school.

"Well, don't stay away too long," he said as he left to pack his bag for the weekend. But he knew she enjoyed spending time with her mother, and he liked Grace too. She was a lively, intelligent woman, full of creative ideas and outspoken opinions that amused him. He loved talking politics and architecture with her. She was the ideal mother-in-law—she was busy and independent, had her own life, was still going full speed, and never interfered. And she was still quite beautiful, even at seventy-four. He was sure that Ellen would be that way too, although her character wasn't as determined as her mother's and she wasn't as bold in the way she expressed her ideas. Ellen's gentler style suited him, as did her willingness to adapt to him. Her mother was never afraid to voice her opinions, whether others agreed with her or not. She was exceptionally bright, fun to be with and to talk to. Her daughter was quieter and more discreet— and probably easier to live with, he assumed.

When they went downstairs to get something to eat, Ellen pulled a large salad out of the fridge that their housekeeper had prepared, and she reminded George that there would be meals left for him every day, and he should let the housekeeper know if he was going to be out for dinner. He usually went out a lot when she was away, and didn't like being home alone. Or sometimes he stopped at his club on the way home and ate there.

"Don't worry, I think I can manage for ten days," he said, as they sat down at the round table that had been set for them, looking out at the garden, in the big comfortable kitchen Ellen had redesigned for them the year before. The house was too big for them, with five bedrooms they didn't need yet. She used one as a home office, had done another as a study for him, and they had two guest rooms, and a gym and home cinema downstairs. They had spread out in the large house they'd bought five years before when they had decided to get pregnant, before they knew how arduous a task it would become, and how elusive their dream.

They chatted through dinner about the two important cases he was currently working on, and the clients she would be shopping for in New York and what she hoped to find. She had just been called by a client to do a house in the South of France and was looking forward to it. It would give them an excuse to spend a weekend there from time to time.

After dinner, Ellen went to put more papers and color swatches in her briefcase. George turned the television to CNN before they went to bed, to check on the hurricane again, which was still making its way across the Caribbean toward the East Coast, and he looked worried. But no dire warnings had been issued yet for New York.

"I wish they didn't have those damn things there, or that you went to see your mother at some other time of year." He looked mildly annoyed, and Ellen ignored him. Until the monster hurricane that had hit the city five years before, no one in New York had given the annual hurricanes a second thought, and even now, most people weren't overly concerned it would happen again. But George didn't like it anyway and wasn't nearly as casual as his wife about it. It seemed foolish to him to go to New York in August or September.

"It's not going to hit New York," she said, as they climbed into bed and he kissed her. They didn't attempt to make love that night, and they hadn't for a while. She wasn't ovulating, so they didn't have to, and it was nice not having to think about it for once, and to just lie next to each other, with no particular purpose in mind. Not making love had become as enjoyable as making love had been in their days before IVF. George was relieved not to have to perform, and he looked relaxed as he turned off the light, and she cuddled up next to him.

"You can miss me a little while I'm gone," she whispered in the dark, and he smiled at what she said.

"I'll keep it in mind," he answered, pulled her closer, and a moment later, they both fell asleep, until the alarm woke them at six in the morning for her flight.

Ellen thought about making love with George as she woke up, but he was out of bed before she was awake enough to do anything about it, and headed for his own bathroom and dressing room, so she threw back the covers and went to hers. It was a sunny day in London, and she was looking forward to the still warm, even hot, Indian summer days in New York. She still missed New York at times. But her life was so different now than it had been when she lived there.

She dressed in her travel clothes, and had breakfast waiting for him when he came downstairs. She had to leave in half an hour, and one of her assistants had arranged for a car and driver to take her to the airport for her ten o'clock flight. She was taking the large A380 Airbus, which she liked for its spaciousness and smooth flight, despite the hassle of competing with five hundred passengers trying to retrieve their luggage at the other end. She was due to arrive in New York at one P.M. local time, and after clearing customs and getting into the city, she hoped to be at her mother's apartment by three or three-thirty, before her mother got home from the office. It would give Ellen time to unpack and settle in. And they would have plenty of time to talk over dinner and catch up in her mother's very comfortable apartment. Ellen loved staying there instead of a hotel, and she knew her mother liked it too. Her mother was resigned about her only child living so far away in England for the past decade, and she was busy with her work. Being with her mother always made Ellen regret that she didn't go to New York more often.

When the car came, George walked her down the front steps, carrying her briefcase, and handed it to her with a serious expression. "Stay out of the way of the hurricane." He kissed her goodbye and looked sad for a moment as their eyes met.

"Have fun this weekend," Ellen said, and kissed him again.

"Not easily done without you," he said with a smile, then got into his own car. Her driver put her suitcase in the trunk and waited for her to get in. She waved at George as he drove away, and they headed to Heathrow in the morning traffic.

She checked in at the curb, put her boarding pass in her handbag, and walked into the terminal looking very tall and young and pretty in beige slacks, a crisp blue shirt, sandals, and a blazer in case she got chilly on the plane. She was planning to watch a movie and do some work. She loved catching up on movies when she traveled, and she headed to the business class lounge to have a cup of tea and read a newspaper before they boarded. Her cell phone rang almost the moment she sat down and put her cup of tea on the table next to her.

"I already miss you," George's voice said, and she smiled.

"Good." She looked happy. They had come through the past four difficult years with a minimum of marital damage, despite the stress of the treatments and hormone shots, exams and sonograms, disappointments and IVF. It had been much harder than they'd expected, but their marriage was still intact.

"I love you," she said into the phone, and then they hung up, and she sat back, smiling to herself as she sipped her tea. She was going to miss him, even if she'd only be gone a little over a week.

Charles Williams arrived at Heathrow a half hour later than he was meant to, to check in. He was afraid he might have already lost his seat, but he hadn't, much to his relief. His only luggage was a small carry-on bag on wheels, so he had no bags to check. He got his boarding pass from a machine, and then hurried to the lounge for something to eat. He had overslept and looked tousled and harassed as he sat down in a bank of seats across from Ellen and nearly spilled his coffee. She noticed him immediately. He was a good-looking man, in jeans, an open-necked shirt, and a tweed jacket, which she knew would be too hot for New York at this time of year. He looked very British and probably in his late thirties or very early forties at most. And there was something nervous and stressed about him. He exuded anxiety as he juggled a newspaper and his coffee. He paid no attention to Ellen and seemed lost in thought after he read the paper. And as they left the lounge to board the plane, she heard him ask one of the ground personnel at the desk if there were any further reports about the hurricane, and if it was likely to cause a problem on the flight. Ellen pegged him instantly as a nervous flyer, and the girl at the desk must have too. She smiled reassuringly at him, as he shoved a lock of straight dark hair out of his eyes, with a worried expression.

"Not at all, sir. We wouldn't be taking off if it was likely to cause a problem. We'd be grounded. So everything is fine. Enjoy your flight." He nodded but didn't seem convinced as he walked away, pulling his carry-on bag and holding his battered briefcase. Ellen noticed that he was wearing dark brown suede shoes, which made him look even more English. She followed him onto the plane and was surprised to find that she was seated beside him. She had the window seat, and he had the one on the aisle. He nodded as she stepped past him, but he said nothing, settled into his seat, and gratefully accepted a glass of champagne as the flight attendant offered it. Ellen asked for only a small bottle of water. She hated drinking alcohol on flights first thing in the morning, and didn't need it. Apparently, he did, and his nervousness seemed to increase as they were told to turn off their cell phones, the doors closed, and they were ferried out to the runway, surprisingly on time, since so many flights were late. He glanced at Ellen then, and nodded.

"I hate to fly, especially on these enormous planes, but everything else was booked," he explained. She smiled pleasantly at him before she answered, sorry for him at his obvious distress.

"I think the big ones are especially smooth. They say you don't feel the turbulence on them," she said to reassure him. He appeared unconvinced and glanced past her out the window as they took off, while trying valiantly not to look as panicked as he felt. After they were in the air, he took another glass of champagne when the flight attendant made her rounds again, and then he opened his computer and focused on it, as Ellen pulled up the screen at her seat and checked the movies. She put on her headphones and selected something to watch she hadn't seen, and spent the next two hours engrossed in the film, then ordered lunch. She noticed that her seatmate had calmed down by then, and he chatted with her for a few minutes as they ate their meal.

"Do you live in New York?" he asked, and she smiled at him and shook her head.

"No, in London." He seemed surprised and had noticed she was American, from her accent, and she looked it.

"I'm going over on business," he volunteered, "and I have two daughters who live there." She nodded and realized that he must be divorced, but she didn't comment. They talked for a few minutes, and then Ellen decided to take a nap after their food trays were cleared away, and she slept for two hours until an announcement from the cockpit woke her, and she felt that they were going through some turbulence. Her seatmate was wide awake and looking scared.

"We're going through a bit of chop," the captain explained over the PA system. "Sorry about that. The winds off the East Coast are causing some turbulence. We should be out of it in about half an hour." She noticed that the man next to her was looking extremely nervous. Ellen closed her eyes to sleep some more. The turbulence rocked her to sleep and then jolted her awake half an hour later when it got worse. By then, her seatmate was nearly wild-eyed, and she glanced at him sympathetically.

"Are you okay?" she finally couldn't help asking him as she sat up. She had slept long enough, and they were about an hour out of New York. She guessed they were probably over Boston.

He hesitated for a minute before he answered, then nodded. "Yes. I hate flying, especially when it's like this. It must be because of the hurricane. I don't know why they said it wouldn't affect us."

"Turbulence isn't usually dangerous, it's just unpleasant." The plane was shaking and pitching, and there was obviously a powerful wind outside, and it was raining. And a moment later the pilot made another announcement.

"Things seem to be getting a little stormy in New York. They've got some high wind conditions at the airport. We've just been given clearance to land in Boston."

"Shit," the man next to Ellen said as beads of sweat appeared on his forehead. And Ellen wasn't too pleased about it either—she had no desire to spend a night in Boston, instead of landing in New York. The captain informed them then that everything was fine, they just didn't want to give them a rough ride into JFK, but they were in no danger. "Every time I get on an airplane, I think I'm going to die," her seatmate explained to her. "It's been a lot worse since I got divorced a year ago," he admitted. "Would you like to see a photograph of my daughters?" Ellen nodded, hoping it would distract him. It was a little unnerving sitting next to someone that frightened, as he blotted his forehead with his napkin, and then took out his cell phone and showed her a vast number of images of two adorable little girls, one of whom looked just like him, with the same dark hair and dark eyes, and the other one was a blonde with big blue eyes, who must have looked like his ex-wife. "I'm Charles Williams, by the way. Sorry I'm such a total twit on a plane. I'm actually quite normal on terra firma," he said with a wry smile, and she laughed.

"I'm Ellen Wharton," she said as they shook hands, and the plane started making a slow bumpy descent toward Boston, and five minutes later they seemed to change direction, and the pilot came on the PA system again.

"Sorry to change plans on you again, folks. They're sending us on to JFK after all, so you'll get to your planned destination tonight. We'll have some chop going in, but we'll be fine."

"It must be the hurricane," Charles Williams muttered to Ellen. "I hope they don't have another monster one like five years ago." He looked panicked.

"Actually, this is pretty common at this time of year, and except for Sandy, it's usually nothing. This is probably just a late summer storm."

"Well, I don't like it," he said firmly.

"We'll be there in about forty minutes," Ellen said in a comforting voice, and Charles Williams kept up a steady stream of conversation thereafter, as though to keep his mind off his own conviction that they would crash on landing, if not before.

"My wife left me for someone else," he said out of the blue a few minutes later. "She was trying to be an actress, and did some modeling. He's a photographer. They live in New York now, with my daughters. I suppose eventually they'll get married." He was clearly worried about that too.

"That must be hard for you, being so far from your children." He nodded, then asked Ellen, "Do you have children?"

"No, I don't," she said quietly, trying to resist the feeling of failure that always washed over her when people asked her. She noticed the turbulence getting considerably worse then, and so did he.

"What do you do?" He seemed desperate for conversation on any subject.

"I'm an interior designer. My husband is a barrister."

"I'm an investment banker," he said, as they heard the landing gear come down, and a moment later, the pilot instructed the cabin crew to take their seats in the turbulence, which by then was pretty nasty. "I've got business in New York, and I'm hoping to see my children this weekend, if they're not too busy." He looked sad as he said it, but at least it kept his mind off crashing. "Are you frightened?" he whispered to her.

"No, I'm okay. I don't love bouncing around like this, but we'll be down in a few minutes."

"If we don't crash first," he said miserably. "We shouldn't have come with the hurricane hanging around. But at least I'll be here with my children. Are you here on business?" She nodded.

"And to see my mother. She lives in New York."

"Thank you for talking to me," he said gratefully with a mournful expression. "If you weren't, I'd probably be running down the aisle, screaming." He had a self-deprecating way about him, and made no secret of his fear, which made him seem very human. She laughed at what he said, and they hit several hard bumps on the way down, as the plane lost altitude in sharp stages. Charles was clutching her arm by then, and didn't seem to notice, and Ellen was beginning to hope they'd land before he broke her arm or fainted, but she didn't say anything to him.

And then suddenly, as they came in over the water, they hit the runway hard, and continued at a great speed, while the pilot fought the high winds to keep the plane steady. She was sure Charles Williams didn't think so, but it had been a masterful landing, and as she glanced out the window, she noticed emergency vehicles on the runway with their lights flashing. It was unnerving to see them, and it was a first for her, but with seemingly enormous effort, the flight crew slowed the enormous plane, and they stopped for a few minutes before heading for the gate. Charles looked near tears, with a panicked glance at her.

"Sorry for the rough landing," the captain apologized. "We had some very strong winds up there tonight. It looks like New York will be meeting Hurricane Ophelia before too long. Welcome to JFK, and thank you for flying with us."

"Were those for us?" Charles asked Ellen in a shocked whisper as he noticed the lights flashing on the emergency vehicles next to them, and he suddenly realized he'd been squeezing her arm, and she had let him. "Oh my God, I'm so sorry. I didn't realize," he said as he released his viselike grip on her.

"It's fine." She smiled at him. "You ought to take one of those fear of flying classes. I hear they help."

"I'm not sure anything will help after last year, since my wife ran off with an idiot named Nigel. I haven't been myself since." He seemed sad as he said it, but less agonized than he had a moment before. He was returning to normal, with some embarrassment over the discomfort he had put Ellen through, clutching her arm. "Do you suppose they thought we were going to crash?" Charles asked her in a conspiratorial tone.

"I don't think so. They just don't take any chances, and the weather looks pretty bad." She could see men in heavy yellow slickers guiding the plane in, and fighting the heavy winds outside. "It looks like we're in for some pretty nasty weather this weekend until the storm passes." She sounded disappointed. She and her mother loved walking around the city.

"This isn't a storm—it looks like a cyclone." He was watching the men in slickers too, and then the jumbo plane rolled the rest of the way toward the terminal and parked at the gate. "What- ever it is, thank you for getting me through it," he said to her humbly.

"I'm sure we've just been through the worst of it," she said con- fidently, as they both stood up and gathered their things when the plane stopped moving.

"Enjoy your stay in New York," he said, still slightly embar- rassed, then hurried off the plane rolling his carry-on bag behind him. Ellen followed the mass of other passengers more slowly. She was thinking about him and the details he had shared about his divorce as she walked through the terminal toward baggage claim. He seemed smart and nice, and he was handsome, but obviously a very anxious person, and it sounded like he'd been through a lot in the last year, with his wife running off with Nigel, and taking their daughters with her to live in New York. Ellen felt sorry for him again as she waited for her bag to appear, spotted it, took it off the carousel herself, and put it on a cart to roll through customs. She had nothing to declare and was out of the terminal quickly. When she walked outside, a long line of people were waiting for taxis, and there were none. She saw Charles Williams at the head of the line, and he signaled to her to join him. She hesitated for a minute, then moved forward.

"Do you want to share a ride into the city? I don't think there will be enough cabs for everyone. Where are you going?" he asked her.

"I'm staying with my mother in Tribeca," she explained, suddenly feeling as though they were old friends after a slightly nerve-racking final hour of the flight and the choppy landing in New York.

"That's perfect. I'm staying at the Soho Grand. I'll drop you off. I owe you something for nearly tearing off your arm." He smiled again as a cab pulled up where they were first on line and got in. She gave the driver her address, and then Charles told him his hotel. Her suitcase was safely in the trunk. And they chatted normally on the way into the city.

"I'm sorry I told you all that about the divorce. It's been a bad patch in my life. It's been a bit of an adjustment, especially to have my daughters so far away and living here. I try to see them as often as I can, and they spend school holidays with me in London." He turned to the driver then. "What news of the hurricane? It looks like it's already here."

"This is nothing," the driver said in a heavy foreign accent. "You should have seen Sandy five years ago. Our garage lost most of our cabs. It was ten feet underwater. I think this will blow itself out when it hits land, like Irene, the year before Sandy. That was a lot of noise about nothing. Everyone got evacuated and nothing happened. But Sandy—that was worse than Katrina in New Orleans. I live in Far Rockaway, and my brother lost his house." Even five years later people spoke of Sandy with awe over how devastating it had been. "They call it the Perfect Storm, you know, like the movie."

"It was pretty awful," Ellen confirmed. "My mother's building was very badly damaged. I wanted her to move uptown after that. But she wouldn't. She loves living downtown."

"It sounds dangerous to me," Charles said, watching the wind whip the trees as they sped along toward the city, but the rain had let up, and as they got into Manhattan, the wind didn't seem as fierce. Charles was just grateful to be back on terra firma. And they spoke of more innocuous things for the rest of the ride. Ellen tried to pay for half the trip when they got to her mother's building in Tribeca, and Charles wouldn't let her.

"Don't be ridiculous—you'll need the money for therapy for your arm," he said, and she laughed.

"My arm is fine. And you're very kind to let me ride with you. I hope you have a wonderful time with your girls," she said warmly.

"And you with your mother," he said with a smile, and seemed like a normal person, and not the basket case he had been on the plane, when he was convinced they were going to crash. "And I hope you're right and there won't be a proper hurricane while we're here." The driver got out, took Ellen's bag out of the trunk, and handed it to the doorman, who smiled when he recognized her and hurried inside with the bag.

"Thank you again," Ellen called out to Charles as she smiled and waved at him from the sidewalk. The driver started the cab again and drove off, as Charles waved back at her. He was grateful to have been sitting next to her on the plane and was sure he would have lost his mind without her.

All he could think of now was seeing Lydia and Chloe. He turned his cell phone on as soon as he thought of it, and called their mother's number, but all he got was her voicemail. He left her a message to say he was in New York, at the Soho Grand, and hoped she'd call him back so he could see the girls over the weekend. And as he headed to his hotel, Ellen used her keys and let herself into her mother's apartment. Grace called a few minutes later and promised to be home soon. Ellen went to unpack, and an hour later her mother walked into the apartment and put her arms around her with delight when she saw her. Grace wasn't as tall as Ellen, but she was a striking woman, with red hair and green eyes, and features very much like her daughter's. She looked distinguished and aristocratic, but in no way snobbish. She was wearing black slacks and a black sweater with her long hair in a braid down her back, which she frequently wore when she was working. And a little white Maltese had come in with her and was barking frantically at their feet as mother and daughter embraced and smiled happily at each other. It was obvious that Grace was thrilled to see her.

"Take it easy, Blanche, it's only Ellen." The little ball of white fur was dancing around in circles, showing off for the familiar visitor. The dog was the love of her mother's life and her constant companion. Blanche even went to the office with her, and Grace took pride in saying she had become a weird old lady with a little white dog, and didn't seem to mind the image. Grace Madison was above all herself and made no apology for it.

Ellen looked around the familiar apartment as they sat down in the living room on the enormous, oversized white wool couch she'd gotten for her mother. There were two large white handwoven rugs on the floor, striking modern furniture mixed in with a few mid-twentieth-century pieces, and colorful contemporary paintings. Grace had designed the apartment herself, on two levels, and it felt more like a house than an apartment. And despite the modern feel to it, it was warm and inviting. She lit a fire in the glass fireplace, and the coffee table was a single block of glass that she had had made in Paris. It was beautiful, as was the rest of the apartment, which was on the ground floor with a spectacular view of the Hudson River and the lights on the other side. It had taken a hit during Sandy, but she had staunchly refused to move afterward, even if there was a risk of it happening again. This was her home. She had had all the post-Sandy damage repaired.

Blanche hopped up on the couch next to Grace, as the two women held hands, and Grace asked Ellen about the flight.

"It was bumpy but fine. I guess the hurricane is coming," Ellen commented, but her mother looked unconcerned.

"It will wear itself out before it gets here. They always do."

After they'd been talking for two hours, Grace asked, "Do you want something to eat?" They wandered out to the kitchen, which was as beautiful as the rest of the apartment, and they nibbled from the fridge, but Ellen wasn't really hungry. It was one in the morning for her by then, and she'd eaten enough on the plane. But she kept Grace company while she ate a salad. And as they sat talking for another half hour, Ellen forgot all about Charles Williams and how terrified he had been on the flight. Talking to him had helped pass the time during the bumpy end to the flight, but now she was home with her mother, and thoroughly enjoying her company.

They were still catching up when Grace left her in the guest bedroom. Grace could hardly wait to spend ten days with her, and share a few easy, relaxed dinners. She kissed Ellen goodnight, and as soon as Ellen brushed her teeth and put on her nightgown, she climbed into bed, sent George a text telling him she had arrived safely, and she was asleep before her head hit the pillow.

* * *

And at the Soho Grand, Charles sent his ex-wife Gina one last text before he went to bed, and hoped she would respond in the morning. This was not a scheduled visit, and he had come at the last minute. He knew she didn't have to answer him if she didn't want to, but all he wanted to do was see his girls and spend some time with them. He felt, as he always did, that he had gotten a new lease on life when the plane didn't crash, and now he wanted to see them more than ever. It was like being resurrected, after he had been so sure he would die on the flight. In his mind, they had been spared. And all he had to do now was get hold of Gina, and see his girls. He missed them constantly now that they were living in New York. Charles always felt as though Nigel had stolen not only his wife from him but his children and his life. And despite being exhausted and the time difference, it took him hours to fall asleep, worried that Gina wouldn't call.

Chapter 2

It was pouring rain outside when Ellen woke up in the comfortable bed the next morning, in her mother's guest room. Her
mother had sold the apartment on Park Avenue that Ellen had
grown up in when she moved to London and married George.
Grace had moved downtown then, and loved the unusual two-
level apartment she had found and reconfigured, in an old ware-
house in Tribeca that had been turned into co-op apartments.
There were twenty in the building, each one different, and Grace's
was the most unusual of all. The building was fully staffed, and
like most of the apartments in Tribeca and the highly desirable
areas downtown, units sold for a fortune. Grace felt totally at
home in the lively atmosphere of the neighborhood, with families
and young people living there, and she enjoyed the views along
the river. She considered the Upper East Side too stuffy now, and
went there as seldom as she could, except for her office, which was

on Fifty-seventh Street and Park Avenue. Everything she needed and wanted to do socially or to relax was downtown, and Ellen always loved staying with her.

Her mother was at her desk, checking her computer and paying some bills, when Ellen walked into the study her mother used when she occasionally worked at home. Since it was Saturday, Grace was wearing jeans and a red V-neck sweater with black ballet flats. She had a slim figure and was very fit. She had done yoga for years and still did. She had the erect posture of a dancer, which she attributed to years of ballet in her youth, before she discovered yoga. She had tried to get Ellen interested in it but never could. She thought it would be good for her and help her relax.

"Nasty weather," Ellen commented to her mother, glancing out the window as she sank into a comfortable chair. "What are they saying about the hurricane? Is it still heading this way?" They could see the slim trees outside swaying in the heavy wind, but it wasn't unusual for end-of-summer storms.

"More or less," Grace said vaguely, clearly not worried, "and no matter what they say now, they'll declare it a tropical storm before it gets here." Grace still kept a "go bag" buried in a closet somewhere, with clothes, a few minor medicines, and whatever she might need if they were ever evacuated again. But storm warnings in August and September were considered more of a nuisance than a serious threat.

The building Grace lived in was in Zone 1, which had been categorized as the prime flood zone five years before, which was inevitable since it was on the river. And the building had added an emergency generator four years before, after Sandy, which was reassuring, and Grace really never gave it any thought. She wasn't a person who dwelled on past hardships—she turned her mind to the future and moved on. She was a practical person with a positive point of view, which had influenced Ellen's outlook on life since her youth.

In her mother's opinion, there was nothing one couldn't do, a view that had fortified Ellen during the past four years as she doggedly pursued pregnancy, convinced that sooner or later their dreams of a family would come true. She kept her mind on the goal, that she and George would have their own baby one day. Although her mother had wondered for the past year if they might be wiser to come up with a more realistic alternate plan, like adoption, she hadn't voiced her concerns to Ellen and didn't want to discourage her. She thought their courage and determination admirable, even if a little desperate at times, and she was impressed that her son-in-law was still willing to go along with the plan, despite the poor outcome so far. Grace thought that most men would have given up by then. She and Ellen's father had tried to have a second child for several years and after numerous miscarriages had decided that one child was enough for them, and she had never regretted not pursuing it further. The thought of what Ellen had gone through for the past four years seemed horrifying to Grace, although she could understand the desire to have at least one child, but adoption also seemed like an acceptable plan to her, and didn't to them. She assumed their aversion to adoption had something to do with George's traditional views about carrying on his own bloodline, as well as with her daughter's stubborn refusal to give up. She was her mother's daughter in many ways, in a slightly modified version. Both women were known for their strong wills, hard work, and perseverance.

"What would you like to do today?" Grace smiled at her daughter across the desk, as they listened to the wind howling outside.

"Whatever you want," Ellen said easily. "I'm just happy being here with you. Do you have any errands we need to do?" They liked going shopping together, wandering around SoHo and Tribeca and stopping at some small restaurant for lunch, although it didn't look like a great day for that. "Do you suppose we should stock up on some supplies in case the stores close and we get stuck at home for several days?" Ellen knew the drill for preparation for big storms.

"Let's not panic yet." Grace dismissed the thought. "The storm warnings on the news will have half of New York lining up at supermarkets today, and then the hurricane will take a sharp turn somewhere and go out to sea at the last minute, and we'll wind up with a mountain of bottled water and food we don't need. I have flashlights, candles, batteries, and everything else. I hope they don't get everyone all riled up again—they do it now every year. Like the boy who cried wolf. It took me months to drink all the water I stocked up last time, and I gave all the food to a homeless shelter to get rid of it. Let's face it—how much canned tuna and peaches can you eat?" Ellen smiled at her mother and decided she was right. "A little shopping?" Grace suggested. "I need a new sweater for Blanche—she ate all the rhinestones off her old one." She looked slightly annoyed, and Ellen laughed.

"She has more clothes than I do. It's a shame I don't wear her size," Ellen teased her. Her mother was unashamed of how much she loved the little dog, and readily admitted that she spoiled her rotten. There were dog toys all over the otherwise pristine living room, and most of the apartment.

"We could do some shopping for us too," her mother said thoughtfully. She was always generous with her daughter, and frequently sent her gifts in London when she saw something she thought Ellen would like.

"I wouldn't mind looking in at some of the vintage and antique stores. I have two clients to shop for while I'm here," Ellen commented. And occasionally she made unexpected finds in some of the shops downtown, of unique items she couldn't find anywhere else. Ellen liked pursuing unusual resources and made frequent trips to Paris, to the auction rooms at the Hôtel Drouot, where she had bought some fabulous things for her clients and even her own home. Going to Drouot was like a treasure hunt—you never knew what you would find. But she had had good luck over the years in SoHo too, although the weather wasn't too conducive to shopping, but neither of them was daunted by it.

Ellen had brought running shoes with her, and she knew she could borrow a raincoat from her mother. She made herself a cup of coffee, and they agreed to leave half an hour later. Ellen thought of calling George, but it would be lunchtime at the country home where he was staying, and she didn't want to disturb them. She turned on a small TV in the kitchen and switched it to the Weather Channel to listen to the news. Weather maps in different colors were showing the hurricane's path and speed, indicating that it was heading toward the shores of New Jersey and New York, but she knew that that could change at any moment, and often did. The announcer on the screen said that the city would be issuing hourly statements, but there were no plans to evacuate residents or shut down public transportation yet. It would be almost inevitable if the path the hurricane was on didn't alter, but the storm was still far offshore in the Caribbean and much could still change, and it could be downgraded to a tropical storm long before it reached their shores. There was no cause for alarm yet, as Ellen switched off the TV and went upstairs to dress. She sent George a text message so as not to interfere with his activities or hosts. She knew he was staying at the crumbling old Tudor manor that had been in their friends' family for years, which lent itself perfectly to the big weekend parties they liked to give, and which George enjoyed so much. Ellen sometimes found them a little overwhelming, among people who formed a tight clique many years before, but everyone was always pleasant to her, even if she wasn't one of them, and she was part of the group now. Most of them had known each other as children, and even married childhood friends.

Sometimes feeling like an outsider among them was a bond she shared with her friend Mireille. They laughed about it privately and made fun of them sometimes. Many of their social group were titled and could trace their ancestry back for half a dozen centuries with ease. It was a frequent topic of conversation among them—who had married and given birth to whom, legitimately or otherwise, and who had been the monarch at the time. It was a little hard to follow, didn't interest Ellen a great deal, and seemed silly to her. But the others all took it very seriously, especially George. Ellen was more interested in the present, her activities, her life with George, and her work.

Grace and Ellen left the building half an hour later and walked through Tribeca in the strong wind, as leaves blew off the trees and papers flew around their feet, but it wasn't particularly unpleasant, and the slight chill in the air was invigorating. The temperature had dropped slightly the night before, and Ellen was comfortable in the sweater she had worn and the raincoat she had borrowed from her mother. Grace was wearing a slicker and shiny black Wellington boots, with her mane of red hair blowing in the wind. She didn't seem to mind it, and they talked and laughed as they stopped at various shops Ellen knew in SoHo, although many of them were closed. No warnings had been issued, but people were uneasy, and some had stayed closed as a precaution and taped cardboard inside their windows. The greatest danger with heavy rains and wind was that branches would break off, flying from the trees, or trees would fall as their roots weakened in the wet earth. Ellen was careful not to walk under any and warned her mother to do the same. They were experienced New Yorkers who lived with hurricane warnings every fall and knew what to do. They had left the dog at home, because Grace said she hated the rain, although she had the wardrobe for it, with several raincoats and a set of tiny boots.

"She won't wear them, but she looks so cute in them." Grace grinned as Ellen rolled her eyes.

"Mom, don't tell that to anyone—they'll think you're nuts."

"What can I tell you? She's good company, and I love her. So what if people think it's silly? I'm not hurting anyone." Ellen knew it was true. There hadn't been a man in her mother's life in at least a dozen years. The last man Grace had dated had been a well-known architect too. They had worked on a joint project together and been quietly involved for several years, until he died suddenly of a heart attack, and there had been no one since. Her mother seemed to philosophically accept that women her age were not in high demand, and men in their sixties and seventies were usually involved with women half their age. "A great mind is no match for young thighs," she said practically, "and I can't blame them." So she lavished her affection on Blanche, enjoyed her daughter when she saw her, loved her work, stayed busy, and had many friends. She was satisfied with her life and had stopped longing for a partner, although now and then she admitted that it would have been nice, however unlikely. And she said men her own age were too much trouble. At this point in her life, she didn't want to be someone's nurse, having missed all the good years with them. She always said she didn't want to appear onstage in the last act. It was easier to just keep things as they were. And her work as an architect was still as all-consuming as it had ever been.

They had lunch at a small French café they both liked, and Ellen noticed that people around them seemed to be in good spirits, and no one appeared to be worried about the hurricane. Enough changes had been effected since Sandy to make people feel safe. At first, there had been a multitude of plans suggested, many of which were impractical and too costly and seemed unnecessary, like a storm surge barrier in the outer harbor, which would be fifteen billion dollars to build, or a sea wall for a billion, but all of it was deemed too expensive and unrealistic. But a few changes had been made, and reasonable compromises effected to improve safety conditions in a hurricane in the future, without going all out with plans the city and federal governments couldn't implement or afford, like beach fill, elevated sand dunes, enhanced reefs, and stricter building codes.

The two women spent a relaxed, easy hour at lunch, then drifted through the fancier shops that had opened downtown, Prada, Chanel, and several other brands they liked. Ellen bought a red skirt at Prada, and Grace bought a new Chanel tote that she said would be perfect to take Blanche to the office with her, or conceal her when she went out to lunch. Blanche was a practiced stowaway and never made a sound when Grace sneaked her into restaurants in bags like the one she had just bought. And they stopped at her favorite pet shop on the way home, where Grace bought her pale blue and shocking pink cashmere sweaters, with collars to match, and half a dozen tiny new toys, as Ellen teased her about it, and Grace endured it with good humor. She was used to her daughter making fun of her about the dog.

George called Ellen on her cell phone as soon as they got home. He had just finished dinner in the country, and he said the news on television was alarming about the hurricane that was about to hit them and the damage it would cause. They were comparing it to Sandy. He had switched on his hosts' TV to check on things in New York.

"I think it's just media panic to make it sound interesting. No one is upset here. They're not evacuating anyone, and it's still a couple of days offshore. A lot could change before it gets here." Ellen sounded relaxed.

"Yes," he said pessimistically, "and it could get worse. Why don't you and your mother go somewhere for a few days, out of harm's way?"

"That's silly, darling, we don't need to do that. The city is very responsible about it. If anything, they're given to overwarning people now. We'll hear about it if the situation looks dangerous. And people are better prepared now for a storm like Sandy. No one's going to get surprised again."

"You can't stop the river from overflowing like last time, and your mother lives in Zone 1," he reminded her. She smiled at what he said—he knew all the language, the geography, and the concerns after the last time.

"Don't worry about us. We're fine. Enjoy your weekend," she told him.

"I'm just concerned if another hurricane hits the city."

"It won't, and if it does, we'll be prepared."

"Have you stocked up on food and water and flashlight batteries?" he asked, sounding almost military about it.

"My mother has adequate supplies. We'll be fine, I promise." She asked him about his weekend then, and who was there, and a few minutes later they hung up. He had said there were fourteen guests staying at their friends' house, most of whom she knew, although not all. She knew it would be a great weekend for him, and she was touched that he had called to check on them in New York. She was happy he had something to do—it would make her absence seem shorter. She always felt a little guilty about leaving him when she traveled, even when it was for work. But during the week, he'd be busy at the office. And she knew he was going to a shoot again the following weekend, before she got back.

Ellen did a little work on her computer after that, and her mother did the same. The dog was asleep at Grace's feet, after she had tried the new sweaters on her, and was satisfied that they fit and were as cute as she had hoped. The rain and wind continued relentlessly outside, but they were cozy in the apartment, with music playing softly on the stereo. Despite the hurricane supposedly just days away from them, it was a pleasant, easy afternoon.

Charles had called Gina as soon as he woke up in his room at the Soho Grand on Saturday, the day after he arrived. His calls continued to go to voicemail, and he sent her an email and a text. He knew she didn't always check her messages, especially on weekends, when she was busy with the girls. Chloe was on a soccer team, and Lydia had just started ballet. They seemed to be enjoying their new life in New York and had told him all about their new friends. They never mentioned Nigel to him—they seemed to instinctively sense that he didn't want to know. And Charles could tell whenever he saw them that they were happy and well cared for by their mother, although it broke his heart to be so far from them. He had been an attentive father from the beginning and loved his wife and being with his family. But the ten-year span between him and Gina, and the difference in their interests, careers, and styles, had proved to be a chasm he couldn't bridge. She hadn't fully settled down yet when they married, and loved going out all the time. Charles was building his career and had already sown his wild oats, and he loved staying home. He tried to keep Gina happy, but not always with great results. She worked in a racier, more exotic world as a model. And the stability he offered seemed tiresome to her. Once married, she found his life and friends incredibly boring. She missed being with people her own age. He had thought she would adjust to a more staid way of life, but she hadn't yet when Nigel came along. Charles's parents had disapproved of the match since the beginning, and their warnings had proved to be right. They said she was too immature to be married and didn't appreciate him, all of which was accurate.

Gina's dreams of being an actress had been eating at her, and the modeling she did exposed her to a very different world from his. She had gotten pregnant with Chloe six months after they started dating, and as soon as they found out, Charles had proposed to her. He felt it was the right thing to do, and he loved her. Gina didn't feel they had to marry and wanted to wait until after the baby, which went against everything Charles believed. He was old-fashioned and traditional and wanted a real marriage and family life with her. He had convinced her to marry him when she was four months pregnant at twenty-four, just as her modeling career took off, and she began getting small roles as an actress, which made married life seem even less exciting to her. Two years later Lydia had been another slip. A second child pulled Gina even further into married life and away from her goals. Charles had promised to pick up the slack with their daughters, with a nanny, and he had kept his word. He had fallen in love with his children, and loved Gina passionately. She loved him but chafed at the restrictions of marriage and the conflict with her career goals. When she turned thirty, she had been seized by a wave of panic that she'd be trapped in domestic life forever, her modeling would end, and her acting career would run aground before it fully took off. Everything Charles stood for became a threat to her. And she blamed him for talking her into marriage when she was so young. Many of her friends had children out of wedlock, which she said she would have preferred. Marriage felt like a prison to her.

Charles had always seen a depth that she was capable of but had no desire to develop yet. She was a good mother to their children, when she was around, but she longed to pursue her career among models, actors, producers, and all the creative types who seemed like more fun and were familiar to her. She tried to explain that being a banker's wife wasn't enough for her. And then Nigel had come along, like an emissary from the world she craved. He was right up her alley, or so she thought—a photographer she had met on a shoot in Tahiti for Italian *Vogue*. Although she said she had never meant for it to happen, their romance had taken off like a rocket while they were on location and caught the attention of the tabloids, since Nigel was well known on the fashion scene. Nightmarish months had ensued, of embarrassment for Charles, public humiliation, and his parents' outrage over what he and the children were going through. And not wanting to engulf him in scandal, within two months of when it began, Gina informed Charles that she was leaving him. She said she needed to be free, to experience the last of her youth. They had both cried when she told him, but she insisted she was sure. And Nigel provided too great a lure. He was far more appealing to her than Charles.

She said she was moving to New York to work with American *Vogue,* who was currently enamored with Nigel, and he had promised her dazzling opportunities if she followed him—possibly even a chance to make a film with producers he knew in L.A. It was all too exciting for Gina to resist, and so was he.

Charles would have tried to stop her legally, but he knew that the court battle would be public and ugly, and she would resent him forever if he deprived her of her dreams. He knew he had to let her go, and he hated Nigel for stealing her from him. He helped her get an agent in New York, and they were clamoring to book her for shoots with other photographers as well. Her career had finally taken off. All Charles could hope was that she would tire of it one day and come back to him. He was gracious about it—and now regretted it bitterly. After a year, Gina loved New York and was still with Nigel, she was a successful model, and the girls were happy with her. It appeared that he had lost them for good and all. And Nigel and his world seemed to suit her better than Charles ever had. It had all worked out as she had hoped, much to Charles's dismay. Nigel's unshaven, unwashed good looks were typical of the milieu Gina had been craving for years. She'd been too young and too ambitious for the ordinary domestic life Charles had offered her. He felt as though his whole life had gone down the drain the year before. The divorce had recently become final, and he wondered if she was going to marry Nigel, or at least have a baby with him. Marriage seemed to mean nothing to anyone in their world. Relationships and alliances appeared to come and go, with children born of their brief unions often trailing in their wake. It bore no resemblance whatsoever to anything in Charles's life.

He hadn't started dating again—every other woman paled in comparison to Gina, despite her betrayal and change of heart about him. She was more beautiful and more exciting than anyone he had ever known, and she was the mother of his children, a role he felt deserved profound respect, although she didn't feel the same way about him and had left him for another man. Charles had been deeply depressed for the past year since she left, suffering from bouts of anxiety, and all he felt able to do was put one foot in front of the other to get through the days. He lived for his visits with the girls and was trying his best to detach from their mother, so far with little success. Every time he saw a photograph of her, in an ad or on the cover of a magazine, his heart took a leap again. He knew it was pathetic, and he had to get over her, but he hadn't yet.

And in her usual casual, haphazard style, she wasn't returning his calls, as he waited in his hotel room, hoping to see the girls, and finally went for a walk to get some air. He was a strikingly handsome man but seemed unaware of it. Women noticed him as he walked past them on the street. As he always was, he was indifferent to their attention and never thought of himself as attractive, particularly since Gina left. It was obvious why Gina had fallen for him in the beginning, to everyone but him. He was good looking, intelligent, had a good job, did well, came from a good family, and adored her. But compared to Nigel, who didn't have Charles's values or attributes, he was serious, conservative, and responsible, none of which seemed sexy to her. And when Charles got nervous, he felt like a bumbler at times. Nigel was so much smoother and more sure of himself, but Charles thought he had no soul, and he questioned how long Nigel would stick around. But he showed no sign of exiting yet.

For all his many qualities, any woman would have wanted to be with Charles, but he didn't care. He was oblivious to them—all he wanted was the marriage he had lost, and even he knew there was no hope of retrieving it. She seemed too happy where she was, with Nigel in New York. Her life there was everything she had hoped for when she left, although Charles wondered how long it would last. Nothing was stable in her new world. But after a year, Gina was still on a high, dazzled by it all.

He walked around SoHo, and along the Hudson River for several hours, and still hadn't heard from her when he got back to the hotel at four o'clock and turned on the TV again, to check on the hurricane. It was a perfect focus for his anxieties, terrified that the city would be destroyed. He had nothing else to do that day. But there had been no major change. The hurricane had made a small detour in the Caribbean but was back on course toward New York again, and had picked up a little speed. He tried to imagine where Gina might be with the girls, but he had done everything he could to contact her, several times. Now all he could do was wait. He ordered a hamburger from room service and sat staring at the TV, watching CNN. Hurricane Ophelia was being compared to Sandy, though seemed less ominous for the moment. But it couldn't be dismissed as a potential threat to the city, albeit a lesser one. Even that didn't reassure him, as he ate the hamburger and worried about his girls. And their mother's lack of response to his messages was as maddening as it always was. And wherever she was, he wondered if she had her cell phone with her, or the battery was dead, which was frequently her excuse for not returning his calls.

On Saturday, Juliette Dubois had been on duty in the emergency room at one of the city's three largest hospitals since noon. She was thirty-one years old, a resident and ER doctor. During Hurricane Sandy, she had been in medical school at NYU and was assigned to NYU Hospital. The hospital had been heavily damaged and had had to be evacuated, and she had helped to carry patients out of the building for transfers to other hospitals, when the backup generators failed. No one had expected the kind of damage they had experienced. No lives had been lost in the evacuation, but there had been some terrifying situations involving preemies in incubators and patients on respirators that had to be manually operated by hospital personnel until they got to the hospitals that took their patients. It had made a lasting impression on Juliette and given her a profound respect for natural disasters. And although Hurricane Ophelia didn't seem as dangerous so far, a chill had run down her spine at the first reports and at the news that it was headed for New York.

She hadn't had time for a break in the five hours she'd been on duty. Saturdays were always busy in the ER. People who got sick during the week and hadn't bothered to call their doctors took a turn for the worse on Friday night and had no recourse except to go to the ER over the weekend. A bad flu had been rampant in the city, which was a particular threat to children and old people. Household accidents abounded on the weekends, as did sports injuries, women who went into premature labor, and people who broke bones when they fell on city streets.

They had two broken hips in the ER now, an eighty-four-year-old woman who had been hit by a bicycle in Central Park, and a ninety-year-old man who had fallen off a ladder while checking out a leak in his ceiling. Paramedics had brought them in, along with the usual assortment of heart attacks, minor injuries, asthma attacks, cuts that needed stitches, and a four-year-old whose mother thought he might have swallowed their pet turtle. Juliette loved the variety of what they treated in the emergency room, from serious injuries to minor ones, although at times the place was a zoo.

At five o'clock she was having her first break of the afternoon when Will Halter, the chief resident, walked by her. He was proverbially tall, dark, and handsome, and they had dated for three months earlier that summer, with poor results. They couldn't stand each other. In Juliette's opinion, he had an ego the size of the building, and since she hadn't been willing to cater to it, he had dumped her. He had dated nearly every nurse in the ER, even some of the married ones. She felt stupid for ever having gone out with him, but he was easy to fall for. Everyone did—patients, nurses, med students. He had a bedside manner that made patients nearly swoon over him, although Juliette was no longer convinced that he really cared about them and thought it likely that he didn't. But she had to admit that technically he was a good doctor, even though she thought he was a miserable human being.

And he liked her no better than she liked him. It made working together extremely difficult, without their mutual loathing becoming obvious to the patients. The nursing staff was well aware of it and, in most cases, of the reason why. And whenever he thought he could get away with it, Will Halter made snide comments to her, although he grudgingly acknowledged that she was a damn good doctor. He just didn't like her as a woman. He knew she saw right through him and recognized him for the narcissist he was. She was fearless in her straightforward comments to him and in her challenges, when they benefited her patients, which drove him up the wall. They were barely able to be civil to each other, which was a problem they had not yet resolved and possibly never would. And as chief resident, he was her immediate boss. Juliette had made the situation clear to her supervisor, the director of the residency program, said they had a "chemical inability to work together," and described it succinctly by saying they were allergic to each other. She had warned the director of it in case Will chose to sabotage her residency, which she thought he might be capable of, but he hadn't so far. He just treated her disrespectfully, but he had never told any lies about her, which was at least something.

"I see God has graced us with His presence today," Juliette said acidly to the head admitting nurse at the desk, Michaela Mancini, after she saw Will in the hall. Michaela laughed at her—she was familiar with the situation and knew who Juliette meant.

"I think he came on at four. We have a shitload of cases today, so it's lucky he came in although he usually doesn't work on Saturdays. Unless you want another dozen patients," she said with a smile, and Juliette shook her head as she grabbed a chart.

"I'm maxed out. Let him do a little work for a change." He didn't work as hard as the younger residents, but even Juliette agreed that his diagnostic skills were remarkable, particularly with their hardest cases. Her beefs against him were personal, not medical, and she knew she had to live with the situation.

Juliette was a pretty blonde who wore her hair in a braid, lived in hospital scrubs, and never had time to put on makeup. She was passionate about her work and her patients and thought of little else. She was straightforward and dedicated, and unlike Will, she never tried to play the charming card, or operated from ego. Juliette came from a medical family in Detroit. Both of her brothers were doctors, as was her father, and her mother had been a nurse before she married Juliette's father. And all of them had said that they had had at least one chief resident like that in their careers. They told her that her big mistake had been dating him, which made it look like sour grapes when she complained about him now, particularly since he had dumped her. And she knew they were right. She had no choice but to suck it up and hope he got bored with torturing her in time.

As though talking about him had conjured him up like an evil spirit, the chief resident showed up at the ER desk five minutes later, and gave Juliette a surly look.

A little while later, as they both consulted charts at the nurses' station, Juliette asked him a question in a monotone, so as not to start anything between them. Whatever she said to him would irritate him and set him off, as the nurses had observed countless times. Sometimes it was almost fun to watch them, like a fireworks show on the Fourth of July. You could count on it every time.

"Are we doing anything to prepare for the hurricane, if the city goes on full alert?" she asked him. She had been wondering about it all day. Having lived through Sandy at NYU Hospital, she knew how important it was to be prepared.

"Hardly. We don't need to borrow trouble. We'll deal with it when they tell us. We don't have time to waste before that. I don't know about you, but I've got double my normal workload without worrying about the hurricane."

"So do I. But someone should at least check the generators *before* we're on full alert. That's what did us in at NYU last time—the backup generators failed."

"Are you working for the Office of Emergency Services now?" he asked tartly, his mouth set in a thin line. "Why don't you call the head of the hospital and tell him?"

She ignored the sarcasm of his comment, but persisted. "We can at least be prepared down here. We're below sea level and close enough to the river to get flooded."

"Then wear your rain boots to work tomorrow. What do you expect me to do? Set up sandbags myself? I'm the chief resident here, not the maintenance staff. Stop panicking—your patients will pick up on it," he scolded her, put back the chart he'd been studying, and walked off, as Michaela raised an eyebrow in silent comment.

"We should be prepared," Juliette said to her in a quiet voice, and Michaela nodded.

"He's right, though. No one has time to deal with it unless we have to. And everyone is aware of what happened at NYU. They won't let it happen here," she tried to reassure her. Juliette nodded and walked into the cubicle where the ninety-year-old man with the broken hip was waiting for the orthopedic surgeon to come and see him. They were going to operate on him that night, and his daughter and grandchildren were with him, telling him for the hundredth time that he shouldn't have been on a ladder in the first place. He was alert and intelligent, not senile, just old.

"Are you doing all right, Mr. Andrews?" Juliette asked, smiling at him.

"I was checking out a leak in the ceiling. The building has very old pipes," he explained to Juliette again. She agreed with his daughter about the ladder, but he was a sweet old man, and she felt sorry for him. His daughter was saying that he had just proved that he could no longer live alone, and he looked devastated. He had passed the mental exam with no problem and clearly didn't have dementia. He was just independent, had wanted to check out the leak, and had lost his balance. His problem was that he was ninety years old, and no longer as steady as he had been, or as agile, and lived by himself. He said his wife had died two years before.

"How are you doing with the pain?" Juliette asked him gently.

"I'm all right," he said, looking embarrassed, as she touched his hand.

"You'll be fine after the surgery," she said quietly, and he nodded, as the surgeon walked in. Juliette asked his relatives to step outside for a moment, and left them as they continued to complain about him in the hallway, that he just wasn't sensible, was much too independent, wanted to do all the same things he had done as a young man, and refused to act his age. That sounded like a good thing to her—he was still full of energy and life.

She went to visit the child who had swallowed the turtle after that.

The little boy was dressing to go home, and his mother looked enormously relieved. He had just admitted that he hadn't swallowed it, as he previously told her. He had flushed it down the toilet and didn't want to get in trouble, so he said he swallowed it. His mother was giving him a stern lecture about lying.

Juliette looked at him seriously, barely able to repress a smile. "Johnny, do you have a dog?" She already knew the answer, as the little boy nodded.

"Yes, his name is Dobie. He's a German shepherd."

"I'll bet he's a really nice dog. Will you make me a promise?" He looked at her with wide eyes and nodded again. "Will you promise me that you won't swallow him? I think that would give you a really big tummyache, and Dobie might not like it." The boy guffawed at what she said, then giggled as his mother smiled.

"I promise. But he's too big to swallow." And the ill-fated turtle probably had been too. It had been his sister's turtle, and he had told the nurse that his sister would be really mad at him. But on other occasions, they had seen children who had swallowed a wide variety of unlikely objects, which the doctors had observed on X-rays and scans with some dismay.

"Well, you just remember that. Don't try to swallow Dobie." He nodded, and she helped him off the table once he was dressed, and she signed the release form and handed it to his mother. And then she reminded him that telling fibs was not a good idea either. He nodded solemnly and waved when they left a few minutes later, and he informed his mother that Juliette was nice and he liked her. And then he promised not to lie again.

Juliette went down the line of her patients, doing triage, and was in the waiting room to see the children of the man who had had the heart attack and was on his way to cardiac ICU for an angioplasty, when she saw a bulletin flash across the TV screen. All eyes in the waiting room suddenly turned toward the TV, as the anchorman informed them that Hurricane Ophelia had been upped to a Category 1 hurricane, had picked up considerable speed, and was headed straight toward them. The city was now officially on alert, the subways would be closed by eight P.M., and designated areas of the city were being evacuated. A list of the zones to be evacuated appeared on the screen, and all other residents were being asked to stay home after nine P.M. that night. Further bulletins were promised, and a live message from the mayor at six P.M.

"Shit," Juliette said out loud, "here we go again." And then she turned back to the family of her cardiac patient.

"Will they close the hospital?" one of them asked her, looking worried.

"No, we're fully prepared to handle emergencies like that. We have a backup generator, and we'll make all the arrangements and accommodations necessary, and it probably won't be as bad as last time," she said, hoping it was true, and remembering the scene at NYU, carrying patients down the stairs by flashlight. She went back to explaining the procedure that was going to be performed on their father.

Afterward she went back to the desk. Several of the nurses were going to have to leave early before public transportation shut down, as they commuted by subway, and relief staff was being called in. Juliette knew just what an emergency of that nature would look like, and realized that her own apartment was in a flood zone.

"What about you? Do you need to go home to get some things?" Michaela asked her, and Juliette shrugged.

"About the only thing I have of value there is my passport. I can always get another one. My apartment is a mess. There's nothing I need to run home and save." Her whole life was at the hospital. She had no belongings at home that were meaningful to her, no pets, no sentimental memorabilia. All that was in Detroit. The place where she lived was nothing more than a crash pad she went to between shifts.

Juliette saw Will Halter rush down the hall in the ER shortly after that, on his way to examine a patient. There was no time for him to be snippy with her, now that the city was on alert and flood zones were going to be evacuated. And all Juliette hoped was that someone had had the brains and foresight to check the hospital generators, but there was nothing she could do about it. She had patients to see, and if the hurricane hit them as Sandy had, they would deal with it. All she needed to think about were her patients and her job—the city officials could take care of the rest. And whatever the chief resident thought about it wasn't her problem, and she didn't care what he said to her.

Ellen had just turned on the TV at her mother's apartment when the emergency announcement came on, and she was stunned for a

moment as she watched. She saw clearly that her mother's neighborhood, in Zone 1, was at the top of the evacuation list, and she
went to tell her mother, who was feeding Blanche her dinner in the
kitchen.

"We have to be out by nine P.M. tonight, Mom. That's in four
hours. We need to get organized, and we have to find a place to
stay. I think we should go to a hotel uptown." Everything north of
Thirty-ninth Street had been untouched in the previous hurricane,
and everything below it had been a war zone. Uptown was the saf-
est place to be. Grace listened to her daughter and thought about
it for a few minutes, as she set Blanche's bowl down on the floor
with her dinner, and then she turned to Ellen with a look of determination that Ellen hadn't expected.

"I'm not going," Grace said in a strong, steady voice. "We did all
that last time, and I lost a lot more because I wasn't here to protect
it." She had had two feet of water on the lower floor of the apartment five years before, which was enough to damage her belongings, even with the additional upper floor. "And if the living room
floods again, I can stay upstairs in my bedroom. It probably won't
be as bad as they say. They're covering their backs. They don't
want people complaining afterward that they weren't warned. The
building isn't going to float away. And there are safeguards in place
now. The co-op committee here already voted to sandbag the lobby
for future hurricanes, in case of an evacuation. I'm not leaving. You
can go to a hotel if you want to," she said as Ellen stared at her.

"You can't mean that. It's too dangerous, Mom. I won't let you
stay." Ellen was as stubborn as Grace was, and Grace smiled at her.

"What are you going to do? Carry me out over your shoulder? Don't be silly. Blanche and I will be fine here." There was a steely expression in her mother's eyes, and Ellen felt panic in the pit of her stomach. What if there was a major flood and her mother drowned in the apartment? Other people had in flood zones during Sandy, unable to leave their homes, or trying to escape too late.

"I can't allow you to do that," Ellen said in a frightened voice. And the television announcer had reminded people that not evacuating could mean requiring the services of rescue workers later, who had more important jobs to do than to rescue those who should have evacuated hours before.

"You can't force me to leave. I'm an adult, of sound mind, and that's my decision. Get yourself a hotel room uptown, if you want to, but I'm staying in my apartment." She left no room for negotiation as she threw away the empty can of special diet dog food and tidied up the kitchen. Then she turned to Ellen again. "I think I'll move some things up to the bedroom, though, just in case." She had at least learned that much from the last time, when many of her belongings had been damaged. "But there's nothing here I can't carry myself."

She walked into the living room then and began putting fragile objects on the coffee table, to carry upstairs. The paintings were hung high enough to avoid water damage, and all she had to worry about were books and objects, and there were some valuable chairs she wanted to move too. She couldn't do anything to protect the couches and heavy furniture, but there were plenty of small things she could move to her bedroom on the upper floor.

As Ellen watched her, all thought of evacuating vanished, and she knew what she had to do. As crazy as it seemed, and she didn't agree with her, if her mother was determined to stay, she had to stay too. She was sure George wouldn't like it, but she knew her mother. Grace wasn't going anywhere. She was refusing to evacuate, and whatever happened next, in the coming hours and days, the die had been cast, and foolish or not, they would face Hurricane Ophelia together, come what may.

Chapter 3

Ellen was carefully removing the kind of things that had been damaged last time, among them her mother's collection of coffee table books and leather-bound volumes, some of them first editions, and carrying them upstairs to her mother's bedroom, and to the guest room she was sleeping in. She had found some plastic sheeting from when Grace had had the apartment repainted after Sandy, and she tried to protect the couches and furniture as best she could, while Blanche ran around barking and getting underfoot. She could sense that something major was going on. And as Ellen wrestled with the plastic sheeting and blue tape, the doorbell rang. It was Grace's neighbor from across the hall. He had a similar apartment, was a pleasant man, and checked on Grace from time to time. He was very fond of her, and Grace liked him. He was a well-known mystery writer and had moved to New York from L.A. Ellen had met him once during one of her visits to New York. Grace talked about him often, and Ellen knew from her that he was quiet and retiring, and somewhere in his late forties. His books were on the best-seller lists for months when they came out. Ellen had read one or two of them, and liked them. Grace had read them all and was a devoted fan, mostly because she liked him so much. Robert Wells was a household name all over the world. But despite his fame, he was an unassuming person, and Ellen had been shocked the first time she realized who he was. There had been many movies based on his work as well. Ellen knew from Grace that he was divorced and had two grown kids.

When Ellen opened the door to him, she was startled to be reminded of how tall he was, and he looked surprised to see her. He seemed younger than she remembered too.

"Is your mother home?" he asked, feeling foolish as soon as he said it, and Ellen smiled.

"She's upstairs putting things away," Ellen explained.

"I didn't realize you were here," he said, feeling awkward for a minute. He had seemed shy when she met him before too. And something about him suggested that he was a solitary, introverted man, but his attention to her mother indicated that he was a caring person too. "I came to see if she needed help. Can I give you a hand?" She opened the door wider so he could come in, just as her mother came down the stairs with Blanche at her heels. The dog wagged her tail when she saw him, and ran over to him, and obviously recognized him, as Grace smiled and invited him in, and was happy to see him.

"Hello, Bob. Ellen and I have decided to stay. I was just taking a few things upstairs, in case we get flooded again." Bob Wells looked startled and disturbed by what she said.

"I don't think that's wise, Grace," he said respectfully. "The building took a heavy hit last time. I don't think you should be here if that happens again. Why don't you protect what you can and go to a hotel uptown, or stay with friends?" He exchanged a glance with Ellen, who clearly agreed with him, but Grace had made up her mind.

"It won't happen again, Bob. Lightning doesn't strike twice in the same place, and all that." But Bob thought that Grace staying in the building was a very bad idea, especially at her age, which he didn't say. He liked her as a friend and neighbor and never thought of her as older, but in an emergency like this one, it had to be taken into account. If the building flooded, she would have to be agile and strong enough to escape.

"If what they say is true, we could have fifteen- or twenty-foot waves on the river, across the street, at high tide. Let's not risk that," he said seriously. It had been enough to convince him to go uptown.

"It'll rush down the street, not through my front door," she said firmly. "Are you leaving?" She was surprised, although the news channels had been urging people to evacuate the designated areas.

"Yes, I am. I'm going to stay with my agent on the Upper West Side. They're turning off the power downtown at midnight to-night. There's no point sitting here in the dark, with no electricity and no heat or air-conditioning. I think you should reconsider. And let me help you in the meantime." He took a quick look at what

Ellen had been doing, wrapping furniture in plastic and sealing it with tape, while Grace stripped the surfaces and shelves. The apartment already looked as though she were emptying it. Ellen had been moving fast, and so had Grace. He had done the same in his own apartment, although most of his furniture was old and battered and was comfortable more than attractive or valuable, unlike the beautiful things in Grace's apartment. He was planning to take only his current manuscript and his favorite typewriter with him. His older manuscripts were in a watertight safe in his den upstairs, with copies in a vault at the bank, in case of fire, flood, or theft. He didn't fully trust the safe and never wrote his books on the computer, which he used only for email.

Bob grabbed the large plastic sheets one by one, and helped Ellen wrap the rest of the furniture, while Grace continued removing smaller objects and memorabilia. Ellen tied up the curtains and lifted them off the floor. They rolled up one of the rugs—the other was too large. And they put Grace's coats from the hall closet on her bed. In less than an hour, they had done as much as they could, and Grace offered him a glass of wine, which he accepted gratefully. They had done good work in a short time, but he still urged her to leave.

"It will be frightening down here if things get out of hand," he told her, but she remained unconvinced. "You don't want to have to wade out of the building, or swim," he said pointedly. "And what about Blanche?" he asked, hoping to sway her, but he could see that he hadn't, and he left them to pack his go bag, and put his ancient typewriter in its traveling case with his current manuscript wrapped in plastic, although he had a backup copy in his safe upstairs.

He rang the doorbell again before he left, and gave them his cell phone number in case they needed it, and they wished each other good luck as he left. He was sorry to see them staying, and reminded the doorman on the way out to check on them. The doorman promised that he would—he was fond of Grace too. And the superintendent was staying in the building to deal with flooding as it happened. No one really believed it would be as bad as Sandy, but nature was unpredictable, and even if it was less extreme, there could still be some serious flooding at high tide. According to the reports on TV, the full force of the storm wasn't due for another twenty-two hours, unless the winds picked up, in which case, Ophelia would be in New York sooner. The police were going through the neighborhood from door to door, to make sure that everyone evacuated that night. They couldn't force Grace to, but they were urging everyone strongly to heed the warnings. Bob noticed as he left that there were police boats parked in the street for use the following night, if the river overflowed its banks at high tide as it had before. It unnerved him seeing it, and he was worried about his neighbor who had decided to stay. But at least she had Ellen with her, he thought to himself. He would have insisted even more, if she had been alone, and offered to take her with him or drop her off somewhere in a neighborhood out of the potential flood zone. But Grace was adamant and had her daughter to assist her, so he left. He hoped that Ellen would make her listen to reason in the coming hours and convince her to evacuate.

* * *

They were sitting in Grace's bedroom, talking quietly that night, when the power went off. It was a precautionary measure by the city, and it seemed strange when the apartment suddenly went dark. The emergency generator in the building was operating only in the halls and for the elevator. Ellen lit candles, and Grace turned on a large battery-operated light that she had bought at a camping store for an occurrence such as this, or for one of the power outages that sometimes happened in New York, mostly in the summer.

"Are you okay, Mom?" Ellen asked her with concern, and Grace smiled. The bedroom was piled high with her fragile belongings and the coats from the closet downstairs.

"I'm fine." Ellen was hoping to convince her to leave in the morning but didn't press the point that night. It was too late to leave now, after midnight. And Blanche was perfectly content, sound asleep in Grace's lap. As long as everyone was there, she didn't care what else was going on, and the dog was exhausted by all the activity with both of them going up and down the stairs all night, moving things. Blanche had followed Grace every step of the way.

They went to bed shortly after the electricity went out, and Ellen took care to fill the bathtubs with water in case they needed it. They had bottled water too, though not a lot of it, and had thrown away any food that might spoil. They were as ready as they were going to be, and as she lay in bed, Ellen thought about George in England. He hadn't called, and she didn't want to exhaust her cell phone battery since she wouldn't be able to charge it now, and they might need it in an emergency. She wondered if George was having fun at the house party. He seemed a million miles from what was happening in New York, and she was glad to be there with her mother. She wouldn't have wanted her to be alone, although Grace didn't seem in the least frightened or concerned. She had been totally matter-of-fact about their preparations for the hurricane and remained convinced that it would be far less dangerous than the warnings claimed. Ellen hoped she was right.

The building on Clinton Street on the Lower East Side looked old and ramshackle, and was in poor condition, but the rents were low, and students had been renting apartments there for years. There were one or two artists, but mostly students from NYU. It was one of those buildings that people heard about by word of mouth, and vacancies never lasted for more than a day or two before someone snapped them up. Peter Holbrook and Ben Weiss had been living there for two years. They were twenty-one years old, and juniors at NYU. The apartment was dingy and desperately needed a coat of paint, and they had furnished it from rejects off the sidewalk and at Goodwill. Their parents weren't thrilled about it, and Ben's mother worried about electrical fires in the dilapidated building, but both boys loved their apartment, their independence, and the fact that it was so cheap. It was a sixth-floor walkup, with no elevator, which only tenants as young as they could endure.

They woke up early on Sunday morning, and met in the living room. Ben was sitting on the beaten-up couch with his dog, a black Lab named Mike, sprawled next to him, as Peter walked into the room and glanced out the window at the rain. The sky looked heavy and dark, and the wind was blowing harder than the day before. They had admitted to each other that they found the hurricane exciting, and wondered what it would be like when it hit New York. They were safe from floods in their aerie on the sixth floor, and Ben had gone to the supermarket and stocked up on food and water. They had everything they needed, and it seemed foolish to evacuate, to both of them. What was there to be afraid of? They could always go to Ben's parents' apartment if they wanted to, but neither of them did. It would be more fun to stay here, and they were perfectly content to remain in the cozy apartment until the hurricane passed. There were public schools in the neighborhood designated to be used as shelters if they had to leave in a hurry and couldn't get uptown, and announcements on TV and in the newspapers had said that people could bring their pets, so they knew they could take the dog. But neither Peter nor Ben wanted to go to a shelter with hundreds of people, maybe even thousands. They were better off at home.

Peter was from Chicago, and was an econ major at NYU. Ben was studying drama at Tisch at NYU, and had grown up in New York. They had met when Peter started dating Anna, a drama student at Tisch, two years before. Ben and Anna had been childhood friends since kindergarten, and Anna had introduced Peter to Ben. The two boys had become best friends and roommates three months after that, and they had been an inseparable threesome ever since. The Three Musketeers, and Mike, Ben's black Lab.

Peter opened a box of doughnuts and peeled a banana as his cell phone rang. He saw that it was Anna. She lived in an apartment in the West Village, with two roommates, and the girls had decided to stay at their apartment after the curfew the night before. Her mother was picking them up that morning and taking them uptown to their apartment, and Anna had wanted the boys to come with them, but they hadn't made up their minds the previous night.

"So are you coming with us?" Anna asked him. "My mom will be here in half an hour. We can swing by and pick you up." Her mother had an Escalade big enough to hold all of them and whatever they were taking with them. The girls had packed go bags to last them for a few days at Anna's parents'.

"What do you think?" Peter asked Ben as he played with the dog. "Do you want to go with them?"

"We can stay at my parents' if we want to go uptown," Ben said practically. He had a younger brother who was fourteen and still lived at home, and his parents had an apartment on Central Park West. "What do you think? Why don't we stay here?" The wind was strong and it was raining, but there was nothing ominous happening. And as long as they stayed indoors, they'd be fine. Ben didn't feel like dealing with his family and all the hullabaloo about the hurricane. It seemed simpler to just remain where they were. "Tell her we'll call her later, if we want to come up." Anna was like his sister after knowing her all his life.

"We're not leaving for now," Peter informed her as he took another bite of the doughnut, and the dog looked at him with pleading eyes. The supplies they'd bought were mostly junk food, water, sodas, and beer.

"That's really dumb," Anna told Peter. "What if it floods down here again? You could be stuck in the building for days with nothing to eat. And nothing will be open."

"We stocked up yesterday," Peter said proudly, and Ben grinned.

"With what? Doughnuts and beer?" She knew them well. "You won't even have electricity. You'll be sitting in the dark every night."

"We'll see how it goes. We can always come uptown if we get bored," Peter told her, and Anna wished him luck before they hung up. Half an hour later the three girls were on their way uptown with Anna's mother, who also thought it was a bad idea for the boys to stay downtown.

"They probably think they're cool and macho not evacuating," Anna said with a disgusted look as the girls chattered in the car on the way to the Upper East Side. Both her roommates were from other cities and were happy to have a place to stay. Their parents had been calling frantically, ever since the first warnings of the hurricane, and had called Anna's mother to thank her for taking care of them. And Ben's mother would have been happy to have Peter stay with them. She loved Peter, and he had become part of the family in the past two years. But the two boys thought it seemed more "adult" and "manly" to stay put, and they were curious to watch the hurricane from their own windows instead of evacuating. Ben had told his parents they'd be fine, had food and water and everything they needed. And his parents reluctantly agreed to the plan and assured Peter's parents the boys would be safe, although they would have preferred that they come uptown.

Peter and Ben went out for a walk that afternoon with Mike, to give him some exercise, and were surprised by how strong the wind was. There were gusts that nearly swept them off their feet. It was exciting, and it was after four o'clock when they went back to the apartment, less than two hours before Hurricane Ophelia was supposed to hit. And even Mike had been happy to get some air. They were tired of being cooped up in the apartment all day. They had finished the first box of doughnuts by then, a can of Pringles, and a bag of chips, washed down with Gatorade.

They made sandwiches in the kitchen before it got dark, and Ben gave Mike his dinner, and then they sat down to eat and talk and wait for the storm to hit. Anna had called them several times that day and told them they were idiots for not evacuating and coming uptown. But at least she knew that in a sixth-floor apartment, they might eventually get hungry when they ran out of food, but they weren't going to drown. She and her friends had watched movies all afternoon, and her parents were glued to the Weather Channel, watching the progression of the storm, which was moving faster than earlier reports had predicted and was gaining speed. Anna and her roommates were tired of watching the same images and interviews repeated again and again on TV. There was nothing to do but wait for the storm to hit, and see how bad it really was.

* * *

It was five o'clock when Gina finally returned Charles's calls. He was nearly frantic by then, wondering where they were. He had been in New York for almost two days, and hadn't heard a word from her. And for once, she apologized profusely the minute he picked up her call.

"I'm so sorry. My phone was dead." She sounded like she was in an airport or a train station, with a huge amount of noise. He could barely make out what she was saying. "Why didn't you tell me you were coming?"

"I didn't know till the last minute. I sent you a text from the airport when I left, and started calling you Friday night as soon as I arrived. Where are you?" He was desperate to see them, and seriously worried about them now, with the hurricane due to hit New York that night.

"We're at a shelter in SoHo. They evacuated our apartment building last night. They just set up a location to charge cell phones, so now I can call you. This place is a madhouse, but the girls are loving it. There are a million kids here, and cats and dogs. They're delighted we have to stay here." Gina sounded relaxed and in good spirits, which was more than he could say for himself after the last forty-eight hours of trying to reach her, with the hurricane bearing own on New York, and no idea where they were.

"Where's Nigel? Is he with you?" Charles sounded worried, but Gina was calm, despite having to evacuate with the girls.

"No, he went out to Red Hook in Brooklyn yesterday, to try and secure his studio and take his cameras and equipment to a friend's. They were planning to be there all last night moving things, and he was going to try to help some of the other guys today. There are a number of famous artists there. And Red Hook was one of the hardest-hit areas last time. He's afraid it might be again. I haven't heard from him since he left yesterday. He said he'd find us. He'll probably show up at the shelter tonight or tomorrow, after things calm down."

"He left you alone with the girls?" Charles was shocked, although he usually tried to refrain from making comments about Nigel to her.

"All the equipment he owns is in his studio. He can't afford to just leave it, and stay with us. He'll turn up sooner or later, and we're fine. The girls aren't even scared. They're happy playing with the other kids. They think it's an adventure." She had packed bags for all three of them, with enough clothes for a few days, toiletries, medicine, and their passports. Hers was important because she had a work visa in it from *Vogue*. And Charles had an idea as he listened to her. He didn't know how she would feel about it, but he would have preferred staying close to the girls.

"Would you mind terribly if I come to the shelter to see them? I don't have to stay if you don't want me to. And if Nigel comes, I'll leave. But I've been waiting to see them all weekend." She hesitated for only an instant as she thought about it, but she couldn't see any harm in it, and she was sure Nigel would understand. He didn't like Charles, but had no real issue with him, since he was the winner in the contest for her.

"That's fine. He'll probably come tonight, but not till late. He couldn't call me either since my battery was dead, so I don't know his plans. But the girls would love to see you."

"Thank you," he said gratefully. "They haven't evacuated my hotel yet, but they might later." She told him where the shelter was located, in a school not far from where he was, and a few minutes later he was braving the fierce winds, and walking toward the temporary shelter three blocks away. It was pandemonium when he got there, with close to a thousand people in the gym and designated classrooms, on cots and in sleeping bags on the floor. Just as she had said, there were dogs, cats, a woman with two parrots in a cage, hamsters, guinea pigs, rabbits, and a boy with an iguana on his head. There were children of all ages running everywhere, and food was being served in the school cafeteria. Charles spent twenty minutes wending his way through the crowd, and then he saw them in the corner of the gym. Gina was talking to a group of women, and Lydia and Chloe were playing tag with their new friends and squealing with delight. Gina didn't see him until he was standing next to her, relieved to have found them. People looked as though they had dressed hastily, and the room was stifling from the heat of a thousand bodies. The smell of food and people was heavy in the air. Gina glanced up at Charles and smiled cautiously when she saw him.

"I can't believe you found us."

"Neither can I." He was wearing jeans, as she was, and a perfectly starched collared blue shirt, with his raincoat over his arm. He looked as respectable as he always did, and she was wearing a

T-shirt with no bra with her jeans, and silver sandals. And by then his daughters had spotted him and came running over.

"Daddy!" they screamed happily, and threw their arms around his legs. "How did you know we were here? Did you come to New York just to see us? A hurricane is coming, named Ophelia."

"There's a girl in my class named Ophelia," Lydia added. "She's mean and I don't like her." Charles smiled at what she said.

"I know about the hurricane," he told them, squatting down with an arm around each of them as he hugged them. "I came on business, and I've been trying to find you since Friday. Mommy just told me you were at the shelter, so here I am." He looked as ecstatic as they did.

"Can we have ice cream? They have some in the cafeteria." A nearby supermarket had donated it to use immediately, before it could melt once the power was off. Gina nodded when Charles glanced at her for her permission. He followed the girls to the cafeteria then, and they were back half an hour later, as the girls finished the last of their ice cream, which had run out by the time they left the cafeteria. He wiped their faces, just as they got to Gina, who was staring at the enormous screen that had been set up, so everyone at the shelter could follow the progress of the hurricane. It had just hit the Jersey shore, and was dragging houses, trees, boats, and several buildings in its wake. The room fell silent as people watched, and knew it would reach land in Manhattan within minutes. The reporter on the screen said that high tide had just been reached. The circumstances had become uncomfortably similar to Sandy in the last few hours. There were weather maps in the corner of the screen, showing where it was expected to hit hardest. Red Hook, where Nigel was, in Brooklyn, was foremost among them, and Charles could see that Gina was worried. It hurt to think it had been a long time since she felt that way about him. She was terrified that something would happen to Nigel. And the weather map showed as well that lower Manhattan was likely to be clobbered, just as it had been before. It seemed incredible that another hurricane so similar to Sandy was about to beat the city to a pulp again. Experts had predicted it as a possibility all along, but no one had believed them. And suddenly the safety measures that had been rejected since Sandy seemed like a tragedy yet again. And without question, people in the suburbs and outlying areas, and even some in the city, were about to lose their homes.

In the next few minutes, they could see on the screen the enormous waves that engulfed the southern tip of Manhattan, Battery Park, the Lower East Side, the Village, Tribeca, the West Side Highway, and Staten Island. It looked like a tidal wave hitting New York. Many of them had seen it five years before, and now here it was again. Charles and Gina stood in shocked silence as they watched with hundreds of other adults in the shelter, while their children went back to their games, oblivious to what was happening on the screen. Watching it made Charles grateful that they were at the shelter, instead of Gina being in their apartment on the Lower East Side, right next to the East River. They could see familiar buildings being battered, and one woman burst into tears watching her ground-floor apartment on the West Side Highway disappear under water, as the river overflowed and swept an entire street of cars away like so many toys, while other vehicles simply disappeared.

"Oh my God," Charles said in a muffled voice, as he instinctively put an arm around Gina's shoulders and pulled her close to him and held her. It was infinitely worse than anyone had expected, and there was no doubt that lives would inevitably be lost as the flood tides rose and swept across the Zone 1 areas that had suffered similar damage before. It was a nightmarish déjà vu for them all. And all Gina could hope, as she watched it with her ex-husband's arm around her shoulders, was that Nigel would survive the waves washing over Red Hook in Brooklyn, and that he had already left his studio. The waves were said to be twelve feet high in some areas, fifteen in others, and the Hudson River had washed over its Manhattan banks again.

The doorman and superintendent came to check on Grace and Ellen again just before the storm was supposed to hit. They were waiting peacefully in the apartment, sitting on the plastic-wrapped couches, with battery-operated lamps around them, and Blanche on Grace's lap. The wind was howling, and one of the trees outside the building had fallen over earlier, but the floods hadn't started. Grace and Ellen heard it distinctly when they did. It was like a roaring and rushing sound, with crashing as equipment fell or was swept along. They looked out the window and saw the entire street of cars disappear beneath the water, and within instants, there was the sound of the doors breaking in the lobby, and they were suddenly standing in several inches of water, which rose to their knees almost immediately, as they escaped up the stairs, while Grace clutched the dog. The water stopped halfway up the stairs for a few minutes, almost as though it were resting, and then continued to climb. All the furniture in the living room was underwater by then, and the flood in her living room was steadily rising. And as Ellen and her mother watched in horror, there was a frantic pounding on the door, and the superintendent of the building and two policemen forced their way in, and pushed open the door. They saw the two women on the stairs, and the men from the rescue unit told them there was a boat outside to get them out, as they waded toward the stairs to reach them.

"You need to come with us," the rescue team told them, and Ellen looked at her mother fiercely.

"We're going with them, Mom." Grace nodded and ran up the stairs. She reappeared with their two small go bags, much to Ellen's astonishment, and she had put on a baby harness and slipped Blanche into it so the dog was secure and she had free hands. The water was to the men's waists, and almost to her chest when she and Ellen came down the stairs. The superintendent grabbed their bags from them and held them high to keep them dry. And the policemen in diving suits half-carried the two women out of the apartment and across the lobby, which had filled with water. The water had reached the dog's collar by then, as Grace pushed the baby harness higher to keep Blanche's head out of the water. They moved through it in total darkness, and as they went through the front door, they saw the boat with the searchlights outside, and the two policemen lifted both women up and heaved them into it. More strong hands grabbed them, and set them down in the boat. Grace and Ellen were soaking wet and barefoot from wading through the water, and Blanche looked like a drowned rat in her harness, but all three of them were alive, and hadn't stumbled or slipped beneath the water as capable hands had guided them through the darkness and water in the lobby out to the waiting boat, which was buffeted by the winds and currents like a toy. There were three other people in it who had been rescued, and the policeman operating it turned up the powerful engine and drove the boat several blocks away to higher land, where they were assisted out, wrapped in blankets, and put in an ambulance to dry off and catch their breath. Someone handed Ellen and her mother towels and dry clothes and rubber flip-flops, which they put on, still shocked by what they'd been through, and then Grace dried Blanche off with one of the towels. The poor dog was shaking. They were led out of the ambulance into a van then, as another boatload of rescued flood victims arrived, and those in Grace and Ellen's group were driven to a shelter close by. They still had their go bags with them, although Ellen was sure that everything in them was soaking wet, and they walked into the shelter looking dazed. Grace murmured something to Ellen about how guilty she felt for not evacuating sooner and taking up the rescuers' time when they surely had more important things to do, but she was grateful they had come when they did.

So much had happened in such a short time that it was hard to absorb or understand. Ellen was holding her mother's arm and guiding her through the crowd at the shelter when she heard someone call her name. She turned in surprise and saw Charles Williams from the plane with a woman and two little girls. But he no longer looked terrified as he had that night—he looked strong, calm, and protective as he reached out to Ellen and gave her a hug. He felt he owed her at least that for nearly breaking her arm when he thought they were going to crash on the plane.

"Are you all right?" he asked, worried about her. The two women looked profoundly shocked.

"I think so . . . we were just rescued from my mother's apartment, in about four feet of water. They got us out in a boat, just in time." They wouldn't have drowned on the upper floor, but they could have on the lower if they had stumbled for an instant, or if they had tried to get out of the building. Even Grace was stunned into silence as Ellen introduced her to Charles, and explained how she knew him.

"And this is Gina, my . . . ex-wife," he hesitated only for a beat before he said it, "and my daughters Lydia and Chloe." The two little girls stared at them with wide eyes, and they were excited to see Blanche, who was still in the harness on Grace's chest that had saved her life while they exited the building. It had seemed like a ridiculous thing to buy for no reason ages ago, but now Grace was grateful she had. Grace took her out of the harness then and cradled her in her arms. Ellen went to get some hot soup and tea for her mother, and left her with Charles and Gina, who led her to the area where the girls' cots were so she could sit down. It had been quite a night so far, and the images on the enormous screen showing scenes of the hurricane were terrifying. Ophelia had turned out to be as bad as Sandy, and was hitting the city and surrounding areas just as hard. And the damage to Grace's apartment that night had been considerably worse than what she'd experienced five years before. Grace looked dazed when she sat down and felt suddenly ancient.

When Ellen returned with the soup and tea for her mother, Grace took it from her gratefully without a word. All she could think of was that they were lucky to be alive, which was what others were thinking as they watched the hurricane's disastrous path.

Ellen insisted that her mother lie down on a cot that Charles was kind enough to get for her, and when Grace fell asleep with Blanche next to her and a blanket over both of them, Ellen went back to the cafeteria with Charles for a cup of tea herself. It had been an incredible, terrifying night.

"I never expected it to be like this," Charles admitted to her.

"Neither did I, or at least I hoped not," Ellen said sadly, thinking of the state her mother's apartment had been in when they left. She was just thankful they had gotten out safely, made it to the rescue boat, and saved her mother's dog. Grace would have been traumatized beyond belief if the dog had drowned. And Ellen was suddenly doubly grateful for the harness.

"I wish I could get my girls out of here and take them home," Charles said in an exhausted voice. "I'd love to take them to a hotel room in the meantime. They were talking about evacuating mine when I left. Gina hasn't heard from her boyfriend yet, and I'm sure she won't want to leave here till she does." His eyes were tired and sad, as Ellen nodded. It was hard to believe what they'd been through, or imagine what still lay ahead.

"Hopefully, the worst will be over soon, and the water will recede again," Ellen told him, still dazed herself. "That's what happened last time. The water went back out as fast as it came in, except in the low-lying areas below sea level, where it stayed." They were still talking about it when they went back to find the others, and Ellen was relieved to see her mother sound asleep on the cot with her dog beside her. They all knew it was a night none of them would forget, and it wasn't over yet. The full force of Hurricane Ophelia, and the destruction she was wreaking, was just beginning.

Chapter 4

The ER got increasingly busy as the night wore on after the hurricane hit. People with minor injuries were brought into the ER, and some with very major ones, among them a man who had been hit by a tree branch that had fallen on him, and he had brain surgery that night but didn't survive it. And the police began bringing people in from the rescue boats by eight o'clock. Some had been injured, and most of them were in shock. Two young children had drowned, swept away by the currents. Others had drowned in their cars, when the waters came up quickly.

Juliette, Will, and the other residents and doctors on duty did triage all night, and raced from one patient to the next. The entire hospital staff had been called in. It was nonstop as they treated triple their normal capacity of patients. They had them lined up on gurneys in the hall—they had run out of rooms and cubicles hours before. And Juliette had just referred a six-year-old to the orthopedic resident for a broken leg when the lights in the ER flickered and dimmed, and then went out, like so many candles that someone had just blown out, and they were instantly plunged into darkness.

Someone said "Shit!" in a loud voice standing close to Juliette when it happened, and she recognized it as Will's but didn't acknowledge she'd heard him. Nurses scurried everywhere, and maintenance men, to set up battery-operated lights, so they could at least see what was around them, but the lights weren't strong enough to treat their most seriously ill and injured patients. It was exactly what had happened at NYU five years before. Then the maintenance men informed them that the backup generators had just died, although no one seemed to know why. It was a serious problem for them in the ER, but a disastrous one in surgery, ICU, and the neonatal ICU (NICU), and for patients relying on respirators or other forms of life support.

As she hurried down the hall to find out what they were doing about it, Juliette could see Will Halter at the nurses' desk, speaking to them tersely.

"Get the boys from the OES in here *now*! Paramedics, the fire department, anyone you can get here. I'm not going to lose patients tonight because the goddamn generator failed." NYU hadn't lost a single patient when it happened to them, and he didn't intend to either. The nurses started dialing everyone they could on their cell phones, including 911, and reported what had happened, as Juliette looked at Will. They were both exhausted, but the real work was only just beginning, with what had happened when the hurricane reached its peak at high tide.

"What can I do to help?" Juliette said to Will in a voice that was calmer than she felt.

"You were right," he said through clenched teeth. "They must not have checked the backup generators. I don't know what the hell we can do now." He looked livid, and scared.

"They managed it at NYU during Sandy—so can we," she said quietly. "We need to send teams of people upstairs when the cops and fire department get here and start bringing people down."

"Where are we going to send them?" He was fighting waves of panic and impressed by how steady she seemed.

"The other hospitals will take them—they have no choice. The cops will help us figure it out. We need to get everyone on respirators out first, and the babies in the NICU, and operate the respirators manually. They're probably organizing teams upstairs already. Thank God we have no code blues in the ER right now."

"Don't say that out loud," he said, worried, as paramedics, uniformed policemen, and firemen started to arrive. The head of the hospital was on site that night and came to talk to them immediately, and a plan was made to get their sickest patients out of the building as soon as possible. With limited power from a few small generators, the decision was made to let the least sick patients stay, so as not to create mass panic trying to get everyone out. All off-duty staff had already been recalled, so they had enough personnel to manage the evacuation.

Juliette didn't see Will again for several hours, and she was talking to one of the nurses about how to handle the patients lining the halls on gurneys when a man in overalls and a fireman's slicker walked in. He had an air of total authority, and moved with lightning speed from one problem to the next. He was in charge of the entire operation of moving their patients to other hospitals that night, and he identified himself to Juliette and the other staff.

"Sean Kelly, OES." He was from the Office of Emergency Services and had an official badge around his neck, and he exuded both tension and calm at the same time. Tension to attend to the task at hand with the utmost precision, speed, and efficiency, and the kind of calm that inspired everyone to do their jobs and give a thousand percent of themselves. He asked Juliette how many patients they needed to move out of the ER. They had just over two hundred people being treated in the unit that night, and she estimated that forty-one needed to be moved to other fully functional hospitals immediately. They would keep the rest. All the ICU had to go, the NICU, and the entire surgical floor.

The OES and NYPD had commandeered all the ambulances they could, and staff from the upper floors were already carrying patients down the stairs, with respirators and without. And she watched Sean Kelly mastermind the entire operation, with all the help he could get from the hospital staff. He ran it like a Swiss clock, and by two A.M. everyone who needed to be was out, and the OES staff on site in other locations radioed back that all patients had made the transfer safely, even their preemies. A cheer went up from the ER staff and on other floors when they heard the news. Will Halter was beaming and high-fived Juliette, then lowered his voice to speak to her.

"Thank you for not saying you told me so," he said sincerely, and actually sounded human. He had been humbled that night.

"Who cares?" She smiled at him. "I'm just happy we got them out safely." It had been the most impressive transfer they had seen, in crisis circumstances, in the dark, with their sickest patients at life-threatening risk. And it had all gone smoothly. It was a modern-day miracle, and Sean Kelly was behind it.

"What are you in real life? A magician?" Juliette said to him when she ran into him in the doctors' lounge, when they were both getting a cup of lukewarm coffee half an hour later.

"Thank you, doctor." He smiled at her. He looked energized, not exhausted like everyone else. He was running on adrenaline and brilliant at what he did. "No, I'm just a crisis junkie. I flunked medical school and should have majored in transportation." She laughed at what he said.

"I was at NYU when it happened there during Sandy. I thought that was amazing. You outdid yourself tonight."

"So did all of you," he complimented her and meant it, and took a sip of the coffee. "It's going to be a long few days for everyone here," he said sympathetically, and she nodded, wondering when she might get some sleep again. Clearly not anytime soon. And something he had said to her had caught her attention.

"Maybe we're all crisis junkies in this business," she said honestly.

"The key word is 'emergency.' In my case emergency 'services,' in yours emergency 'room.' You could have specialized in dermatology or plastic surgery. You didn't. So here we are, running around like lunatics turning disaster into victory. It's a high like no other." He smiled at her again. He was a good-looking man, with powerful shoulders and electric blue eyes that saw everything, and he had a very humane quality to him. He was practical and down to earth, and all he cared about was the lives they saved.

"I guess you're right," she said, looking pensive. "I never thought about it that way. Actually, one of my brothers is a plastic surgeon, the other one is an ENT, he treats runny noses, and my father is an obstetrician. That's kind of a high too."

"Not like ER though," Sean Kelly reminded her, and she nodded. "See ya," he said, waved at her, and went back to work, checking each floor before he left. He wanted to make sure himself that they hadn't left anyone behind who needed to be moved.

Sean Kelly had nailed her as a crisis junkie, and she couldn't say he was wrong, when she thought about it. Not in her personal life, which had been comatose since she entered medical school; but working in the ER, she got her highs. It was a thrill to come to work, and she liked the tension and fast pace. He was right, she admitted to herself, as she threw her empty Styrofoam coffee cup away to go back to work. And he claimed it was true about himself too. It took a special breed to do what they did.

She went back to the nurses' desk then, and they assigned her to a supply closet with a cot in it for two hours, so she could get some sleep. With the hurricane having hit its peak that night, they had a long day ahead of them tomorrow, and probably a long many weeks, and it would be months before the city returned to normal again. One thing was sure—countless lives had been changed irreversibly when Hurricane Ophelia hit New York that night. New Yorkers and the world would remember it forever. And heroes would emerge from it, like Sean Kelly and the rescue teams of the OES.

Peter and Ben hadn't heard from Anna again after midnight—they couldn't reach her on their cell phones, and their landline no longer worked. They sat up and talked for most of the night, listening to the sounds around them, and looking out the window at the flood rushing through the streets below. Cars had been swept along and disappeared. Police boats came by, traveling through the streets, watching for people to rescue, and whenever possible removing them from the places where they were trapped. The engines of the police boats had become a familiar sound through the night. And the building creaked so eerily in the gale-force winds that at times they thought it might be coming down. And they knew there was nothing they could do to get out that night. They were the only tenants left in the building. Everyone else had evacuated, and by morning, they both knew they had made a mistake. They could almost feel the ancient building swaying in the wind. And sensing what was happening, Mike had sat and watched them all night, nervous and alert. Ben stroked him to calm him down and the big black Lab whined as he looked at him with worried eyes.

"It's okay, boy, everything's fine," Ben reassured him, and Mike whined nervously.

As daylight came, after the heavy rains that had continued through the night, the groaning of the building seemed to grow louder, and Mike barked several times as though trying to tell them something, and Peter looked at Ben.

"Do you think we should try to get out?" he asked cautiously.

"I'm not sure we can. The street is still flooded." And they were close enough to the river that the currents would be strong and hard to fight. The water was moving fast. "We could wait for a police boat to come by." But they hadn't seen one in a while, and the building was beginning to sound like a ship trying to break loose from its moorings. Peter didn't like the sound of it, and neither did Ben, or the dog.

"I don't think the building will hold for long," Peter said nervously. "It's beginning to sound really bad."

"Yeah, it is," Ben agreed.

"I was the captain of the swim team in high school," Peter said, wondering what they should do—try to make a run for it, or stay and wait for the floodwaters to recede, which could take a long time. And if the building collapsed, they'd be killed for sure. "What about you? Want to give it a shot?" Peter wasn't sure, but trying to escape was beginning to seem smarter than staying.

"I'm a pretty strong swimmer, but I've never swum through anything like this. And I'm not sure he can make it either." Ben glanced at Mike, who had lain down on the floor with his head between his paws and was whining piteously, as though he didn't like the sound of their plan at all.

"Dogs are smart—he'll probably let the current carry him along, which is what we'd have to do too," Peter said seriously. "We don't have to go very far to get to high ground, as long as we don't get caught somewhere, or smashed into a wall." Nothing that Peter was saying was appealing to Ben, but the sound of things breaking in the building and outside was unnerving, and they watched a tree come down a few feet from their front door and the rushing waters sweep it away like a twig.

"That's what we'd have to watch out for," Ben said thoughtfully, and as he said it, they heard a crash and the sound of breaking glass somewhere in the building, as the wind blew a window in. Theirs had been rattling for hours. "I think maybe we should get out of here," Ben said, looking worried, and then glanced down at his dog. "I guess we could try to leave Mike here."

"What if something happens to the building? We might not be able to come back for him for days," Peter said, and Ben nodded. It felt as though they had no choice. Anna had been right. It had been dumb to stay, and they both regretted it now. The two boys looked at each other and nodded. They were young and strong and in good shape, and figured they could make it to safety, or be rescued by a passing boat. It was better than sitting there waiting for the building to come down around their ears, which sounded like what was about to happen. The groaning sounds had gotten worse just in the last few minutes.

"Let's make a run for it and get the hell out of here," Ben said as he stood up, wondering what they should wear so they wouldn't get dragged down by their clothes. In the end, they decided on jeans and T-shirts, which was what they had on.

They let themselves out of the apartment a few minutes later, and Mike followed them down six flights of stairs to the front door. There was a steep staircase up from the street, and a foot of water in the front hall, which they waded through to get to the door.

"It must be about twelve feet deep out there," Peter commented as Ben nodded and patted the dog, and Peter opened the front door. Ben had put Mike on his leash so he could control him better and wouldn't lose him in the fast-moving water. He could always let go of it if he had to, but it seemed a better way to start out so Mike didn't swim too far from his reach.

Once Peter opened the door, the wind was so strong that it pulled the door right out of his hand and slammed it against the wall behind them. The glass broke and fell into the water they were standing in, in the hall. The two boys looked at each other and exchanged a smile. They both were nervous but sure now that they were doing the right thing and should have done it hours before. But the tide was lower now than it would have been the night before, and it was better trying to escape in daylight, where they could see what was around them in the water.

"Good luck," Peter said to Ben, then walked out onto the front stoop and stepped into the floodwater, and an instant later he was gone, swept away with the force of the current, moving at high speed as he tried to stay on the surface and not get pulled down.

He didn't have time to turn around and watch Ben jump in behind him, holding tightly to Mike's leash. Peter was already out of breath from the struggle when he saw a lamppost coming toward him, and thought it might help slow him down. He tried to maneuver himself toward it, and with a superhuman effort, he grabbed it and hung there for a minute, fighting the powerful forces that tried to tear him from it. Then he saw something dark race past him, and instinctively he reached out with one hand and grabbed Mike's collar. It was the Lab hurtling through the water. Peter turned and tried to see what was behind them, but there was no sign of Ben, just the dog.

"It's okay, boy!" Peter shouted at him, holding tightly to his collar, keeping his head above the water with one hand and his other arm wrapped around the lamppost with all his strength. He didn't even feel a piece of metal slice through his arm as he saw a boat heading toward them. They had seen Peter hanging on, and they sped toward him. The dog was frantic as Peter refused to let go of his collar to keep him from being swept away. The boat was next to him seconds later, and two Emergency Services officers grabbed Peter and the dog and dragged them into the boat. Peter was breathless and nearly unconscious as they wrapped him in a blanket and laid him on the floor, and the dog whined as he lay beside him. Peter waved a hand at them before they could move on.

"No . . . my friend . . . he's in the water . . . we were together, he was with the dog . . ." They looked around the swirling waters, but saw nothing. They headed backward for a short distance, but there was no sign of anyone in the water, and without saying anything to Peter, they moved on, as he slipped into unconsciousness. He had swallowed a lot of water and threw up when he came to again. They brought him to a makeshift dock they had erected for emergency boats, and had ferried the people they rescued to it all night. They signaled for an ambulance for Peter, and as they put him on a gurney and slid him in, he waved wildly at them for the dog. The two men who had rescued him glanced at each other, and one of them nodded and helped the big, exhausted Lab climb into the ambulance, and he lay down on the floor. His leash was still attached to his collar, but there was no sign of Ben anywhere. Peter laid his head down on the gurney and was crying when they got to the hospital. He tried to explain to the paramedics what had happened, and that Ben was still in the water back there somewhere where they had found him.

"Maybe he got ahead of you, son, and you didn't notice. The water was moving pretty fast. We'll tell the boys in the boats to go back and take another look. Just take it easy now."

"It's his dog," Peter said, crying like a child, feeling as though he had stolen Mike instead of rescued him. The Lab barely managed to crawl out of the ambulance and followed the gurney into the hospital. But no one stopped him as he dragged his leash behind him and followed Peter. The nurses in the ER had seen stranger things that night, as the paramedics rolled Peter down the hall, and left him there crying, when they went to fill out the admission forms. Mike lay down next to the gurney with a mournful look, and a little while later, the nurses came to check on Peter. He had his face turned to the wall and he was still crying, as he thought about Ben, and worried about him. All he could hope was that someone had picked him up by then.

"Is this your dog?" the nurse asked gently. They both looked as though they had nearly drowned, which was the truth.

"He belongs to my friend," Peter said, turning to look at her. "They went back to find him."

They had heard a hundred stories like it as the rescue teams brought people in. And not all the stories had happy endings. Many of them didn't. The death toll so far had been higher than they feared. "What's the dog's name?" she asked to distract him as she took his vital signs, and saw the cut on his arm, as Peter continued to cry. She asked Peter his name, how old he was, his address, and if there was someone he wanted them to call. He gave them Anna's number because he didn't want to frighten his parents if the hospital called them directly, and the nurse jotted down the number. "The doctor will take a look at you in a minute," she reassured him, and Mike watched her go, as Peter leaned down and patted him. All Peter could think about was Ben and what might have happened to him after he jumped into the water. The current had been a lot stronger than he had expected, and he hadn't even noticed he had a gash on one arm from when he'd been hanging onto the lamppost. The nurse had made note of it on his chart and was telling Juliette about him as she handed it to her.

"The paramedics said he nearly drowned. I think he may need stitches in the arm. He came in with a dog. He said he was in the water with a friend, but they brought him in alone." Juliette nodded somberly. It was easy to spot him down the hall, with the black

Lab lying next to the gurney, and she could see that Peter had been crying when she stopped next to him and smiled. They had put heated blankets on him to keep him warm. The OES had gotten a series of generators working for them a short while before. Peter was shaking violently from the cold water and the shock.

"How are you feeling, Peter?" she asked him gently. He was badly shaken, very pale, his lips were blue, and they had treated him for shock in the ambulance and when he came in. Like everyone else she'd seen since the hurricane hit the city, he had been through a lot, and from his appearance, so had the dog. She examined Peter's arm and decided it didn't need stitches, and his vital signs were better than she'd expected. He had youth on his side. Anyone older than he wouldn't have been able to survive and resist the powerful force of the water. He told her about Ben while she examined him, and she told him Ben might have been taken to another hospital, depending on where he'd been found, and by whom, and she asked about the dog. Peter was in fairly decent condition, all things considered, but she wanted to keep him for a few hours to observe him, possibly overnight, to make sure he didn't have any more serious secondary reactions from nearly drowning. And he told her he was a junior at NYU.

"Would you like us to call your parents?" she offered, and he shook his head.

"They're in Chicago, and it'll just scare them. I'd rather call them myself and tell them I'm okay. My mom was worried about the hurricane." He felt for his cell phone, but it was no longer in his pocket, and his wallet was gone too. It made him realize that Ben might have lost his too, and if he was injured or unconscious, they wouldn't know who he was. He said something about it to Juliette, and she promised to let him know if a young unidentified male came in, in the next few hours, and he thanked her. He told her what Ben looked like, and then she asked him if he'd mind if she put Mike somewhere out of harm's way, in case one of the patients objected to him, or was scared of him, although he was very well behaved.

"There's a supply closet with a couple of cots in it that the ER docs have been using to get some sleep. I'll put him there and give him something to eat," she promised, and Peter sat up and watched as she led him away. Mike didn't seem to object, and she came back a few minutes later and told Peter she had given Mike half a turkey sandwich and a bowl of water, and he seemed peaceful and was lying down. Peter smiled and lay down on the gurney and thought of Ben again, and drifted off to sleep.

When he woke up, Juliette asked one of the nurses to bring him a phone so he could call his parents. He was already crying before they answered. He told his mother where he was and what had happened, and she burst into tears. He was sobbing as he listened to her. Getting through the water was the hardest thing he'd ever done, and just thinking of it now made him shake harder. He knew he had come close to dying in the water.

"I don't know where Ben is, Mom. He was right behind me, and I grabbed on to Mike. But I didn't see Ben anywhere, and they didn't find him when they picked me up. They said he might have gotten ahead of me, but he was behind me when we left the

house." He couldn't stop crying, nor could his mother, and his father had burst into tears the minute his wife had signaled that it
was him. It had been an agonizing wait for word of him.

"He's probably okay, and they took him to another hospital," his
mother tried to comfort him. It was what Juliette had said to him
too.

"I hope so. It sounded like the house was going to collapse, so
we got out." He tried to explain to her, and she didn't blame him
for not evacuating when he should have—she was just grateful
that he was alive and had called her. They had been trying to reach
him since the night before, but cell service had been poor or non-
existent, and they were worried sick when they couldn't get
through. There was almost no cell phone service downtown by
then, and Ben's mother had called them several times too. Jane
Holbrook wasn't sure now what to say to her when they called her,
but if Peter had turned up in a hospital, Ben might have been
picked up too, by another rescue boat, and taken somewhere else.
If one of them had survived it, the other probably had too. But it
would be hard telling her that Peter had been rescued and Ben was
missing.

They talked for a few minutes, and Peter spoke to his father too.
They wanted him to come home to Chicago as soon as he could fly
and the airports opened. It had already been announced that parts
of NYU had been severely flooded and would be closed for months.
Their buildings extended over a broad area, and those in the worst
flood zone had been badly damaged. And the airports were still
closed or the Holbrooks would have flown in. They wanted him to

come home to recover from his ordeal as soon as he could. Peter didn't comment, but he wanted to go home too, once he knew Ben was okay.

He called Anna after that, and she cried as soon as she heard him, and they both sobbed when he told her that Ben was missing. "I grabbed Mike when he went past me, but I didn't see Ben anywhere. Has he called you?" Peter asked her, and Anna said he hadn't. She promised to come to the hospital if he stayed there, and she said she could take Mike home with her until Ben got in contact with them. After they hung up, Anna's mother called Ben's parents, to see if they'd heard from him. They had just spoken to the Holbrooks in Chicago, and Ben's father was calling all the hospitals to see if they had anyone matching Ben's description who had been rescued from the flood. It was agony waiting to hear from him, and getting through to the hospitals and obtaining information was hard. Everything was chaotic, and information was sparse.

Anna's mother went to see Peter that afternoon, and brought him some clothes and a pair of her husband's sneakers, which fit him, and he clung to her like a child and cried. There was still no news of Ben, and no sign of him at the hospitals his parents had called. All they could do was wait until he reached out to them, or they located him at a hospital.

Juliette decided to keep Peter for the night when he ran a fever, and she checked on him several times. She told him that Mike was doing fine, that one of the nurses had taken him for a walk on her break, and everyone loved him and was feeding him. Peter had asked Anna's mother to leave the dog with him. He liked knowing he was there, like a piece of Ben he had with him, and the hospital didn't mind. When Peter went to check on him in the supply closet, Mike was ecstatic to see him. Peter sat on the floor next to him with his arms wrapped around him until a nurse made him go back to bed.

"What about his friend?" the admitting nurse asked Juliette while she made a note in his chart about the fever.

"We don't have him here, and I gather no one has heard from him," Juliette answered quietly, and the nurse nodded. There was nothing else she could say. It was a familiar story by then, of people who had lost track of each other in the flood. And Juliette knew that sooner or later, they would find Ben's body, or he'd call home. Until then all anyone could do was hope.

Chapter 5

The noise level where Ellen and her mother were was deafening, the lights were on constantly, children cried or played and ran around. Conditions were crowded, people were upset, and it was like trying to sleep in an airport or a train station, and between the stress of what they were all going through and the chaos around them, no one could get any rest. Grace looked exhausted and every bit her age on Monday morning, after the hurricane hit the city the night before. It had arrived with lightning speed in the end, much faster than predicted, and with greater force. Ellen felt no better than her mother, and Gina and Charles were wiped out too. There was almost no cell service, with very rare exceptions downtown, so Ellen could no longer reach George. And just as had happened with Sandy, the news channels reported that the city was virtually untouched uptown. All the serious damage and flooding had occurred south of Forty-second Street, only a few blocks higher than the last time. Charles told Ellen that he would have liked to find hotel rooms uptown for all of them, if possible. His hotel had been evacuated too. But Gina had already told him she wouldn't go. She still hadn't heard from Nigel, and he had agreed to meet her at the shelter whenever he could. Most of the bridges into the city were closed, and she suspected that he hadn't been able to leave Brooklyn yet, and Red Hook had been one of the places hardest hit. She thought he might still be trying to salvage the equipment in his studio. She didn't want to just disappear to a hotel uptown and leave him worried sick when he came to look for her. It didn't seem right, however tempting Charles's offer of comfortable accommodations was.

"If you can even get a hotel room uptown," Ellen commented when he told her. "Lots of people are trapped in the city. The hotels uptown must be full." They were talking as they got trays of food for the others in the makeshift cafeteria. He said his kids were living on potato chips and popcorn and he was letting them. The Red Cross and restaurants and hotels uptown were donating food to the shelters. And Ellen said she had drunk enough coffee to keep her awake for a year. They exchanged a smile. Ellen would have liked to get her mother to a hotel soon, but the word on TV and around the shelter was that there wasn't a hotel room to be had anywhere in the city. Those who could organize it quickly enough had gone uptown the day before, some even before the evacuation was announced, fearing what would come. And now it was unlikely they could find a hotel room anywhere. All the hotels were full with people who couldn't leave the city, tourists who couldn't go home when the airports closed, and anyone who had fled the trendy neighborhoods downtown. For many of them, money was not an issue, and they had filled the hotels the day before.

"So I guess we're stuck, at least until Nigel shows up in our case," Charles said, as they juggled the food trays back to their cots where the others were waiting for them. Ellen was impressed by how calm he was. The basket case he had been on the plane, clutching her arm, bore no relation to the man he was now. He had his wits about him, was wonderful to his children, and kept them entertained, playing games with them and telling them stories for hours. For lack of anything better to do when they were bored, he walked them around the shelter so they could count how many dogs they saw, or how many cats, or black or white dogs, anything to keep them distracted and amused. And he was patient and respectful of his ex-wife, despite her obvious concern over the man she had left him for. Ellen admired Charles for how protective he was of her and said as much to him.

"I loved her for a long time, and I guess my heart has taken a while to catch up," he said ruefully. "And she's the mother of my children after all." The way he said it made Ellen wonder, as she often had in the past four years, if she would have that noble role one day. Being a mother seemed like the highest honor of all. It made her sad thinking about it, as it always did, but for now they had other things to worry about. And her mother was already asking when she could go home, at least to take a look. There were police lines threaded throughout all of downtown, which no one was allowed to cross, with electric lines down, in some sad cases drowning victims in the streets, trees still liable to fall with weakened roots, and buildings at risk of collapsing. By Monday morning, the floodwaters had begun receding, but not enough, and some buildings were reported to be flooded with ten or fifteen feet of water, filling the basements and part of the ground floor in many cases. And there was no telling when Grace would be allowed to check out her home. Ellen was nervous about the shock Grace would experience when she did. She had been through it once before, after Sandy, but this seemed like a lot for her to go through a second time. She was, after all, seventy-four years old.

"How's your mother holding up?" Charles asked her as they wended their way through the crowd and passed the boy with the iguana. It had remained on his head most of the time since he'd arrived, and Ellen made a face as they passed him, and the lizard stuck out its tongue as Charles laughed. They felt like old friends now. "She seems remarkably plucky, after all she's just been through." And Grace had been very sweet with his children and let them play with her dog. Blanche was shaken up and nervous too, but still sweet with the children.

"She was convinced it wouldn't be as bad this time, and the apartment was already underwater when we left. The lower floor at least." Wading out of the building in water to their waists and chests had been an unforgettable experience for Ellen and her mother. "I think it's going to be pretty bad when we go back. Possibly a total loss, and she loves her home." It was a bit like living through a war. Natural disasters took everything with them, with no regard for what one loved, or what one did or didn't have, or how well one had prepared. Ellen had a strong sense that all her mother's neighbor's help with the preparations had been in vain, despite his good intentions and theirs.

When they got back to the others, Gina was worried, and talking about Nigel again. They had just shown scenes of Brooklyn on the screen that was powered by a generator, and all of Red Hook looked as though it had been destroyed. Fourteen people had drowned there, and Gina was terrified that Nigel might be one of them. Charles put an arm around her and comforted her, like a brother or a friend, without taking advantage of the situation, or whatever lingering feelings he had for her. Ellen admired him more than ever. She talked to her mother quietly when she insisted that she wanted to at least try to get back to her building and see if the police would let her in for a look.

"I think it's too soon, Mom," Ellen said gently, feeling bad that she hadn't been able to call George. He must have been worried sick about them, and would be in his office by then. But there was no way she could call him, until they got to an area where her cell phone would work again. Their cell phones had worked sporadically in the beginning but less well now, with lines vastly overloaded by people calling in and out.

"It just said on CNN that the floodwaters are receding," Grace insisted. "Last time they let me in to look ten hours after the storm. It's been sixteen now. We can always come back here if they won't let us in." She was determined to try and was stressed all day, waiting to go home, while Ellen worried about contacting George, and Gina cried every time she thought of Nigel. It was an unnerving day for them all.

And almost like the vision of a romantic hero, a handsome, fiercely disheveled man with long hair and an unkempt beard, but a taut athletic body, in rough boots and jeans, cut through the crowd and strode toward them. The moment she saw him, Gina screamed and threw herself into his arms, as Charles turned away discreetly and looked at Ellen. She raised a questioning eyebrow, and he nodded. It was Nigel. He held Gina in his arms for an instant, then peeled her away from him, and paid no attention to the two little girls or anyone else around them.

"Thank God . . . I was so afraid something happened to you . . . ," Gina said breathlessly, and together the two of them were a striking image of youth and beauty, however bedraggled they both were. "It said on the news that fourteen people drowned in Red Hook." She had been terrified for him.

"I lost all my equipment. The studio is ten feet underwater," he said, looking devastated, without asking how she and the girls had fared, or expressing relief that they had survived too. It struck both Ellen and Charles simultaneously, though neither of them commented. "Do you realize what that means to me?" Nigel went on. "And of course I have no flood insurance. I spent the entire night helping all the artists out there load their canvases into vans. We managed to save a lot of their work, but none of mine. My negatives are gone too. It's a tragedy." He was nearly in tears as he said it, and Gina expressed her heartfelt sympathy with her arms around his waist.

"I'm just grateful you're alive," she said in a deeply moved voice.

"It will take me years to replace that equipment, and the negatives are irreplaceable. Thank God I left my old negatives in England," he said as he looked around, noticing their surroundings for the first time. "My God, what a dreadful place this is. So many children and old people." He made a face as Grace and Ellen watched him with interest, almost like a character in a movie, which was what he seemed like. There was an unreal quality about him, and his blatant narcissism came right through his pores. "Why didn't you go to a hotel?" he asked Gina in surprise.

"We didn't have time. The police evacuated us, I had to leave everything at the apartment, except some clothes for the girls. All the hotels downtown are flooded. And I didn't want to leave here until you came—I didn't want you to worry if we just disappeared and went uptown." She didn't tell him that Charles had been begging to find them a hotel room uptown, whatever it took to get one.

"You should have. I've got a ride back to Brooklyn in a few minutes. I came over to drop some artwork off at a friend's." He hadn't even come especially to see her, which wasn't lost on Charles. "I've got friends in Red Hook I still want to help." And a woman and two children at a shelter in Manhattan, whom he supposedly loved. There was no evidence of it in his eyes or his words. "You really ought to try and get out of here as soon as you can. The noise alone would drive me insane." They weren't enjoying it either, but Gina had insisted on staying for him, so he could find them. And then it was as though he remembered her children as an after-thought and looked down at both of them. "Having fun, girls? It's an adventure, isn't it?" He didn't wait for their answer but turned back to Gina with a distracted look. "I've got to go. They're waiting for me. I'll see you back at the apartment whenever I can get back in. It won't be for a few days."

"Take care of yourself out there—it's still dangerous. Where will you be staying?"

"God knows, most of Red Hook was destroyed last night. I'll find a bed somewhere. I'll call you when I have cell service again." And with that, he gave her a peck on the lips, forgot to say good-bye to the girls, ignored the others, and pushed his way through the crowd to the exit, with a look of irritation and disdain as peo-ple blocked his path by virtue of sheer numbers, and without a glance back at Gina, he was gone. It was all about him, and he hadn't even bothered to tell her to take care, when he went back to his friends waiting for him outside. And he hadn't offered to take her with him, which Charles would have objected to anyway, for the safety of their children. But Nigel apparently had no interest in them at all, and no concern for Gina.

Seeing him there had been a somewhat shocking experience that illustrated who he was, and Gina wasn't oblivious to it either. There were tears in her eyes when he left, and she turned away from Charles so he wouldn't see her cry. He made no comment and chatted with the girls, but he had gotten a full on view of who and what Gina had left him for, and so had she. She went to get a cup of tea then, or so she said, and when she came back, she said to Charles quietly that maybe they should try to go to a hotel, if they could find one anywhere. She didn't say it, but there was obviously no point waiting for Nigel here. And Charles no longer had business to conduct in the city, since all the Wall Street firms were closed, and Wall Street itself and the stock exchange were underwater. All he had to do in New York now was help Gina and their girls. It was his only mission there.

"I'll see what I can do," he said quietly, and went to stand on line for one of the landlines they had just set up for people at the shelters. Ellen had tried that to call George, only to discover, after she'd stood on line for two hours, that the phone lines were set up only for local calls, not international, so she couldn't call him. In one fell swoop, they had lost all the conveniences of modern technology and civilization. It was like camping out in the dark ages, as someone said while she'd waited on line. But for the most part, they were relieved to have a place to go, however noisy, uncomfortable, and limited it might be. It was better than being in danger in their homes, and all the children seemed to enjoy it, far more than the adults, who were uncomfortable, stressed, and exhausted.

Gina was quiet and looked distressed, thinking of Nigel's visit, after Charles left them to use the phones, and Ellen said nothing to her. She sat quietly talking to her mother, as she held Blanche and fretted about seeing the damage to her home.

Charles was back an hour later, and announced that he had

found a hotel room in the East Fifties. "It sounds pretty awful," he said honestly. "It appears to be a second-rate hotel, but someone told me to try it. All the decent ones uptown are booked. I tried those too, and this one as a last resort. It's called the Lincoln East, and they only had one room. They'll give us rollaways for the girls, and I can sleep on the floor, if it's all right with you. I don't mind. Or you can just take the room, and I'll stay here, although I'd rather be close to you and the girls. I don't want you wandering around the city alone right now, even uptown. What do you think? I reserved it and paid with a credit card, so we've got it if we want it." Gina looked immensely thankful and relieved. The shelter was wearing on all of them after nearly forty-eight hours. Two days of noise, discomfort, and chaos among a thousand people was rough on anyone at any age.

"Let's all go," Gina said gratefully. Charles had taken the situation in hand, and was taking care of them, and made her feel protected, instead of Nigel making her feel abandoned. There would be a lot to say about it, after the hurricane was over. She didn't like the way he had left her to her own devices, and seemed not to be worried about her or the girls. They weren't his children, but she had expected more of him, and he was disappointing her severely. This was the first time she had seen such extreme evidence of his selfishness. He had always been sweet to her before. But Nigel had never taken care of anyone in his life, or been responsible for anyone. And he clearly cared more about his artist friends than about Gina and her girls. She was suddenly deeply grateful for Charles, and remembered how he had always been there for her, and he still was. And he seemed stronger and more in control than ever now, and she knew that she and their girls were in good hands. Charles had risen to the occasion like the gentleman and kind human being he was. She had forgotten just how reliable he was till now, and how reassuring that could be. "Let's get out of here." She smiled at Charles. "And I don't mind your sleeping on the floor in the same room, or I will. I can share a cot with one of the girls, and you can have the bed."

"We'll figure that out when we get there. Gather up your things. We'll need to find a cab outside, which may take a while." There was no public transportation, and many of the garages that housed New York taxis had been flooded, but there were a few on the streets. And traffic heading uptown, with many of the streets flooded downtown, was said to be ferocious. The news had said that getting from the devastation of lower Manhattan to the unaffected areas uptown could take as much as four hours, with streets blocked and flooded, no traffic lights, and power lines down.

Charles said a quiet goodbye to Ellen. He had given her his cell phone number for when their phones worked again. He told her to call him if he could do anything to help her, even after the storm. He had asked her if she wanted him to find a hotel room uptown for them too. Ellen asked her mother, but Grace was adamant that she wanted to stay downtown, even in the shelter, and move back into her apartment as soon as possible, whatever the damage. She was very firm about it, so Ellen thanked him and said no.

They kissed the children goodbye, and both little girls kissed Blanche before they left. Ellen wished Gina luck, she would need it with Nigel, although she didn't say that. And she and Charles hugged.

"Take care of yourself, Ellen," he said, looking moved, and sorry to leave her and her mother at the shelter.

"You too," she said, thinking how strange it was that they had become friends on a turbulent flight from London and now in the hurricane in New York. Crises of this magnitude brought people together as nothing else could.

It seemed lonely at the shelter to Ellen once Charles and his family had left, and her mother commented on Nigel's appalling behavior.

"It's amazing the foolish choices we make in life, some of us anyway. Her ex-husband seems like such a good man. The boyfriend is sexy, but he doesn't give a damn about her," Grace said wisely, and Ellen concurred.

"I think she saw that too. But I think Charles is a little too square for her. She's a beautiful girl, she's ten years younger than he is, and he seems like kind of a traditional businessman. The poor guy was terrified on the flight from London. Nigel is gutsier and more masculine in a sexy way, but he clearly never gave a thought to her or the girls." Ellen had been shocked and could say it now.

"The more traditional choices last a lot longer, but they're always less exciting," Grace said philosophically. It was what Ellen had figured when she married George. There was no one more conservative or classically British. She had had her share of racy, irresponsible boyfriends, but George was the kind of man one married, even if she had had to adapt to his ways. It had been an adjustment for her at first, and he wanted everything done his way, but she had accepted that as part of being married to him, and she loved how solid and dependable he was.

It was still surprising to her how different the British and Americans were. The differences between them were vast, but she had come to like their ways. And they were always loyal to their own, and now she was one of them. She wanted to introduce Charles to George when they went back to London—she was sure they would like each other, and were very much alike in some ways. Solid, traditional men with conservative values, who believed in the right things.

The afternoon dragged as they watched the same images on the news over and over. Flooded streets in Tribeca, Red Hook destroyed in Brooklyn, Staten Island less decimated than the last time due to safety features they had put in place, New Jersey a scene of mass destruction, Coney Island leveled yet again, the Rockaways as vulnerable as before with the loss of many homes, and the East River and Hudson having flooded everything on their shores. It was tiresome and depressing watching it, and Grace took Blanche for a walk to get some air. She had just joined Ellen again when they both saw a tall man wend his way through the crowd toward them. It was Bob Wells, Grace's neighbor, and he was clearly looking for them. He gave Grace a warm hug when he reached her, and she was thrilled to see him.

"What are you doing here?" she asked with a look of surprise. It was a miracle that he had found them but he had been looking for hours. He was wearing rubber fishing boots that he said his agent had lent him, and rough clothes, but he was a sight for sore eyes in the noise and chaos of the shelter that had become their temporary home, along with a thousand others.

"I can't get through on your cell phone," he said simply. "They said on the news a little while ago that the police are letting people through in some parts of Zone 1, among them Tribeca—not to move back in but to assess the damage in their homes, retrieve documents, and salvage what they can. Some buildings are still too flooded to enter, or too dangerous if walls collapsed, but in some cases, they're letting residents go in. I want to give it a try, and I wanted to know if there's anything you want me to bring back to you." It was a kind offer and nice of him to stop by on his way. He had rented a large, solid SUV, and Grace gave him a grateful look.

"I'll go with you," she said quietly.

"I don't think you should," he said respectfully, glancing at Ellen, and she agreed. "It's pretty rough, Grace, worse than last time. The water level is higher in some places, and the sewer lines have broken again." The last time he and Grace had both found open sewage in their apartments when they went back, it had seeped into everything, and the stench had been sickening. He wanted to spare her that, and the shock of what they would see. But Grace refused to be convinced to stay at the shelter, while he went back to their building to observe the damage and salvage whatever he could.

"If they're letting people back into some buildings," which they hadn't heard yet, "I'm going, with or without you, Bob, even if I have to walk." Grace wasn't a woman to be daunted, by natural disasters or anything else, no matter how tired she looked, and her red hair, the fiery color it always had been, was a tangled mass, and she looked as big a mess as everyone else. Bob was neater and cleaner, staying in the comfort of his agent's apartment uptown, and there was no way he would let Grace go to their building alone. He wanted to be there to help.

"You're sure?"

"Of course." She gathered up her things before he or Ellen could stop her, and looked like a soldier ready to march, as she clutched Blanche and put her back in the harness she'd worn. Bob smiled at her. He had always liked her, and had strong feelings of affection for her now.

"You realize it will probably be pretty bad. Prepare yourself for a shock, Grace."

"I will," she said, as they followed him out. They had decided to take their belongings with them, so they weren't stolen while they were gone. It was much like staying at a homeless shelter, where the people might be good or bad.

He had left the SUV he had rented double-parked with the lights flashing, and he helped Grace get into the high vehicle, for the ride to their building. The roads were so blocked by police lines, deep water, overturned cars, and debris that it took them an hour to travel the short distance to their building, and it was after four o'clock when they got to their block and were stopped by police. Bob explained that they lived in a building just down the street. He showed them the address on his driver's license as proof. The police were keeping out journalists and the curious, and all three of them noticed two ambulances with firemen around them, which meant that they had removed bodies from the street. It was a sobering scene.

"We just want to go in to get a few things, officer. Some important documents we left behind and will need." The young policeman hesitated, nodded, and waved them through. He was wearing heavy rubber boots himself, and there was evidence of sewage in the street even before they got to the building. Ellen tried not to be sickened by what she saw, so she could be fully functional and helpful to her mother when they arrived. This was not a scene for sissies—she knew she had to be strong. And her mother was, with her face set in hard lines, looking straight ahead as they drove past the policemen to her building, parked the car among the debris outside, and got out. Everywhere they looked were broken objects, shattered glass, overturned trees and shrubs on the sidewalk, and unrecognizable objects that the floods had carried along. There was a crane hanging crazily at the end of the street, and the area had been roped off. And all three of them were careful not to step on any electric lines—it was impossible to say which were live wires. Nothing was safe or secure right now.

When they got to the entrance of the building, the familiar superintendent was standing outside with a devastated expression. He explained that one of their favorite doormen had died, drowned in the basement, and his body had just been removed. They sobered further at the news, as they entered the darkened lobby and made their way past a crumbling wall. All the lobby furniture had disappeared and had floated into the street the night before. It brought back instant memories for Grace and Ellen of their exit from the building in water past their waists. There were still several inches of water, to their ankles, as they walked to the apartment, and Grace took out her keys, while Ellen held her breath, and Bob stood with them to lend his full support. There was a short flight of stairs up to the apartment, so Ellen assumed the water would have receded, but there was still a foot of it inside. And once they opened the door, they waded through it between furniture that had been moved and overturned, couches and chairs that had become sponges for sewage and floodwater. The smell was evil and the destruction downstairs complete despite the pieces carefully wrapped in plastic, which had been torn off by the force of the floodwater. The apartment was dark with no electricity, and the three of them made their way upstairs, where broken windows had allowed the water to enter freely, but most of what they had put away upstairs was safe, except for the beds, which had turned into sponges as well, and all of Grace's coats and furs were soaking wet. Most of the clothes in the closets looked like they could be saved, and the paintings high up on the walls were intact, but objects were found helter-skelter in every room. Some had even been transported downstairs, and most of what they saw looked unsalvageable. It was easy to believe that Grace could have drowned if she'd stayed there, particularly alone. Tears rolled silently down her face as she observed the scene, and touched favorite objects like people who had died. It was heartrending, and Bob and Ellen cried with her, as even Blanche hung silently in the little harness on Grace's chest. For several moments Grace said not a word.

"I think it might be worse this time," she said simply, and Bob agreed. It was an overwhelming feeling of helplessness to see almost everything you owned upended and destroyed. Ellen suspected that like the last time, some favorite objects could be saved, with diligent restoration work, but it wouldn't be easy. And most of what she owned was gone. Grace had always been a big believer in insurance, so Ellen knew that once again her insurance company would help, and they had been wonderful the time before. But there would be treasures and things of sentimental value that could never be replaced. And it would be hard to start all over again, and would take enormous energy and courage.

Ellen hated what she saw around her for her mother's sake, and knew how long it would take to restore and rebuild the apartment, repair what could be fixed, and replace so many things, and she'd have to find someplace else to live in the meantime for several months.

"Well, it won't be easy," Grace said, drying her eyes, as she unconsciously patted the dog, "but we'll get there." She smiled weakly at Bob and her daughter. It was sad to see all that she had lost, and then they went next door to Bob's, and it was even worse. Since his furniture wasn't of great value, he had done less to protect it, and almost everything in his apartment had been demolished. He had left his clothes in the closets downstairs, and they were a sopping mess, and almost everything in the apartment looked unsalvageable. Only some of his books and manuscripts on a high shelf upstairs were intact. Nearly everything else in his apartment looked like it belonged in a Dumpster. Both Grace and Ellen knew from the aftermath of Sandy that there were companies that restored nearly everything. Special book restorers who froze volumes while still wet, then dried them page by page. Remarkable furniture restorers. Others who handled furs, although all of Grace's had been irretrievable before. Dry cleaners who worked on leathers and fine fabrics. Her insurance company had helped Grace with all of it before, and it had taken months for the final results, but looking at the contents of Bob's apartment, it was hard to believe that any of it could be saved, and there was the same stench of sewage as at Grace's, and his living room walls were so saturated that they looked as though they might come down. There was little they could do now. They would have to do triage to figure out what had to be thrown away, and what should be sent to restorers, which was minute, meticulous, time-consuming work that would take months and cost the insurance company a fortune. Ellen had helped her mother with it before and would again, and Grace looked at Bob and patted his arm.

"We'll help you, Bob," she said gently. "It may not be as bad as it looks." He sighed and smiled at her, and wiped a tear from his cheek. It was upsetting for him too, and would have been for anyone.

"It's worse than I thought," he admitted. There were framed photographs of his children underwater, and all of his books other than his own. "I guess we have our work cut out for us, don't we?" He smiled at his neighbor, and after a few more minutes of the depressing scene, they left and made their way through the lobby and back to the SUV. Ellen was particularly grateful that they had gone there with him—it had been comforting to share the shocking first sight of the damage with him, and they supported one another.

Ellen assumed he would drive them back to the shelter, and he looked at them as soon as they were in the car again.

"Won't you come uptown with me? My agent has an enormous apartment on Central Park West. He would love to help out, and he's a nice man. He told me to bring you with me if you were willing. At least you can get some rest, instead of at the shelter with all that noise and all those people. I'm going to stay there for the duration, and you can stay as long as you want."

"I would hate to impose on him," Grace said, looking uncomfortable, but the shelter was undeniably exhausting, and she had barely slept since they got there. "Maybe for a few days," she hesitated, "until we can get a hotel room, or I can find a temporary furnished apartment. It took me almost four months to set everything to rights last time," which was too long and too costly to stay at a hotel.

"Seriously, he won't mind. I think he enjoys the company. He's a widower with no children, and he likes to help his friends." But they were strangers to him, which Grace found embarrassing. Ellen was willing to do whatever her mother wanted. At this point, it was unlikely they would find a hotel room, or even a furnished apartment, anytime soon. And she thought it might be a relief to stay with Bob's agent for a few days, even though Bob wasn't a close friend. But they were all in the same boat now, and Bob was a kind man, and obviously fond of Grace, and Ellen by association.

"All right," Grace said in a soft voice, still overwhelmed by what she'd seen. She had lost her home again. "We'll go uptown to your friend. But we won't stay too long, I promise," she said, looking apologetic. And both Ellen and Bob were relieved. They didn't want the shock and hardships she was enduring to impact her health, and they easily could.

It took them two hours to reach Forty-second Street in the chaos of downtown, having to make constant detours, and getting stuck in traffic, as people tried to get to or from their damaged homes, on streets that were impassable or destroyed. And it went more quickly after that, once they were in the unaffected part of town. It was nearly seven o'clock when they pulled up in front of a well-known building on Central Park West, with a uniformed doorman waiting outside. It was like being transported from hell to heaven, as Grace stepped out of the car looking tired, and Bob and Ellen followed. Bob handed the doorman the keys to the car and asked him to put it in the garage. The doorman recognized him immediately. He had the keys to James Aldrich's apartment and said that Mr. Aldrich was expecting them. They were familiar with Bob and knew he was staying there.

Bob let them into the apartment, and it was like stepping into another world. It was enormous and handsomely decorated in a masculine style. He had beautiful antiques, important paintings, and it was obvious that both an architect and a designer had worked on the apartment, which looked more like a house and occupied two floors. Grace recognized immediately that she had seen it in several architectural magazines over the years, but didn't know who it belonged to. And its owner had collected unique treasures and works of art on his travels. Like bedraggled victims of a shipwreck, Bob led them into the library, while Grace suddenly hoped Aldrich wouldn't mind the dog. This was a very impressive home, and she and Ellen both felt lucky to be there. Jim Aldrich was the most important literary agent in New York, and his art collection was famous in the art world.

Bob preceded them into the library, and strode across the room to a man quietly working at his desk. Their host looked up as soon as they arrived, and came to greet them with a welcoming hand and a warm smile. He looked thrilled that they were there, as though it were a long-awaited visit and not an imposition, and he went straight to Grace, thanked her warmly for coming, and patted the dog.

"I had an English bulldog I adored for thirteen years. I lost him two years ago, and I miss him dreadfully. I haven't had the heart to get another one. I'm so glad you brought yours—it will put a little life in the place. Thank you so much for coming." He smiled warmly at Grace as she stared at him. They were intruders, and he was treating them like greatly anticipated, welcome visitors, and was even nice about her dog. Jim was obviously as kind as their mutual friend. He chatted with Ellen as he showed them to their bedrooms, both of which were elegant and as beautifully decorated as the rest of the apartment, and Ellen felt as though they had landed in some kind of fairyland after what they'd been through at the shelter, and just seen at her mother's apartment. And in the elegant atmosphere of comfort and discreet luxury, Grace looked and sounded more like herself again and not like the victim of a disaster.

"We have food for you in the kitchen whenever you're ready," Jim told them. He was anxious to ask Bob how things were in his apartment, but was afraid to do so in front of Grace, in case she had suffered terrible damage in hers. A few minutes later Bob filled him in, that both apartments had been destroyed and very little could be saved. He said it had been a terrible blow to Grace, and he thanked Jim for letting the two women stay with him.

"I've always been an admirer of her work as an architect," Jim said candidly, looking relaxed. "And I'm happy to do whatever I can to help. From everything I see on TV, downtown looks like a nightmare. I'm glad you're all right at least. You can always get another apartment. But there's only one Robert Wells," he said warmly, and Bob smiled.

"I think this one did me in," Bob admitted. "It's too traumatic living down there, if this could happen again. I made a decision when I saw my apartment today. I'm going to move uptown."

"There's an apartment for sale in this building, if you're interested," Aldrich said easily, and Bob looked doubtful.

"This is a little grand for me. I like the bohemian side of Tribeca, but not the risk of natural disaster. Maybe a small apartment somewhere, even in this building, but not as big or elaborate as yours. I'd get lost in it, and my kids hardly ever come to New York, so I don't need a huge apartment," Bob explained to him.

"Neither do I," Jim admitted, and he had no children or family at all. "But I like it anyway. I guess it's the show-off in me. But I'll ask if there's something smaller in the building for you. I think you've made the right decision to move, and I'm relieved to hear it. Drowning in a hurricane in lower Manhattan would be such a stupid way to die." And it could easily have happened, and had to others. The hurricane had turned out to be far more dangerous than many people had wanted to believe.

Jim and Bob talked about business for a moment then. Jim had had an interesting offer for him that afternoon to sell another of his mystery novels for a film in L.A., not to write the screenplay, which Bob never did, but simply to sell the book for a major movie with first-rate stars in it, and Jim thought he should agree. The two men had become good friends in the twenty years Jim had represented him and initially launched his career. And Bob attributed his considerable and very impressive success to him. Jim had unfailing judgment in the business, was a master negotiator, and had represented Bob well, with rewarding results for them both. Bob had recently turned forty-nine, and Jim was twenty years older than Bob, although he didn't look it. But over the two decades he had represented him, Jim had gracefully shifted into the role and appearance of a distinguished older man. He was as tough as ever in business, but a little mellower privately than he had been in his youth, when he had been known as something of a firebrand. Bob loved that about him too, and had a profound respect for him as an agent and a friend. And he was very touched by his offer to let

Bob's neighbor and her daughter stay with him in the aftermath of the storm, which was so typical of Jim, who never failed to help a friend, even someone he scarcely knew.

Bob went to call his children then. He had called them the night before to reassure them and tell them he was at Jim's. But after seeing the destruction in his apartment, he wanted to call them again. They were both sad to hear how much he'd lost, and grateful that he was willing to sell the place and move uptown. It sounded like a sensible decision to them.

As Ellen unpacked the pathetically few items she had brought in her go bag, and thought of the suitcase of clothes that were now soaking wet in her mother's apartment, she wanted to call George immediately and tell him where she was. She could well imagine that he must have been frantic trying to reach her for the past two days. It was midnight in London by then, but even if she woke him up, she knew he would be relieved to hear from her, and upset if she didn't call as soon as she was able.

She used the landline in the spectacular guest bedroom she'd been given, told the operator to bill the call to her mother's home phone, and listened as the phone rang in their house in London. George sounded sleepy when he answered.

"I'm sorry, darling, I haven't called you in two days. We've had a hell of a time, and my cell phone didn't work downtown. We had to evacuate from my mother's apartment, after she initially decided to stay. We waded out in water almost to our chests, had to go to a shelter, and we just went back to her place today. She lost everything. I just got uptown so I could finally call. I'm sorry if you were worried." She told him all the pertinent information rapidly so he could understand her silence.

"When I didn't hear from you, I assumed you were fine," he said, sounding very British and half asleep. "I tried to call you a few times, but nothing went through, and I heard on the news that cell phones weren't working in the affected parts of the city. I knew you'd turn up eventually. How's your mother?" he asked, seeming surprisingly matter-of-fact. Ellen had expected him to be panicked about her, and even Grace. This was the first time she had ever heard him sound so calm, while knowing she might be in danger.

"My mother is being very brave," Ellen answered, "but understandably very upset. She just lost everything, or close to it. The apartment was nearly destroyed."

"She'll just have to move," he said simply, as though it wouldn't matter to Grace, which Ellen knew it would, and the way he said it seemed a little heartless to her. Grace was very attached to her apartment, and loved living in Tribeca, which George knew, but she had to be sensible about it now, even if it was painful for her. Ellen suspected that it was going to be a battle, but she intended to try to force her to listen to reason. "You're all right?" he asked, sounding cool, which seemed strange to Ellen, since he had been so worried about the hurricane when she left. But sometimes he was that way and got very British and unemotional. He seemed to be in that mode now, and appeared to be neither affectionate nor concerned. She had thought he would be worried sick about her, especially with no word from her.

"I'm fine, but it's been pretty rough. The shelter was a mad-house."

"You really shouldn't have gone to New York," he said almost coldly. "You should have changed your plans and stayed here. It's a bit ridiculous to fly into New York in a hurricane, don't you think?" He seemed irritated, and far less sympathetic than she'd expected.

"Of course not. What about my mother? I couldn't leave her alone to face that. I'm glad I was here, even if it was scary and a mess. And I never thought it would be this bad when I left. But I'm glad I was here for her."

"She's a lot tougher than either of us. She would have been fine." He wasn't the least bit worried about them, or even compassionate, and she was upset. He acted as though she had just been in some minor summer storm, while he enjoyed his weekend with his friends. And his lack of concern for her mother didn't sit well with her either. It wasn't totally uncharacteristic, but seemed unusual, extreme, and particularly inappropriate in the circumstances. She had envisioned him frantic about them, while she had agonized over not being able to call him. And she had the impression that he couldn't have cared less. "Where are you now?" he asked her dispassionately.

"Staying with a friend of my mother's neighbor. He was very kind and took us in. New Yorkers are wonderful in a crisis. We're uptown, and it's totally normal up here, so I could finally call. We just got here half an hour ago."

"You mean the famous mystery writer who lives next door to

Grace?" George knew his books too. The whole world did, and he had read some of the ones her mother had given her, and thought he wrote extremely well, and was impressed Grace knew him.

"Yes, his agent. Bob is staying here too, and I was relieved for my mother. The shelter was too hard for her. I don't want her to get sick, and there isn't a hotel room available in New York supposedly, or damn few. We're going to have to find her a temporary apartment. I'm afraid I may get stuck here for a few weeks while I help her sort it all out, and deal with the insurance. I don't want to just leave her alone to face this on her own," she said apologetically.

"Whatever you need to do," he said, sounding unworried and practical, which wasn't like him. He usually complained vehemently if she stayed away too long.

"Are you mad at me?" she asked him bluntly. She wondered if he was jealous that she was staying at Bob's agent's home, but he didn't seem it. Mostly, he seemed indifferent, which came as a shock to her.

"Of course not," he said quickly. "I think we need a break anyway. When you're home, the baby-making thing always becomes an issue. It's exhausting." They hadn't tried in three months, but he still felt worn out about it. She hadn't told him she was planning to see a specialist in New York, for another opinion about her chances. The last doctor they'd seen in London had been pretty bleak. And since adoption and surrogacy weren't options for them, and she didn't want a donor egg, they had to pull it off on their own, with IVF and the hormone shots she gave herself. She had heard great things about the doctor in New York and was hopeful again.

"We haven't pushed it for the last few months," she reminded George, and he sighed in answer.

"I don't know, Ellen. I just can't do it anymore. It's too depressing. We need to make our peace with it, and accept the status quo of being childless." It was the first time he had said that to her, and she was shocked, and tears sprang to her eyes. He sounded utterly fed up as he said it, with her as well as the process. "You don't always get everything you want in life. And things don't turn out the way you plan. You think you can control everything down to the last detail—well, it doesn't work that way. Nature has its own plan."

"That's a big statement to make over the phone," she said, crying. "When did you decide all that?" And why now, when they had just survived a hurricane and she hadn't slept since yesterday, which he could have guessed.

"Oddly enough, I thought about it a lot this weekend, although I've been thinking about it for a while. But several people there this weekend don't have children and don't want them. I'm not so sure that's a bad thing. And even if we have them, they'll go to boarding school at seven or eight, so what will we really be missing? A few years of nappies and bedtime stories, and then they're gone?" They would be if they did it his way, and their sons went to Eton. In his family, even girls had been sent away to boarding school by nine or ten, and he was adamant his children would do the same. It was his way or no way on that score, and he had made it clear to her right from the beginning. If she wanted to be married to him, she would have to adopt all his British traditions, and she had till now. But she expected him to compromise about their children, and it didn't sound like he would. He had never been that clear before. "And we're a lot freer without children. We can do whatever we want, travel, pursue our careers. Maybe it's a blessing it hasn't worked." She considered it the greatest heartbreak in her life, and the worst disappointment, not a blessing. She had been pumping herself full of hormones and undergoing unpleasant procedures, and enduring crushing disappointments, to have a child. Their failure to have a baby was far from a blessing to her. She was shocked by what he'd said.

"I don't see it that way," she said, with an ache in her heart, and changed the subject. "How was your weekend?"

"Great fun!" he said enthusiastically, wide awake now, since they'd been chatting for a while. "It was marvelous! Lots of good people, old faces and some new ones. You would have loved it." It was clear he'd had a ball, while she and her mother had gone through hell in New York. Her feelings were hurt as she listened to him go on about his weekend.

She gave him the number at Jim Aldrich's then, and told him her cell phone would work uptown once she charged it, but not when she was downtown at her mother's, helping to clear the apartment.

"Call me at a good time for you," he told her. "I have a busy week, and I don't want to be chasing you and catch you at a bad time." He didn't seem anxious to speak to her, and she felt her heart sink as they hung up. Something was wrong—she knew it. He didn't sound like himself, he had been cold on the phone, and his no longer wanting a baby and being willing to accept defeat on that score was bad news to her. He had cooperated with the plan until then, but now he gave her the impression he was done, and didn't mind not having children. That was a 180-degree change for him, and a heartbreak for her. And what would it mean for their marriage? She wasn't sure.

Her mother walked into the room a few minutes after she hung up and saw the look on her face.

"Something wrong?"

"Not really. George is just being very English," Ellen said sadly.

"He always has been. You never seem to mind it, but he has very traditional ideas, and he's not exactly warm and fuzzy. You turned yourself inside out for him, and said that was what you wanted. But he's always going to be who he is. You're not going to change him, if it's bothering you now. And after ten years, it's a little late for you to complain about it." Ellen nodded, not wanting to explain it. Her mother knew how hard she had struggled to have a baby and thought she should either have adopted or given up years before. She thought Ellen was wrong to force nature's hand to that degree to have a child. It was too stressful for her and even for her husband. And apparently now George agreed with her. Ellen felt suddenly entirely alone in her pursuit of a baby. She had just lost her last and most important ally, and if he was no longer willing to cooperate, then her battle to have a child was over. She couldn't do it alone.

Ellen's heart was in her shoes when she went to join Bob and Jim Aldrich in the kitchen. Bob could see that she looked troubled and assumed it was everything she'd been through in the past few days. Jim didn't know her well enough to see it. And the four of them had an easy, pleasant dinner at the big round table in the kitchen. The meal was delicious and impeccably served, and the refugees enjoyed the blessing of normalcy in lovely surroundings, and a relaxed evening with a gracious host. After the chaos of the shelter, it all seemed so civilized.

They all went to their rooms after that. Grace and Ellen languished in the bath in their respective bathrooms, Grace even shampooed Blanche, and Bob read his most recent manuscript and made some corrections. It was the kind of evening they all needed, before they faced the next wave of challenges. And without a doubt, there would be many in the days ahead. Of that each of them was sure.

Chapter 6

On Tuesday morning, before Peter even woke up at the hospital, Ben's parents, Jake and Sarah Weiss, heard their phone ring. Adam, their youngest son, was already awake, playing video games, and picked it up. He was in his parents' bedroom a moment later, as his mother sat up in bed. They had been up until very late, calling hospitals again, trying to find Ben. No one had seen him.

"Mom," Adam said in a hoarse fourteen-year-old voice. "It's the police." It was the call they had both dreaded and longed for for days, hoping to hear that he was in one of the city's hospitals, alive, even if injured. They had talked to Peter the day before, and they were relieved that he had made it. They knew he had Ben's dog, and agreed to let Peter keep him until they heard from Ben.

Jake was awake by then, and sat up in bed next to Sarah when she answered, while Adam watched them, as anxious for news of his brother as they were.

"Yes, this is Sarah Weiss," she responded to the officer on the line. He and a dozen other officers had been assigned the detail of calling next of kin, to tell them where their relatives were and in what condition. Only the most senior officers in the unit made calls like this one.

Her husband watched her face as she listened and squeezed her eyes shut briefly, and then nodded. "Yes . . . yes . . . I understand . . . where is he now?" It was torture for both Jake and Adam listening to her, not sure of what was being said at the other end. She said very little. "Where do we find him?" It sounded as though he was at a hospital, and then she thanked the officer and hung up, as uncontrollable sobs seized her, and she looked from her younger son to her husband.

"They found him on Henry Street, several blocks from his house. He died from a blow to the head, probably when he was pulled under the water and struck by something. The cause of death is listed as drowning . . . oh my God," she said, looking at both of them. "He's dead . . . Ben is dead. . . ." She couldn't believe it and didn't want to, as she sobbed in Jake's arms, and Adam joined them on the bed and wrapped his arms around them, holding on for dear life for fear he would drown too, just like his brother.

The three of them lay in bed for an hour, crying, holding on to each other, trying to understand what had happened to the boy they had loved so much. And why had Peter made it and Ben hadn't? How could life be so cruel?

After a while they got up and went to the kitchen together. Sarah made coffee for herself and Jake, and toast for Adam. She told Jake what the police had said, that Ben was at the morgue, and they would have to identify the body and claim him later and make "arrangements." She couldn't imagine it. And after they had coffee, Jake called John Holbrook in Chicago to tell him, and Sarah called Anna's mother, Elizabeth, to tell them the news. The two women cried on the phone for a long time, and then Elizabeth went to tell Anna. They decided that Elizabeth would tell Peter in person, and he could stay with them until he went back to Chicago. She was sure that once he was released from the hospital, he would want to see Ben's parents, but they had enough to deal with right now, planning a funeral for their son. They all knew that Ben's death would be an unbearable blow to Peter too, and he would have his own private agony to live through, not just the loss of his beloved friend, but also the inevitable guilt that he had survived the flood tides and Ben hadn't.

Anna cried piteously when her mother told her, unable to believe the news. And Peter's parents were devastated. They were waiting for the airports to open, to bring Peter home, and now they had even more reason to come to New York. There would be a funeral for Ben, which they would attend with Peter.

The hurricane had turned into a nightmare for Ben's family, and Adam was inconsolable and couldn't stop crying. His brother Ben was his hero, and now he was gone. And Ben's parents acted like zombies as they moved around the apartment, trying to decide what to do next. They could barely think as they wandered into Ben's room and sat on his bed. It was inconceivable that he would never come home again.

*   *   *

Anna's mother was standing next to Peter's bed in the emergency room when he woke up. They had put him in a back room in a small cubicle, and had gotten him out of the hallway the night before. Elizabeth was grim-faced and solemn as she looked down at him, and all he could think of with a wave of panic was that something had happened to Anna, but she had been all right when he last spoke to her the night before, and she had promised to come and see him that morning. Her mother had told her that he needed to rest and get over his ordeal the day before. And once they heard about Ben, Elizabeth had decided to come alone. Anna was distraught at home.

"Is Anna okay?" he asked, sitting up, as Elizabeth nodded, her eyes filling with tears as she looked at him.

"She's fine . . . they found Ben this morning," she said in a tragic voice, as she gently took his hand in her own.

"In a hospital somewhere in the city?" He was both panicked and hopeful all at once.

"A few blocks from the apartment. They think the flood carried him there. He was struck on the head and drowned." They had found his body between two overturned cars on the sidewalk, but she didn't tell him that. What she had said was hard enough.

"Oh my God," he said, looking as horrified and grief-stricken as she did, as she put her arms around him and they cried together. "The doctor said you can come home with me. You can stay with us until your parents get here from Chicago. I talked to your mom this morning—they're going to come as soon as they can."

"I want to see his parents and Adam," Peter said with desperation. He wanted to explain to them how it had happened, and tell them he had wanted to search for him and told the rescue workers to go back and find him. He didn't want them to think he had forgotten. He explained it all to Elizabeth again, and she nodded. She believed him. "I tried to do everything I could to find him." And Elizabeth realized better than he did that Ben might already have been dead by the time they rescued Peter from the lamppost. He might have died very quickly, and she said as much to Peter as they waited for the doctor to sign him out.

"I'm sorry about your friend," Juliette said quietly when she came to examine him, change the dressing on his arm, and sign the release form. His eyes filled with tears in silent answer, and he nodded.

"Yeah, me too," he said hoarsely, and after he left the cubicle, he dressed in the clothes Anna's mother had brought him, went to get Mike, and met her in the waiting room. She looked as pale and shaken as Peter as they left the hospital together and took a cab uptown to the apartment, where Anna was waiting for them. Ben had been like a brother to her, and she couldn't believe he was gone. She reached out to Peter the moment she saw him and clung to him for dear life as they cried together over their lost friend. Mike watched them, whined, and lay down near them with his head between his paws.

The atmosphere in the house was somber, and as soon as Peter had eaten something, he and Anna took a cab to the Weisses' apartment. The Weisses had just come back from the morgue after seeing Ben, and were sitting silently in the kitchen, looking dazed, when Anna and Peter walked in with the dog, who was excited to see them. Adam had asthma and wasn't supposed to get too close to him, but he loved him anyway. Ben had gotten Mike when he moved into the apartment, since he had never been able to have a dog because of Adam. But Peter wanted to bring Mike back to them now. It was right that they should keep him, in memory of their son. Adam wrapped his arms around the dog and started sobbing, and Peter cried as he watched.

Ben's parents hugged Peter, and listened as he explained what had happened, why they hadn't evacuated, which he readily admitted now had been a mistake, but they had thought they didn't have to. And he explained how they had left the building the morning before, afraid that the building might collapse around them. Risking the floodwater had seemed like the lesser of two evils, which had turned out to be the gravest mistake of all.

"You couldn't know that," Jake Weiss said kindly, with an arm around his shoulders. "You did the best you could, and so did Ben, in a bad situation. I probably would have done the same thing you did. Waited it out to see how bad it got, and then made a run for it."

"We should have come uptown with Anna and stayed with you," Peter admitted, as tears rolled down his cheeks, and Adam sat watching them. He knew he would regret all his life that they hadn't.

"No one thought the hurricane would be this bad," Jake said sadly. "And he might have made it—you did. You can never predict what's going to happen in life." He was trying to be philosophical about it, and kind to the boy who was clearly consumed with guilt for surviving. "We're glad you made it," he said softly, as Anna and Sarah cried, and they went to Ben's childhood bedroom. Sarah wanted Anna to have something of Ben's to take with her, and Adam sat looking devastated and stroking the dog, even though he knew he wasn't supposed to touch him, he was so allergic to him.

"I brought Mike back for you," Peter told Jake quietly after the women had left the kitchen. "You should have him. Ben would want you to. He loved him."

"I know he did, but we can't, because of Adam. I think Ben would want you to have him. It's a piece of Ben you can keep with you, a part of your life together." A life that was over and would never come again. Ben would never go back to NYU, or graduate, or grow up, or marry, or have children. They had thought of it all morning. His life had ended at twenty-one, at the end of his boyhood, and he would be young and healthy and vital and handsome in their hearts and minds forever, just as he had been the day he died. "You should keep Mike, and take him back to Chicago with you, if your parents will let you." Peter knew they would, since they had a golden retriever at home and loved dogs, and his father had loved Mike when he'd seen him at the apartment.

"They won't mind," Peter said tearfully, touched by the gift of the dog he had rescued and loved for all the time he'd known him.

"Do you think you'll come back from Chicago?" Jake asked sadly. An era was over. The school would be closed for many months, and he suspected that the memories of the hurricane and how it had all ended would be too painful for Peter to return.

"I don't know," Peter said honestly. "I don't know what I'll do now." It was all too new and too fresh to try to make decisions. "My parents want me to come home for a while."

"I think that's a good idea," Jake said, as Peter melted into his arms and started sobbing.

"I'm so sorry . . . I'm so sorry I couldn't save him . . . I didn't know where he went, and I couldn't see him anywhere, just Mike as he went past me. I would have saved Ben too if I could have."

"I know you would have," he said, crying himself as the two women walked back into the kitchen, Ben's childhood friend and his mother.

They stayed for a little while longer, Peter kissed them all good-bye, and he and Anna left with Mike and went back to her place in a taxi. Peter was silent on the ride home, wrung out by the emotions of seeing Ben's parents and Adam. Even Mike was quiet as he sat at Peter's feet on the floor of the cab. He acted as though he knew bad things were happening and he was mourning Ben too. Peter had never seen him as quiet. And when they got back to Anna's apartment, the two friends sat together for a long time, talking about Ben and everything that had happened. Like all the other students at NYU, she had the rest of the semester off now too, and hadn't given any thought to what she would do in the meantime. Maybe nothing.

There was suddenly no sense of romance between them, although they had been dating for nearly two years, but it was as though they were too powerful a reminder to each other of all they'd lost with Ben.

"Is it over with us?" she asked him softly, when there was no one else around. The question had haunted her since they had learned of Ben's death that morning. She wanted to be with Peter now, for the comfort it offered both of them. Her romance with him seemed both superfluous and inappropriate now. It was a time for mourning, not love.

"I don't know," he said, as honest with her as he had been with Ben's parents about their leaving the apartment. "It feels weird now, doesn't it?" he admitted, looking at her sadly. They had had a good time together, but now it felt like part of the distant past, a time they had shared with Ben and couldn't anymore without him. They had lost too much.

"It does to me too," she admitted, confused by the fact that it seemed so over now, to both of them. She had thought it was only her, when she first realized it, but now she knew that Peter felt that way too.

"Do you mind my staying here?" he asked cautiously, feeling awkward with her.

"Of course not. Where else would you go?" And he had stayed there with her before.

"My parents should be here in a couple of days when the airports open. I can stay at the hotel with them when they get here." The funeral was set for Friday. He was glad they hadn't asked him to speak at it, he knew he couldn't have. Just being there would be hard enough.

Elizabeth ordered pizza for everyone. Peter and the three girls had dinner together that night, and afterward the girls watched a movie but Peter went to bed. He was exhausted. None of them had commented on the ugly gash on his arm, when he took the bandage off—they knew only too well how he had gotten it. Mike lay down next to Peter's bed in the guest room, and Peter let his hand drop down so he could touch him. Mike was his dog now, a gift from Ben and his parents. And he wished with all his heart that he wasn't, that Mike still belonged to Ben, and he was here to claim him. Peter rolled over in bed and looked down at Mike with tears in his eyes again. "I'm sorry, boy," he said softly. "I miss him too." Mike whined and licked his hand, and then laid his head down on his paws, as they both thought of the friend they had lost, the boy they loved so much.

By Tuesday night, the seriously ill and injured had gone to other hospitals, and the moderately ill as well, due to their lack of enough generators to function fully, and having to rely on battery-operated equipment. And the less seriously ill patients were starting to go home. They still had overcrowded conditions in the ER, as people continued to come in, but it was a little less insane than it had been. And they were still operating at full staff, with everyone's time off canceled. Juliette had been there since before the hurricane, sleeping in the supply closet, usually with another resident or one of the nurses on the second cot. She would have slept on the floor in a train station by then. It no longer mattered, and she could have slept standing up. The few hours of rest she was able to grab in the supply closet were enough, although she missed the dog when Peter took him home. She had been sad to see him so distraught when he got the news that his friend had died, but it wasn't surprising. There had been too many other stories like it, and she knew that it would take Peter a long time to recover. More than likely, he would be traumatized by the memory of it forever. She and her medical colleagues could treat their injuries and their bodies, but how the survivors' minds reacted to what they had experienced was harder to treat or predict.

She was on a dinner break at ten o'clock that night when Sean Kelly came by to check on things at the ER and get a sense of how many patients they were treating and for what, to add to their statistics for a federal report to FEMA. More fatalities were being discovered every day, and bodies were turning up in apartments, on streets, and in basements and garages, particularly old people and children who had drowned, but there were many adults too, people who had tried to swim for it, stayed too long in their homes, or tried to rescue others without the resources, expertise, or equipment to do so. And as always, heroes had emerged, and remarkable stories were being related by the media. Juliette had begun to feel as though there had never been a time when Hurricane Ophelia wasn't a part of their lives. It was all they talked about or thought of.

"Have you been home since the hurricane?" Sean asked her as they walked down the hall together, while she described her caseload to him for his report.

"No. I haven't been out of here in days," she said. "It doesn't matter. I'm sure the place is a mess if it got flooded, but it wasn't so great before that." She smiled at him, and he laughed. He could easily guess that homemaking wasn't her strong suit. She was too dedicated to her work and too focused on it to care about much else, or her apartment, and residents in the ER had crazy schedules and more important things on their minds. He could sense the kind of doctor she was.

"I feel the same way," he admitted. "If my apartment got bombed, I'm not sure I'd notice." She laughed at what he said—they had that in common. "Where do you live?" he asked, curious about her.

"A few blocks away, on Twentieth Street. I got the place for convenience, not its beauty. I'm never there anyway, except to sleep." She didn't seem to mind it.

"That's what I meant. You're a crisis junkie. So am I. We all are in this business. It's not a crime. Do you ever think about having a personal life?" She laughed out loud at the question.

"Yeah, like when I retire. Even my father was never around when we were kids. He was always delivering babies. And ER is even crazier. I figure I'll have kids maybe in my fifties or sixties."

He smiled as he looked at her. She was a pretty woman and would have been even more so in street clothes, makeup, and combed hair, which he suspected she never bothered with either.

"You can manage to do both, or so I'm told," he said ruefully. "You can actually have a life and work in emergency services."

"Really? Let me know how when you figure that one out," she said, although she knew that some of the residents were married, usually to doctors who worked as hard as they did, and then they never saw each other. And she also knew that a lot of the regular ER docs cheated on their wives with the nurses, or other doctors, and she didn't want to be a candidate for that life.

"Do you date?" he asked her when they got to the cafeteria, even more curious about her. She didn't seem to care that she didn't have a life, and had made her peace with it. He thought she was too young to do that. But so was he. At thirty-five, he hadn't had a serious relationship in four years. He just went from one natural disaster to the next, with little time to breathe in between.

"Sometimes. I dated the chief resident on the ER service for about five minutes. He was a jerk." She didn't know why she was telling Sean that, but he was easy to talk to, and he'd asked her.

"Oh, that," he said, smiling. "I've had my share of those too. What we do doesn't give one a lot of time to shop around." And then he surprised her. "After you grab something to eat, do you want to take a ride to your apartment, so you can have a quick look around and see how bad the damage is, if you have time? I can get you back here pretty fast, and lend you a hand if you need it." It was a kind offer, and she was touched by it.

"That would be nice. I'm a little scared of what I'll find."

"You might be able to save something you couldn't otherwise if you go now. And you'll probably be on double duty for a while." She nodded her agreement, said she'd run in and grab a sandwich, which was all the cafeteria had for the moment anyway. They had brought in more generators to keep the refrigerators running so they could feed the staff and the remaining patients. And she said she could be ready to leave with him in five minutes. He waited for her, and with her sandwich in a bag in her pocket, she followed him outside. His OES truck with the light on top was parked at the curb, and she got in next to him and gave him her address.

"So what brought you here from Detroit?" he asked, as they drove the few blocks to her apartment. She had told him in a conversation earlier and forgotten about it.

"I didn't get the residency I wanted in Chicago," she said honestly. "And I got a great one here, so I took it. It's worked out fine. I like New York. What about you? Where did you grow up?"

"In New York. In Queens. I'm a local boy—maybe that's why I care so much about the city and the people in it." She knew they both had to care about people to do what they did, and care for strangers who were in distress or extremis.

They were at her apartment by then, and she took her keys out of her wallet. He parked the truck and followed her inside. It was a depressing building, and her apartment was on the ground floor, which didn't bode well for possible flood damage, although she was far enough from the river that she might have been spared.

He had brought a powerful flashlight with him so they could look around, since the whole lower part of Manhattan was still without electricity, and he could see clothes and clogs on the floor, a stack of medical books on the table. Her bed was unmade, and there was nothing on the walls.

"Ah, I see Martha Stewart is your decorator," he said, teasing her. She had a large fruit bowl on the table with two stethoscopes in it, and a salad bowl full of medical samples to give away, as Juliette looked around, surprised at the lack of damage.

"It looks pretty much the way I left it," she said, gathering up a pile of hospital scrubs in embarrassment and tossing them on top of the hamper in the bathroom, and she tried to make order of the clogs.

"Do you spend any time here at all?" Sean asked her, startled by how spartan it was. It was worse than he'd expected. It looked like a crash pad, which was all it was to her. They checked the fridge, and there was nothing in it except a shriveled lemon and a Diet Coke.

"Not if I can help it," she said, laughing, in answer to his question. "All I do is sleep here, and change the sheets when I have time. Sometimes I sleep at the hospital, if my breaks between shifts are too short. And I never eat at home."

"You're actually worse than I am," he commented. "I have two Classic Cokes in my fridge and a Pellegrino. You beat me on the lemon. But I think I might have a three-year-old frozen pizza in the freezer." And then he startled her even more. "Any interest in having dinner with me sometime? A real dinner, not my antique pizza. It looks like we both need it." He was smiling at her in the eerie light from the flashlight.

"That would be nice," she said softly, although she couldn't see how either of them would maintain a relationship. It wasn't in their job descriptions, but maybe they could be friends.

"Do you ever dress like a girl, when you're off duty?"

"Sure, at my first communion. I had a white organdy dress. And my sister-in-law gave me Victoria's Secret underwear for Christmas." He laughed at what she said. "It still has the tags on it."

"I think we'd be good for each other," he said bluntly, as they got ready to leave. There had been nothing to do in her apartment, but he was right, she'd been relieved to see that it hadn't flooded, and she hadn't lost the few things she had there. She would have hated to lose her medical books and even her favorite clogs. It had taken her two years to break them in.

"How do you figure that? Wouldn't you rather go out with a girl who wears real clothes, high heels, and makeup? I've been kind of saving all that for when I finish my residency. I don't like being distracted from my work." That much was true, and dating had never seemed as exciting to her as her medical studies.

"Maybe we both need more of a life," he said, looking at her intently.

"True," she agreed with him, and she liked him. She liked his honesty, the career he had chosen, and his apparent lack of ego, unlike egomaniacs like Will Halter at the ER. "But why me?" What was it that he saw in her? She couldn't imagine. She never thought of herself as a femme fatale, or even particularly attractive to men. She was so used to working side by side with them that she no longer thought of them as potential romantic partners, just as colleagues and buddies, and she knew all their failings and flaws.

"Easy answer to that one," he said as she locked her front door and put the keys in the pocket of the doctor's coat she wore over her scrubs. "You're beautiful and smart, and kind. That's an unbeatable combination, and hard to find," he said, as they got back in his SUV.

"Yeah, nice guys are hard to find too, and smart ones." She smiled at him as he turned the key in the ignition. "And most doctors have such huge egos. It's hard to take them seriously, or want to spend five minutes with them." Sean wasn't like that, she could tell, despite his good looks. But like her, he was oblivious to his own attributes.

"So what do you think? Dinner sometime when things calm down?" he asked as they drove back toward the hospital.

"Sure. Why not? Just give me enough warning to borrow a dress from one of the nurses," she teased him, and he shook his head.

"No, I like you fine the way you are. Don't bother. You look great in scrubs," he commented. "Just wear the underwear your sister-in-law gave you, if we get to know each other better." Despite the baggy hospital clothes she wore, he could tell that she had a great figure.

"Maybe I've been saving it for you and didn't know it," she said playfully, and then turned to him after he parked the truck outside the ER. "Wouldn't it be weird if something nice happened to us as a result of this fucking awful hurricane, which has done terrible things to so many people? Maybe there's a blessing in it some- where. I haven't thought about my personal life in years."

"Me neither. Meeting you the other night woke me up, and re- minded me that I'm thirty-five years old and we're not dead yet. We help people survive catastrophic events, but we have a right to some joy ourselves. Do you ever think about that?"

"No, but maybe we should," she said seriously. "It's their catas- trophes, not ours. It would be nice to have some fun together."

"Now you're talking." He smiled at her and had an overwhelm- ing urge to kiss her, but he didn't. When and if it happened, he wanted it to be special and meaningful to both of them, not a ca- sual throwaway, which it would have been then. "I'll come by to see you tomorrow," he promised, as she hopped out of the truck and turned to smile at him.

"Thank you. I had a great time. And thanks for letting me check on my apartment. I'll try to remember to buy a new lemon the next time you come by."

"Fantastic!" She waved at him, and walked back into the hospi- tal as he watched her. He had never picked up anyone he had worked with before, but there was always a first time. And he had known the moment he laid eyes on her that there was something special about her, and now he was sure he was right.

"Where have you been?" Michaela asked her when she walked back into the ER. She was twenty minutes late coming back from her break, which was rare for her.

"I went to check on my apartment," Juliette said as she took the sandwich out of her pocket and took a bite before she went back to work.

"How was it?" Michaela asked, looking concerned, ready to offer sympathy for flood damage in her home.

"About as bad as it was before the hurricane. But no worse. It was dry as a bone. I really have to do my laundry when we get some time off. I must have fifteen sets of scrubs lying on the floor." The head nurse laughed and shook her head.

"Why don't you just throw them away and take some more? No one will know or care."

"Great idea!" Juliette said, tossing the rest of the sandwich away as she grabbed a chart and headed down the hall. She was smiling to herself, thinking about Sean, and looking forward to their date, if they ever found the time and it ever happened. But suddenly she hoped it would. He was cool. It made her wonder where the Victoria's Secret underwear was, and if she'd given it away. Or hung on to it and buried it somewhere. She'd have to look, just in case.

Chapter 7

The hotel Charles had found for Gina and his daughters turned out to be better than he had thought it would be. It was small and certainly not elegant, or as pleasant as the apartment that Gina had rented on the Lower East Side, with her own money and support from him, but it was adequate for what they needed now. Gina still hadn't gone to check on her apartment, and didn't know if the police would let her. Many areas were considered dangerous and inaccessible, and she wasn't sure about the status of hers, and Charles didn't want her to go there yet anyway. It was still chaotic downtown, where the power hadn't been turned on yet, so she'd be checking out her apartment in the dark, like so many others. He told her he'd help her when they knew it was safe.

The hotel they were in was in the East Fifties, not too far from Central Park, and he took Gina and the girls there to play and go for walks around the model boat pond, which Lydia and Chloe loved, and then they had tea at the Plaza, and he bought them the book about Eloise. Gina wasn't surprised—he had always been a good father, just not exciting enough for her. When they'd married eight years before, she had been forced into a life she wasn't ready for and hadn't wanted at the time. But after a year in New York with Nigel, she was less enamored with the fast life than she had been when she met Charles. And the people in that world could never be relied on, as Nigel had just demonstrated.

Charles took them out for every meal, and thought of fun things for the children to do, and he stayed with them when Gina wanted to do some shopping. She was still worried about Nigel, although she was upset with him. She hadn't heard from him since he'd come to see her at the shelter. She was half annoyed about it, and half concerned for him and the dangers in Red Hook described on the news. She would have liked to hear from him, and had tried to call him, but he still had no cell service where he was.

And true to his word, Charles was sleeping on the floor in their hotel room, and a good sport about it. She had offered to take turns with him, every other night, but he'd bought a sleeping bag, and said he was perfectly comfortable on the floor, and he had bought some jeans and casual shirts to go out with the kids, so he didn't look ridiculous in the business suits he'd brought for work. And as usual, Gina looked spectacular in whatever she wore, mostly T-shirts and tank tops, miniskirts and skintight jeans. She could put on rags and look great, although he was dismayed to see that she had gotten a tattoo on her back. It was a flower, but it wasn't his thing, and he didn't comment when he saw it. She was no longer his wife, as he had to remind himself when they went out together. Sometimes when they were with the girls, it felt like the old days when they were a family, and he had to tell himself again that they were divorced, and she was in love with someone else.

But in spite of that, one night when the girls were asleep, he asked her if she would consider coming back to England for a few weeks—not to get back together, which he knew she didn't want, and it was obvious she was still in love with Nigel, whether he was worthy of it or not. But he wanted her to come home with him so she and the girls could recover from the ordeal they'd been through, and to avoid the mess in New York right after the hurricane.

"Just so you and the girls can catch your breath. Their school will be closed till Christmas anyway." It was being used as a shelter for hurricane victims, so they had no school until January.

"I don't know." Gina looked surprised by his suggestion. "I might. But I want to be here for Nigel," she said honestly. "I don't want to just run off and leave him." Yet he was doing exactly that to her, with two children, and not even checking on her. From what Charles could see, Nigel was concerned only about himself. And Gina and her daughters were not high on his list of priorities.

"Just keep it in mind," Charles said easily. "I have no ulterior motive. I just think it would be good for you and the girls, and I'd love having them in London for a few weeks, while New York gets put back together."

"Maybe they could go back with you," Gina said thoughtfully.

"Let's see what Nigel says when I hear from him again." Charles nodded, still trying to be fair to a man he loathed and had no respect for. He thought his behavior at the shelter had been deplorable, but he said nothing to her. And Charles wondered when Nigel would show up again. He seemed to be in no hurry for news of her, and assumed she could take care of herself. She probably could, Charles realized, but why should she have to if Nigel was in love with her? Charles's views on the subject were far more traditional than Nigel's. And yet it was men like Nigel who turned Gina on. Although Charles could tell she was upset by Nigel's lack of communication with her after the hurricane, he could also see that she was clearly not ready to give him up. Whatever his failings in Charles's eyes, all that mattered was what Gina thought about him.

Ellen had spent the first morning in Jim's apartment calling her mother's insurance company and reporting what had happened. They had promised to get an appraiser there as soon as possible to assess the damage, but said it might not be anytime soon. Everyone in lower Manhattan was calling their brokers to have them come and assess flood damage and their losses. But at least now they were in line. And she called several real estate brokers Grace knew, and told them that her mother would need a temporary furnished apartment of some kind for several months. Grace was still determined to repair the damage, however long it took, and go back, and Ellen was hoping to reason with her in the coming days. She couldn't see her mother taking the chance that a hurricane could wipe her out for the third time, in two years or five or ten. It was too dangerous and too stressful. Ellen thought it was time for her to get sensible and get out of Zone 1, but she knew it was too soon to broach the subject with her. And for now what Grace needed was a place to stay. She couldn't stay at Jim Aldrich's forever, they hardly knew him, no matter how kind and hospitable he was, and Grace was the kind of woman who needed her own space and own life. She was too independent to be a houseguest for many months, no matter how generous her host.

The realtors told Ellen that half of New York was looking for temporary furnished apartments, and it wouldn't be an easy task to find one, but they would check through the listings they had and get back to her. And in the meantime, Grace was comfortable at Jim's, and they had their work cut out for them. They had to empty the unsalvageable debris from Grace's apartment, send whatever they could to restorers, and put the rest in storage, until the apartment was livable again. And that could happen only when the building was habitable, the electrical systems had been restored, and Grace had had the apartment repaired. They had been through it all before. And Ellen and Grace both knew the entire process would take months and cost a fortune, but Grace was undaunted by it, and insisted she was an architect and used to restoring homes, and might even make some changes. Her mother loved her apartment, the neighborhood, and the building where she lived, and she was not ready to give it up, no matter what her daughter said.

Ellen met her mother after lunch at the apartment to clean up what they could. Bob helped them drag debris into the hallway, with a handyman from the building who put it in a Dumpster. They stopped for a break, as Grace stood ankle deep in water, impervious to the stench of sewage, and wearing rubber gloves to deal with whatever she picked up or threw away. Bob said he was definitely going to sell his apartment once he got it cleaned up. Two hurricanes in five years were enough for him.

"Are you serious?" Grace looked shocked. He had mentioned it once before, but she hadn't believed him.

"We could have all drowned this time, Grace," he said sensibly. "I'm too old to start again from the ground up, every five years." And he had lost some first editions and mementos that he loved. "You have more energy than I do," he said admiringly. She had told her office that she wouldn't be in for two weeks until she got her apartment cleared and organized and dealt with the insurance. But she was more than willing to start again. "It's too depressing," he said. "It's like living on the edge of a volcano. And sooner or later, this is going to happen again. Climactic conditions are such, and changes in the planet, and the city can't afford to put all the necessary safeguards in place to protect us down here. They've been talking about them for five years, and they've implemented a few, but not enough, and not the important ones, which are too costly. This mess is an even bigger one than Sandy was. I can't go through it again. I talked to my kids about it the other night, and they think I was nuts to stay after Sandy. So I guess I'm done. I'm going to look for a place uptown. And I think you should think about it too. I know Ellen worries about you, and if she hadn't been here the other night, you might have stayed. And none of us want to lose you," he said gently, and she smiled.

"You won't. I would have left in time," she said confidently.

"You nearly didn't," he reminded her. "It would be a tragedy if something happened to you. You can't always gauge it that closely. And do you really want to risk going through this again?" He glanced around her apartment, and Grace didn't answer for a minute.

"I don't want to move uptown," she said sadly. "It's so stuffy. I used to live there and don't want to anymore. I love it downtown." Grace was wistful as she said it.

"It's too risky for me," Bob said with a sigh. And the Village, Tribeca, SoHo, all the areas they loved looked like a war zone and would for a long time. None of them even had electricity yet, and some wouldn't for many months. And their building was severely damaged. All the tenants had to move out for at least six months, even those on higher floors, while the electricity and mechanical functions were replaced.

Grace was quiet as they continued throwing things away that afternoon, some of them beautiful and expensive, others irreplaceable. Her white mohair couches were unsalvageable, as well as her beautiful rugs, all the upholstered chairs, and they were going to send them to restorers, but Ellen knew that many of her wood pieces, even antiques, had suffered irreparable damage. A great many things went into the Dumpster, and Grace looked tired and a little beaten when they went back uptown. It had been a depressing afternoon for all of them, and the work to clear the apartment was by no means done. Ellen had taken photographs for the insurance of what they had to throw away. The smell of sewage was so strong from the soaked upholstered pieces that they couldn't keep them to show the appraisers, and put them in the Dumpster after photographing them.

Grace went to lie down when they got back to Central Park West. Ellen called Phillippa, her assistant in London, to report on what was happening, and then Bob and Ellen went out to the kitchen for a cup of tea. They were both exhausted, and Ellen was worried about her mother insisting that she wanted to repair the apartment and move back in.

"It's too dangerous," Ellen said unhappily, and Bob agreed with her.

"Maybe it's too soon for her to give up." He smiled at Ellen. "She's a fighter. She doesn't concede easily, but she's not foolish. She may come around eventually. Right now she wants to fix what she lost. Sometimes it's hard to move on," he said, looking thoughtful. "It took me a long time to give up the life I had in California, and let it go. My wife and I got divorced, I was hoping to convince her to try again, and then she died. I wanted to stay there and live in a shrine. And then I finally realized I was hanging on to the memory of a woman who didn't want to live with me, didn't like being married to me, and didn't like me very much. Her dying allowed me to create a fantasy for a few years, about how much we loved each other. But I'm not sure we ever did. The marriage never really worked, right from the beginning. I finally gave it up, sold the house, got rid of everything, and moved here. I was a lot happier when I did. We waste a lot of time sometimes, crying over what we never really had in the first place.

"The hard part here is being far from my kids. They like California better, but they're grown up, they have their own lives. They both live in L.A., my son is a filmmaker, my daughter is an attorney in the entertainment business, and if I lived out there, I'd just be hanging around annoying them waiting for them to see me. This way I have my own life, and I'm much better off in New York. I have a life here. I never liked L.A. when I lived there, even if they do. We can't hang on to our kids. We're on our own after they grow up. It's hard to accept sometimes, but that's the way it works. Look at you, you live in London, your mother's here. She's not trying to hang on to you, just like I can't with my kids." Ellen looked pensive as he said it, as though he had told her something she didn't know. It was rare for him to talk about himself to that extent, but he felt comfortable with her. Normally, he was a man of few words and kept his private life to himself.

"Somehow I always thought children were forever." She was thoughtful as she said it.

"Not really. Technically, that's true, but in reality, they grow up and move on, and they should. And I can't complain about mine. I was never really there for them when they were growing up. I was always writing, and busy with my work. There's no reason for them to stick around now. And they should have their own lives.

So I live and work here, and they're busy and happy in L.A. We enjoy seeing each other, but it's all very brief and temporary at this age. We don't get them for long. I wish I'd known that when mine were young. I might have been around more."

Ellen could see the regret in his eyes and felt sorry for him. But he had made her realize that the babies she wanted so badly wouldn't stay babies, and wouldn't be hers for long, especially if George had his way and sent them to boarding school at seven and nine. And they were children for all too brief a time.

"It's up to us to fill our lives once they grow up," Bob said quietly. "And that's not always easy to do. It makes our adult relationships even more important, our life with our partners, and our work, like in my case. I live in a world of fantasy," he said with a rueful smile. "My books fill my life. In a way they always did," he admitted to her, "more than my children or my wife. She was right to divorce me. I was a lousy husband. All I cared about then was my career, and being at the top of the best-seller lists. I managed that nicely, but blew my marriage. You can't have it all, I guess." And he was without question one of the most successful writers in the world. But it sounded like it had come at a high price. "Sometimes we make the wrong choices," he said with obvious regret. Her mother had said that too.

"Did you ever remarry?" she asked, as she poured them both a second cup of tea. He shook his head in answer.

"No. After I gave up the illusion of the perfect marriage I never had and faced the truth, I figured it wasn't my strong suit and stuck with the books. It seems to work for me." But it didn't sound like enough to Ellen. He sounded like a lonely man to her. She wondered if that was the nature of writers, if they were solitary people, like sailors who were in love with the sea. Bob sounded like he was in love with his work, although he wasn't very old, and at forty-nine he was still liable to meet someone else, even if he hadn't so far. But his comments about children had caught her attention. He made it all sound so ephemeral, so temporary, and so brief. They grew up and left. And in George's world they were sent away as babies. She thought she could change his mind about it, but maybe she couldn't. And she'd have been miserable sending away a child of seven or even ten, especially after all it took for her to have them. She would want to keep them around for as long as she could, which would have been a travesty to George, not sending a son to Eton.

They had dinner with their host again that night, and the conversation was interesting and lively. Jim Aldrich knew a great deal about architecture, and he and Grace had a serious discussion, and he took her to his library after dinner and showed her some fascinating books he had collected. He was a very erudite man, and he seemed as intrigued by Grace as she was by him. They were still in the library talking, when Bob and Ellen gave up and went to bed. They laughed about it on their way to their bedrooms.

"They both make me feel like I'm ancient," Bob commented to her. "I can hardly move after all the work clearing the apartments today. Your mother worked hard too. Those two look like they could talk all night." And Ellen couldn't help thinking that it was fun living in community, with people to have dinner with and talk to about interesting subjects. Grace was obviously enjoying it immensely, and Ellen liked it too, despite their reason for being there. She said goodnight to Bob outside her room, and wanted to call George, but it was too late again. She was going to call him in the morning and let him know how things were going.

"See you tomorrow," Bob said pleasantly, and a few minutes later, she could hear him on his ancient typewriter in the next room. It was a nice old-fashioned sound, and she fell asleep listening to it, marveling that he still wrote his books on a typewriter rather than a computer. She thought about the things he'd confided to her about his marriage and children. He seemed like a deep and introspective person, and she could see why her mother liked him and considered him a friend. He didn't open up easily, but when he did, he was honest, without artifice, and obviously sincere.

Ellen called George at his office before she left her room the next morning. It was one in the afternoon for him, and he said he was just leaving to go to his club for lunch. He sounded like he was in a hurry, and he was unusually distant on the phone. She still had the feeling that he was mad at her about something, but she didn't want to press him and ask again. She told him about everything she was doing for her mother. And once they got the apartment cleared, sent her mother's things to storage, and found a temporary apartment, she thought she could come home. They were both very organized, and she hoped it wouldn't take too long.

"Well, no need to rush," he said vaguely. "Absence makes the heart grow fonder," he teased her. It was the first time he had ever said anything like it, and she was shocked.

"It doesn't sound like you miss me very much," she said, letting him know that she was more upset than she intended.

"You really haven't been gone that long. Not even a week," he pointed out, although so much had happened that it felt like ten years to her. They'd been to hell and back since she'd left London, but George almost seemed like he was enjoying being on his own, which was unusual for him.

"Where are you going this weekend?" she asked him. He'd had no plans for it when she left.

"To the Warwicks'," he said simply. They were yet another couple who gave great house parties in a fabulous house they had inherited. Ellen was starting to feel left out of his London life, after less than a week. He told her he was going to be late for lunch then, and they said goodbye and got off. She sat in her room and thought about how disconnected he sounded. She was sure something was wrong, but she had no clue from George what it might be.

Ellen and her mother went downtown again after breakfast, and worked on clearing the apartment with the help of the handyman and the doorman. And Ellen thought they were almost ready for the movers to come to box up what could be sent to storage in a few days. The restorers were coming to pick up the damaged but hopefully salvageable pieces soon too. They were moving ahead at a good pace, and Ellen told her she had to leave for an appointment that afternoon.

"Are you seeing a client?" her mother asked her, feeling guilty for all the time Ellen was devoting to her. She knew she had intended to do some work for clients while she was in New York, but Ellen shook her head. She had the meeting with the fertility specialist, and she didn't want to change the date she had set for it months before. All her files had been digitally sent ahead for him to study before he saw her.

"No, it's someone new," she said vaguely, not wanting to tell her what it was. She hadn't told George about it either. She knew how tired he was of new specialists, and Ellen wanted to see what he said first. She was hoping that an American doctor would be more optimistic than the ones she'd seen in London. She was hoping that a fresh pair of eyes on her chart would give rise to new hope.

She gave herself an hour and a half to get uptown and arrived five minutes before the appointment. After she filled out a dozen forms, she was ushered into his office. He was young and energetic, and highly respected in his field, and known to be very innovative. But as soon as she sat down, he told her that he had studied her records carefully, and said that unless she was willing to consider a donor egg, there was absolutely no hope of her carrying a fetus to term. He concurred with her specialists in London that although she was only thirty-eight, her hormone levels were poor and the quality of her eggs inadequate for a successful pregnancy, as experience had shown. Reproductively, she showed signs of premature aging, and even with a donor egg, he wasn't convinced her body could sustain a pregnancy to term. He suggested that she consider surrogacy or adoption if one attempt at a donor egg didn't work. She told him that she and her husband didn't consider those possibilities an option and they wanted their own baby genetically. He looked at her honestly across the desk and gave her the answer she had been dreading.

"That's not going to happen, Mrs. Wharton. I would be lying to you if I said I thought it was possible. It isn't. I think surrogacy or adoption are your only options. You're torturing yourself with these repeated attempts at IVF that are doomed to fail. It must be very hard on you psychologically," he said sympathetically.

Her eyes filled with tears. What he had just said sounded like a death sentence to her, and she didn't want to tell her husband that it was over. They would never have a baby unless they adopted one, or used someone else's eggs, which meant that genetically the baby would be his, but not hers. And George wouldn't like that idea either. They had reached a dead end, after four years of attempts for nothing. It had become her obsession, and she had made it George's. They had made love by schedules, and their life had been a constant round of sonograms and hormone shots. And undeniably, no matter how patient he was, it had taken a toll on them. The thought of trying to have a baby was agony for both of them now. They had endured four years of crushing disappointment, never made love spontaneously, and every hormone test felt like a life-or-death pronouncement, every miscarriage a tragic event.

"I think you need to give some serious thought to what route you want to take in the future," the doctor told her. "As I said, you can try a donor egg once, but if it fails, I wouldn't do it again. And I don't think your chances are great for that either. And if you and your husband aren't open to adoption, it may be time for you both to face the reality of your situation, and consider a future without children. Some couples prefer that to adoption, if you feel that strongly about it." He brought the interview to a close then after she asked him a few more questions, and she nearly stumbled out to the sidewalk, blinded by her tears.

She cried all the way back to Jim Aldrich's apartment, and was relieved that no one was home when she got there. Her mother and Bob were still downtown, and Jim was at his office. Ellen got into her bed in the guest room after locking the door and cried herself to sleep. Her last hope of a baby had just been snuffed out, and she dreaded telling George, but it wasn't fair giving him false hope. Their baby-making days were over. They would be childless forever. To her, it was the worst fate she could imagine. And she knew a part of her had died that afternoon.

Chapter 8

Once Gina was uptown with her cell phone working again, she tried to call Nigel whenever she could, and sent him several texts, hoping he would get them and respond. She hated to be out of touch and was worried about him. And it seemed reasonable to assume that he would want to know how she and the girls were. She had been living with him for a year, after all, and had left her marriage for him and moved to New York. She considered the bond they shared akin to a marriage, or just shy of it. And she had asked him to call her just to check in, in the texts she sent him. In the aftermath of the storm, she didn't even know where he was staying. Since their apartment was in a flood zone and the building was still evacuated, she knew he wasn't staying there, and assumed he was still in Brooklyn with the artists he'd been helping, although he had said that all their apartments and studios had been washed out too.

He called her finally on Thursday night, while she was at a restaurant having dinner with Charles and the girls, and Nigel sounded irate when she answered. She went outside to talk to him, away from Charles and the children.

"Why the hell are you sending me all those fucking texts? Don't you know I'm busy? I don't have time to answer you," he snarled at her, and she was taken aback by the tone of his voice.

"I'm worried about you, that's all. I don't even know where you are, or where you're sleeping," she said plaintively, which made him even madder.

"What difference does it make? I told you, I'm busy. I'm helping my friends, and pulling their art from underwater. I don't have time to worry about you. And I'm staying at a motel in Brooklyn." For a moment she wondered if he was cheating on her, but it didn't seem likely. He was on a mission. "I'll come back when I'm finished. You've got that idiot you were married to, to help you—why do you need to hear from me too?" She was offended on Charles's behalf—he had been extremely nice to her and the girls, in spite of what she had done to him, and he was genuinely concerned with their well-being and safety, with no apparent ulterior motive.

"He's just concerned about the children. And I'm not his responsibility. I live with you, not with him."

"You're not my responsibility either," he said harshly. "I'm not your mother or father, Gina. I can't worry about you all the time, and they're his brats, not mine. He should be taking care of them. Why do I have to?" He sounded incensed that she wanted anything from him, and everything he had said to her was offensive, about her, Charles, and her children.

"Presumably you would want to take care of us because you love me." And she had hoped that he liked the girls better than he seemed to. She was furious that he had called her daughters "brats." They were well behaved and had always been nice to him, and respectful. And thanks to Charles's discretion, they weren't old enough to know what Nigel had done to their parents' marriage, or resent him for it. They were well-behaved, loving, good kids. "You can't just dump us in the middle of a hurricane, while you help a bunch of artists in Brooklyn, with no thought for us," she said reproachfully to Nigel, and she was starting to get angry at him. She didn't like the tone he had used with her, or what he said.

"Well, that's what I'm doing, whether you like it or not. And you're fine. What are you complaining about?" Nigel said, sounding furious.

"I was in a shelter for several days. We were evacuated from our apartment. We can't even go back there yet. We're living out of a suitcase. My girls are frightened, Nigel, and so am I. Or at least we were. I'm not just some bimbo you picked up last week. I left Charles for you. You have some responsibility to us, just as a human being, if you care about us at all."

"Don't get me confused with Charles," Nigel said, shouting at her. "I'm not some prissy little wimp who's going to hang around to wipe your ass or your daughters'. Put on your big-girl panties, Gina, and take care of yourself. I'm not your nursemaid, and I don't want to worry about you all the time. You left him because you wanted to—you were bored to death with him. But that doesn't mean I have to be responsible for you, or your children. I'm busy right now—figure it out for yourself." She had been seriously worried for his safety in the hurricane, and she realized now that he hadn't been worried about her. And Charles might be traditional and less exciting than Nigel, but he would have never let her go through a hurricane without coming to her aid. He had been remarkable ever since he came to the shelter. And he would never have said the kind of things Nigel had just said to her. He was too decent to do so.

"Is this all I am to you, a piece of ass when it's convenient, and when things go wrong, you expect me to fend for myself? Is that all I mean to you? I was *worried* about you, Nigel. I love you. I was afraid you'd get killed out there or drown. I was worried sick all night. And you didn't give a damn about us."

"I'm not the Red Cross, for chrissake. And you were fine at the shelter."

"Maybe so, but we were scared in the middle of a hurricane."

"Nothing happened to you. I lost my goddamn cameras and equipment and my negatives. That's a lot more important!" He had just spelled it out for her. His cameras and equipment meant more to him than she did. "I can't deal with this bullshit. I'm not going to cater to you because you think you're some kind of superstar now."

"I'm not a superstar. I'm a woman and a human being, and we needed you with us to help us."

"I'm not going to ride in on a white horse because you're scared. I have better things to do," he said bluntly.

"What if something had happened to one of my children? There were kids washed away in the flood the other night."

"That's not my problem. And they looked fine to me when I saw them at the shelter. That's not who I am, Gina. We're not married. They're not my kids, and I'm not going to play knight in shining armor to fulfill your romantic fantasies. I was helping *artists* save their *work*. That's a lot more important than sitting around a shelter holding your hand." He had made that abundantly clear. As far as he was concerned, she could take care of herself and her children, and he would come back when he was ready to, and not before. He didn't even feel inclined to call her. "I came all the way into Manhattan to see you. I didn't have to do that." He had also been delivering art to safe locations for his friends. He had said that.

"You should have wanted to, because you love me," she said with tears in her eyes. He was all about himself, his friends, and whatever he thought was important at the moment. And for now, she wasn't it. And whatever she needed from him was of no importance to him.

"I love you, but my studio is important to me too. And right now, my friends out here need me more than you do."

"That's good to know," she said quietly. Suddenly the fight had gone out of her. He didn't want to get it, and he was never going to. She was someone he cared about, but she was never going to be his first priority. He didn't have the same kind of values that

Charles did, or that she had grown up with, where you expect a man to be there for you. She suddenly realized what she had given up, in exchange for something fun and flashy. And when the chips were down, the flash vanished, and she was on her own. She didn't expect anything from Charles now, but she did from Nigel, and he didn't play by the same rules.

"I'll see you when I see you," he said somberly, as annoyed with her as he had been when he got her messages to call her. "And don't expect me to call you. I don't want that hanging around my neck while I'm doing what I can out here. I'll probably stay here for a few weeks."

"I think I'm going home for a while," she said quietly. "It's a mess downtown, the girls don't have school, Charles wants to spend time with them, and I want to see my parents. It's too stressful being here right now. And there's no work for me anyway. The agency is closed too because of the flood. And if you're not coming back for several weeks, I don't see why I should sit here waiting for you to show up, while you take care of your friends in Brooklyn and don't give a damn about us."

She was angry at him, possibly irreparably. She didn't know yet, but Nigel had shown a side of himself she had never fully understood before. And with his attitude, he was never going to be there for her in a crisis, or maybe even in day-to-day life as time went on. He had made things plain to her that night, and she didn't like anything she'd heard from him. She had been a fool to fall for him in the first place. He had dazzled her with his charm, when he felt like it, but there was nothing behind it to back it up. She could see that now, and it had been an unpleasant revelation and a huge disappointment. He was not someone she could count on, in a hurricane or at any other time. Nigel took care of one person, himself, and he would never be any different.

"Do whatever you want," he said tersely. "When are you leaving?"

"I don't know yet. Maybe this weekend. I have to find out when I can get tickets." She had been waiting to talk to him first and see what he said. Now she knew.

"Have a good time in England, if you go back," he said blithely. She wasn't going for a good time, if she did. She was going to provide a little peace for her girls and herself, after the shocking experience they'd been through. She didn't bother to explain it to him, because she knew he wouldn't get that either. As long as he was fine, that was all that mattered to him.

They hung up a few minutes later, after he reminded her again not to bother calling him. He'd be in touch when he was ready to be. Gina was pensive after the call, trying to absorb all she'd heard from him. When she went back into the restaurant, Charles could see that she was upset. He didn't ask her about it. He knew the call had been from Nigel. It had been obvious to him the minute she answered and her face lit up. But she looked different now, unhappy and sad, and he could see it had gone badly, as he continued chatting with the children. And as they walked back to the hotel, she told him that she had thought about it and maybe it would be a good idea to go back to London for a few weeks, since the girls couldn't go to school anyway, and it would be a nice treat for them.

And she couldn't get back into their apartment yet. Her whole street was shut down, and her building.

"I can stay with my parents," she volunteered, which he knew was an inconvenience for her since they lived an hour outside London. "The girls can stay with you, if you like. I can come and take care of them in the daytime when you're at work. Or they can stay with me at Mum and Dad's, and I'll bring them into the city at night to have dinner with you."

"You can stay at my apartment with us, if you want to. I have a guest room, and a pullout couch. I can sleep on the couch, and you and the girls can have the bedrooms. And I'm not trying to start anything with you," he said solemnly. "It would just be nice to have them around while you're there. And you can come and go as you please. I can watch the girls at night, if you want to go out." It sounded like a respectful arrangement, and she believed that he wouldn't "start anything." He had been nothing but polite and pleasant to her while they shared the hotel room, and entirely appropriate. It had been a year since they had lived together, before she left him, and she had forgotten how kind and thoughtful he could be, and she was sure he would be equally so in London. And staying with him would be easier for her than staying in the suburbs, at her parents'.

"That would be very nice," she said quietly. "When are you going back?" She'd have to go to the apartment to pick up some things, if the police would let her. If not, she could buy clothes for the girls and herself in London.

"I was thinking about Saturday," he answered. "Now that the

airports are open. Is that too soon for you?" He didn't know if she wanted to see Nigel before she left. And Saturday was in two days.

"That would be fine. I'll see if I can get into the apartment tomorrow, and grab whatever's dry."

"If not, we'll figure it out in London," he said simply.

"That's what I was thinking too." She smiled then. "My parents will be thrilled to see them." And Charles could hardly wait to have his daughters with him for a few weeks, and Gina too.

They walked into the hotel arm in arm, and for a minute it almost felt like the old days, and then as he always did, he remembered that they were divorced, but she was still the mother of his children. It was enough, and all he had a right to now.

He made the plane reservations for them when he got back to the room, and she told him she wanted to pay for her own ticket. He could pay for the girls, which he had intended to do anyway. "I don't mind paying for yours," he said gently, but she shook her head and declined the offer.

"It wouldn't be right," she reminded him. Just as Nigel had said, she was an independent woman. But she was happy to be going home with him, and so were the girls when they told them. Charles explained that they were going to London for a visit for a few weeks, so they wouldn't be confused and think they were coming back forever, although he had a feeling they would have liked that too. They seemed to like living in New York, but they were still typically English children. He told them about all the fun they were going to have, and the things they were going to do, and they squealed and jumped on the big bed in the room. Gina and Charles had a hard time getting them to bed that night. And after they finally fell asleep in the small hotel room, Gina rolled over in bed and looked at him in the sleeping bag on the floor.

"Thank you," she whispered so as not to wake the girls.

"Thank you for being willing to do it." He smiled at her.

She was thrilled to be leaving New York after the horrors of the hurricane, and after her conversation with Nigel that night, she knew she had nothing to stay for, or maybe even that she wanted to come back to.

"Goodnight," she said and then rolled over again and went to sleep, while Charles realized that as frightening as it had been, the hurricane had been a blessing. He was going home with his children. And even if it was only for a few weeks, it was a gift, and meant the world to him.

Ben's funeral on Friday was as agonizing as everyone had expected. The Holbrooks had flown in from Chicago the night before, now that the airports were open again. Peter walked into the church with his parents. They looked serious and solemn, and Peter sat down next to Anna and her parents, with his parents on his other side. There were countless friends and fellow students, teachers from Dalton, and people who had known Ben since he was born. All their friends were there, after they had seen the notice of the funeral in the newspaper. In lieu of flowers, they had asked for donations to the Hurricane Relief Fund, to help those who had lost their homes. FEMA was contributing to them, but not in amounts that were significant enough to help them, and most people didn't have hurricane insurance, certainly not to the degree they needed.

Adam, Ben's younger brother, started crying almost as soon as he sat down, and Ben's mother was inconsolable as her husband kept an arm around her for most of the service. Ben had always been such a good boy that they had never expected anything bad to happen to him. He wasn't a big risk taker, had never taken drugs or been an excessive drinker. He had been an exemplary child and a brilliant student, and the eulogies by his favorite high school teacher, and several of the Weisses' close friends, reflected that. Ben's father was Jewish, but his mother wasn't, and he had been brought up in the Protestant faith. Peter sat stiff and pale throughout the service, and he almost expected someone to scream at him, "Why are you still here and Ben isn't? Why didn't you save him?" His shoulders were shaking by the time the congregation sang "Amazing Grace" at the end of the service, and Peter couldn't make eye contact with Ben's parents, and lowered his eyes as they filed out behind Ben's casket. They had asked him to be one of the pallbearers, but he knew he couldn't do it. He felt too broken and too guilty, and he looked like he was about to faint as he and his parents left the church and stood outside on the sidewalk, and the men from the funeral home slid the casket into the hearse.

He realized that Anna was standing next to him then with a look of concern. "Are you okay?" she asked, and he nodded and watched as the hearse drove away. They were burying him at a cemetery in Queens, with only the family present. They had invited the Holbrooks to come, but Peter knew he couldn't do that either. He felt sick and dizzy as he looked at the faces around him, as though everyone were accusing him in silence. He knew he had no right to be there and felt as though he shouldn't have survived. He felt his mother touch his arm then, and saw her watch him with worried eyes. She had spoken to their family doctor in Chicago, and he had said that Peter might suffer from post-traumatic stress disorder for a long time, and he had suggested therapy to help him deal with it. They had the name of a therapist for him to see when he got home.

He went back to the Hotel Pierre with his parents after the service, without speaking to any of his friends. And he hadn't wanted to talk to Anna, who was as distraught as he was. She had never lost a friend before, and couldn't imagine her life without Ben in it. They had gone all through school together, and college.

Peter lay down on the bed at the hotel for an hour, while his parents sat and talked quietly in the living room of the suite, and then they all went to the Weisses' apartment, where everyone had gathered for an enormous buffet, and friends and relatives congregated all over the apartment. Ben's father cried constantly, and his mother looked as though she were moving underwater. She disappeared and went to her room before the gathering ended, as Jake thanked the guests for coming, and Peter was sure she had left so she wouldn't have to say goodbye to him. He hugged Ben's father and brother on the way out, and he felt like a murderer when he got in the elevator to leave. He hadn't even said goodbye to Anna, although he was leaving the next day. It had become too painful to be with each other. It reminded them both all too agonizingly of their lost friend, and there was nothing left to say.

Peter followed his parents into the hotel like a zombie, and took off his suit. He put on jeans and a sweatshirt, lay down on the bed again, and turned on the TV. He didn't want to talk to anyone, or even think.

"Are you doing all right, son?" John Holbrook asked him, when he walked by Peter's room to his own. Mike was lying on the bed next to him, and Peter had his arm around him. Mike was wearing the same collar he had worn the day that Peter saved him. Peter didn't want anyone to take it off. It was the collar Ben had always used for him, and it was now a sacred relic to Peter, who had inherited the dog. Mike had his head on the pillow next to Peter, and looked like he was enjoying the hotel.

"I'm okay, Dad," Peter confirmed. What else could he say? He knew he would never forget the service or everything that had led up to it since the morning they had left the apartment. And he bitterly regretted it now, and blamed himself for their decision to leave the building when they had. Ben hadn't been as sure he wanted to, and Peter felt as though he had talked him into it. And the building hadn't collapsed after all. They would have survived if they had stayed there, but it hadn't seemed that way at the time.

He had gone back to the apartment with Ben's father and helped pack his things and carry them downstairs, and then he had gone back to pack his own. He had left everything in boxes, and his father was having it all sent to Chicago, and they'd agreed to donate all the battered furniture to Goodwill. Peter never wanted to see any of it again. He didn't know where he'd live when he came back to New York, but he never wanted to see the building again either. The pain of it was too acute, and the memories too sweet before that. Ben had been the best friend he'd ever had, and they had had such good times there. And Anna had been part of it. She was mourning it now too. She had not only lost Ben, she had lost Peter, and the good times they had shared.

Peter's father ordered him a hamburger for dinner from room service, and Peter fed most of it to the dog. And finally he fell asleep with his clothes on, and with Mike lying next to him, after John took him out for a walk. Peter was barely able to function, and looked stiff and solemn when he got into the car to go to the airport the next morning. He didn't even notice how worried his parents were as he kept a firm grip on Mike's leash.

When they got to the airport, John checked them all in and made arrangements for Mike to go in the cargo. They had a large plastic crate big enough for him, and John told Peter to put him in it. The moment he said it, Peter shook his head.

"I won't do that to him, Dad. I'll rent a car and drive him to Chicago if I have to. He's not going in the cargo. He doesn't deserve that, and he'll be too scared."

"There's no other choice, son," John said, lowering his voice so the woman at the counter couldn't hear him. "He's way over the weight limit to take him in the cabin, and he's too big. He's got to go underneath." He was worried about the stubborn, almost desperate look in his son's eyes.

"Is there a problem?" the woman at the desk asked in a nervous voice. She had seen Peter's face too. He looked as though he was about to freak out.

"I won't put my dog in cargo," Peter said loudly.

"Is he a service dog?" she asked, as John answered for him. It was a problem he hadn't anticipated. But it was clear that Peter was not going to give in, and his father didn't want to argue with him and create a scene.

"No, he's not a service dog," John said, looking embarrassed. The first sign of Peter's trauma and stress had just reared its ugly head, and he was beginning to think they might have to drive.

"Is he an emotional support dog?" she questioned them further, looking straight at Peter when she asked.

"What's that?" Peter responded to her directly, as the dog watched them with interest and cocked his head.

"If you're afraid to fly, sir, and feel you need your dog with you for emotional support, if you can give us a letter from your doctor to that effect, he can fly with you, not in a crate, and sit at your feet."

"Even a dog that size?" John asked, stunned. He had never heard of it before.

"Of course," she said as though it were a common occurrence.

"I don't have a letter from my doctor," Peter answered her in a sullen tone.

"Do you need him with you?" she asked as Peter looked down at Mike, whose tail was wagging and his tongue was out in the excitement.

"Yes, I do," Peter said, looking her in the eye again.

"My son has been through an awful lot," his father intervened. "He just survived the hurricane, he saved the dog, and they were in the hospital together until a few days ago. We'd really appreciate it if you could get by without the doctor's letter. We didn't know we'd need it." He was giving it his best shot, and Peter glanced at him gratefully. His father was doing all he could for his son, as Peter's mother watched the scene with nervous approval, hoping it would work.

"You're an Ophelia survivor, sir?" she asked Peter, and he nodded, although he wouldn't have phrased it that way, but it was true. "One moment, please," she said, suddenly very official. "I'll be right back." They could see her go straight to her supervisor, and two minutes later she was back. "There will be no problem. This time we'll be happy to accommodate you, under the circumstances. But in the future"—she smiled at them—"try to bring a letter from your physician. And as long as he's an emotional support dog, he flies for free." Peter was beaming as she handed them their boarding passes, and a special one for Mike, and they walked through security without a hitch, and went straight to the gate with Mike trotting along happily next to Peter. And the men in security patted the dog. They boarded the plane without a problem, and Mike lay down at Peter's feet. He seemed completely at ease being on the plane and watched the passengers with interest as they walked down the aisle. Several heads turned when they saw him, and no one complained. Peter thought some of them might assume he was a seeing-eye dog, but he wasn't wearing the harness for it. He had just become an official emotional support dog, and Peter knew he would get a letter from their doctor, so he could always travel with him. Peter had vowed to himself that Mike would never leave his side.

"Thanks for helping me, Dad," Peter said to his father as the plane took off a few minutes later. Mike was sound asleep by the time the flight attendants came by offering them drinks. All the Holbrooks declined for the short flight. They'd be landing at O'Hare in an hour.

Peter sat staring out the window for most of the flight, as Mike slept happily at his feet. The big black Lab got up and looked around when they landed, and Peter petted him.

"It's okay, boy, we're going home." He loped off the plane next to Peter, whose parents exchanged a smile and looked relieved. Mike's first flight as an emotional support dog had been a resounding success, and Peter was safely home at last.

While they waited to board the plane to London, Charles made one last call on his cell phone. He wanted to tell Ellen he was leaving and wish her luck. He felt a strange bond to her after their flight together on the way over, and the time they had shared in the shelter, and he wanted to say goodbye.

"We're at the airport now," he said softly when she answered. "Gina and the girls are coming with me for a few weeks, since they don't have school."

"That's a lot different than when we arrived, isn't it?" She smiled, listening to him, and remembering his terror at the turbulence on the flight.

He wasn't nervous this time—he felt surprisingly calm, as he used to, traveling with his family. He had nothing to fear now—he was with them.

"I'll be going home soon too," she told him. She had to finish helping her mother empty the apartment and find her a place to live. She was hoping to wrap up everything in the next week.

"Stay in touch. Let's have lunch sometime when you get back," he said to her.

"I'd love that. I'll call you when I get home," she promised, although she knew she'd be busy with her clients, and it sounded like she had fences to mend with George. "Take care of yourself, Charles. And good luck with however you want things to turn out," she said cryptically.

"I'm just looking forward to some time with my girls." She realized again that it was a joy she would never know, spending time with her children, and watching them grow up. She felt cheated whenever she thought of it, particularly after the discouraging news from the doctor in New York. She knew that she had to accept it now, without staring longingly at new mothers holding their babies, or women walking down the street with their daughters, or fathers and sons. She had to give up the dream. "I'll call you," he promised, as the passengers started to board, and he had to shepherd Gina and the girls onto the plane.

"Have a safe flight," she said.

"I know I will," he said, and ended the call.

"Who was that?" Gina asked him as he caught up to her with their boarding passes.

"Ellen. I wanted to tell her we were leaving. She was very kind to me on the flight over. I had a panic attack in the turbulence from the hurricane." But he looked nothing like that now. He was calm and collected and relaxed, as they boarded the plane and found their seats. He was thinking about watching a movie or playing card games with the girls. Gina smiled at him as she sat down in the seat next to him, with their daughters right behind them. He seemed very different to her now. He was happy and at ease and confident. He acted like a normal person, like any other business-man or family man on the plane, which no longer seemed like a crime to her, or even a failing.

The flight attendant wished them a good flight as they both ac-cepted a glass of champagne. There was nothing particular to cel-ebrate. But they had survived Hurricane Ophelia. For now, that was enough.

Chapter 9

The day after Charles left for London, Jim organized a brunch for his houseguests in the apartment on Central Park West. It was a rainy Sunday and a perfect day to stay in. They met in the library of his elegant apartment at noon, with several copies of the Sunday *Times,* and *The Wall Street Journal,* and he was working on the *Times* crossword puzzle when they walked in, and set it down with a smile when he saw Grace.

"Sorry, it's a terrible affliction. The damn thing tortures me all week. I wake up in the middle of the night, trying to figure out the ones I missed."

"So do I," she said, laughing. "There's always a trick to it. It's a special mindset, like learning Chinese. I tried to do that when I was young, to impress Mr. Pei when I worked for him. I finally gave up, but I still wrestle with the *Times* crossword puzzle myself, with only slightly better results."

"I know just what you mean," he said, reaching for the paper again, "like this one. 'Nineteenth-century Napoleonic architect influential in Paris.'"

"That's easy," she said immediately. "Haussmann." He looked up at her, vastly impressed. "Does it fit?"

He counted the boxes. "Perfectly. Maybe we should do this together." He showed her the ones he was missing, and she got two of them right off the bat. They were congratulating each other when Bob and Ellen walked into the room at the same time a few minutes later.

"What's all the noise about?" Bob asked innocently. He could hear them laughing and celebrating down the hall, and Ellen was amused.

"I've found a partner in crime for the crossword puzzle," Grace answered, smiling broadly. "The damn thing drives me crazy, but I can't stay away from it."

"I don't go near it," Bob said, picking up a copy of *The Wall Street Journal*. "I have some sort of learning disability about puzzles. I can't do them to save my life. I gave up years ago. My wife and I used to fight about it. She was usually right, I screwed the whole thing up and drove her nuts because I did it in ink." Jim looked sheepish as he said it, and admitted that he did too, and as a result, the whole thing was a mess by Sunday night, as he crossed things out and wrote over it all day. Grace was having fun as she studied his empty spaces again and came up with another one. They were a good team. And she appeared surprisingly rested and relaxed despite the shock and horrors of the last week. Ellen had lined up the movers and spoken to the insurance adjusters several times. She was planning to clear the apartment for her in the next few days. Having been through it before, they knew what to do and had moved very quickly.

"And now I have the unpleasant task of finding a temporary apartment," Grace said with a sigh. "I might have to look uptown. Downtown is in total chaos, half the buildings are shut down and will be for a long time, and all the people who want to take advantage of the hurricane victims will raise the rent on short-term furnished apartments sky high. I went through all that last time. I might just expand the search to uptown too. It'll be easier than fighting the wars downtown."

"You can always stay here, for as long as you like," Jim said generously, but she didn't want to impose. She knew Bob was planning to stay there for several months if necessary, but the two men were close friends. And Grace liked having her own space and not being beholden to someone she barely knew, however gracious or good company he was.

"Thank you," Grace said, smiling at him. "I don't want to be a burden. Houseguests get tiresome very quickly. And Blanche likes having her own apartment," she said, patting the dog, as he laughed.

"Well, she's welcome to stay, and so are you." He was impressed by how calm Grace seemed, despite all she'd been through. She'd been in close communication with her office, and was upset about missing a week of work. She was planning to go back as soon as she and Ellen got the apartment squared away. Ellen had been in regular contact with her office in London too, since they moved to Jim's apartment and her cell phone worked again, and she still needed to look around the vintage shops and antique stores for her clients, although many of them had been closed all week due to the hurricane. Even if they were in unaffected areas north of Forty-second Street, employees were trapped in the suburbs, or flooded out of their homes, and the bridges to Manhattan had only opened a few days before. But no one could get into the city with fewer than three people in a car. Carpools were mandatory to try and reduce the number of vehicles coming into the city, in an attempt to diminish the fierce traffic downtown in areas that were already severely damaged and hard to get through.

Jim picked up the *Book Review* then, and handed it to Bob with a smile. They both knew what was in it, since they always got the best-seller list in advance, on Wednesdays for the Sunday ten days later. Bob's new book was number one that week, and he smiled as he looked at it and handed it back to Jim, who passed it to Grace. His publisher had taken out a full-page ad for the book, and Bob looked attractive in the picture from the back of the book, in a tweed jacket and open shirt. It was a reminder of just how famous and successful Bob was, although he made no fuss about it.

"I'll pick one up this week," Grace promised, as Bob told her not to, saying he would give her and Ellen free copies if they liked.

"I never press my books on people," he said modestly. "It still embarrasses me after all these years."

"Don't give us any—we'll buy them," Grace insisted, as Ellen looked at the best-seller list and smiled at him too.

"Well done," she congratulated him, although no one was surprised. And she could see from the ad that it was his forty-fifth book and a best-seller on the *Times* list. He was number one on the *Wall Street Journal* and *USA Today* lists too, and on the eBook list as well.

"I never get blasé about it. I always feel lucky that people still read my books," Bob said honestly.

"You and Agatha Christie," Grace said generously. "You'll go down in literary history." He wrote very clever mysteries, always with a surprise ending and a psychological twist. Grace had loved them for years. And unlike Agatha Christie, whose books were shorter and lighter, his were long, solid novels that kept the reader mesmerized and intrigued for four hundred pages. There was real merit to their success, and his. "We should be celebrating today," Grace said as she smiled at him again. "Or is that the reason for our brunch?"

"No, but perhaps it should have been," Jim said, smiling at his friend and favorite author. "I just thought you all needed a bit of civilized relaxation after a hard week." They were called into the dining room by his maid then, where they discovered a sumptuous buffet, and she told them that they could have crepes, homemade waffles, and omelets too.

"This is why I can't stay here for very long," Grace said with a sigh as they sat down. "You're much too good to us, and I would be the size of this table in no time." Jim laughed at what she said. She missed her yoga class and needed it desperately for stress, but there had been no time in the chaotic aftermath of the flood, and the yoga studio she went to in Tribeca had been flooded as well, and was closed. She had checked as soon as they got to Jim's, but their phone didn't answer, and she'd driven by on the way back uptown one night. The person cleaning up the mess inside said they would have to move. She'd have to find a new yoga studio too, or contact her favorite teacher once all their phones worked again. For now, communication was mostly impossible with anyone downtown. And she had no time for yoga, or anything else, anyway. She had to clear her apartment, put things in storage, the damaged pieces had already gone to the restorer, and above all she had to find a place to stay until her home was habitable again, probably not for many months.

The conversation over brunch was easy and intelligent. Bob talked about his children in California, Ellen about life in London, and Jim and Grace had a lively exchange on a variety of subjects. Bob and Jim talked politics, and then the women joined in. Jim was five years younger than Grace, but he made her feel like a woman for the first time in a long time, which seemed strange to her. He was a very attractive, successful, erudite man, and she was sure he had a bevy of women in his life. Why wouldn't he? And he had been widowed for fifteen years, so he was accustomed to being on his own, and undoubtedly had many opportunities for companionship—he didn't need her. Which was how she saw it, and thought she was surely too old to catch his interest. She had put that behind her years before, when relationships just began to seem complicated and too much work, and she felt past the point of wanting to put up with someone else's neuroses, baggage, and quirks. She had enough with her own, and preferred to focus on her career, which was still booming, time-consuming, and rewarding, more so than dating could have been. But for the first time in ages, someone was sparking her interest. She felt almost foolish about it, and had no intention of flirting with Jim and appearing idiotic. She did her best to treat him as an intelligent man, an intellectual sparring partner, and a potential friend. But he appealed to her more than she wanted to admit, and he seemed to be interested in her too, as more than just a houseguest. But she didn't want to open that door again, to relationships and romance. In her view, it was too late.

Ellen had noticed it, and said something when they went to their bedrooms. Ellen had some work to do and emails to answer from her office, and Grace wanted to read memos from hers. They had a busy week ahead. The lazy Sunday afternoon was a welcome break.

"He likes you, Mom," Ellen said pointedly, smiling at her.

"I like him too. And don't give me that look," she scolded her. "I'm much older than he is." She tried to squash the notion before anything started, in Ellen's mind, or her own. She sounded like she was trying to convince herself.

"No, you're not. Maybe a few years, but no more than that. You're great together, and you're having fun with him. And he's very impressed with you."

"That's all very nice," Grace said dismissively. "But I'm too old for all that. I don't need the headache of getting involved with someone. It's too distracting. And I'm sure he's not interested in me that way."

"He'd be good company for you," Ellen insisted, "at least for dinner sometime. See what happens."

"Nothing is going to happen," Grace said firmly. "And I'm sure he has younger women in his life. He's a very attractive man."

"Maybe not," Ellen said about other women. "And even if he does, you're pretty remarkable, Mom. He'd be lucky to have you."

"Thank you for the vote of confidence," she said tartly. "But I'm not up for grabs, thank you very much," Grace said through pursed lips. "Don't even think about it." Ellen went to her own room then and called George. She thought he'd be back from his weekend away by then, but he didn't answer, and the call went to voicemail. She tried him again before dinner, which was late for him, and got voicemail again. She'd only been gone for nine days, but it seemed like a year. She felt strangely disconnected from him, and their calls had been unpleasant since the hurricane, as though he was annoyed with her about something but didn't want to talk about it. She had an uneasy feeling, and decided to answer her emails instead of calling again. She'd be home soon enough, and everything would go back to normal then, she was sure. She hadn't decided yet if she was going to tell him about her visit to the doctor in New York. It was another nail in the coffin of her hopes to have a child, and she didn't know if she wanted to spell it out to him quite that clearly, in case he wanted to give it one more try, or was willing to. Maybe they'd get lucky if they tried one last time. Stranger things had happened to others once they gave up. It was a little bit like gambling in Vegas—she hoped to win the jackpot every time, convinced herself she might, and came away broke. The roller coaster of their reproductive life. She wasn't sure whether to give up completely as they'd been told, or pray for a miracle and talk him into one more round of IVF, knowing that it was a long shot. And what if they never won the baby lottery? What if it really was all over? What would their life be like, and their marriage, without children forever? She still couldn't imagine never having children, although they had managed ten years of marriage without them so far, but they had always been sure they would have them one day. Now that hope was disappearing, or had already disappeared. She didn't say anything about the doctor's visit to her mother, who thought she should have given up and made her peace with it years before. She had a child—she couldn't understand what it was like to accept the fact that you would never have any. People complained about their children, but they wouldn't have given up the experience for anything in the world, and Ellen wasn't ready to either. She didn't know how to give up the dream—it had been part of her, and a driving force within her for too long.

Jim and Bob went out to dinner with a literary group that night, and Ellen and Grace were happy to stay home. They had much to do to prepare for the week ahead. Ellen made to do lists, and Grace sent a memo to her office by email, for a presentation that had to be delayed because of the storm. And there had been several calls from people whose houses had been severely damaged, mostly in Connecticut and New Jersey. It was going to be a busy year ahead.

For an architect, hurricanes were good for business. And bad for everything else.

On Monday morning, two handymen from Grace's building helped them put the last of the debris in the Dumpster. "Debris" that had once been the handsome furniture Ellen had ordered for her in Italy, and delicate items that had been smashed to bits. Everything they dumped was soaked beyond recognition and smelled of sewage. It was a relief to get it out of the apartment. And the movers came to pack all her breakables, china, crystal, objects that had survived. All her lamps had to be rewired and sent to an electrician, after being soaked where they were plugged in. They were working by the light of large battery-operated lamps that the building had bought for her, since there was no electricity in the building and wouldn't be for a long time.

And by the end of the day, the movers had loaded boxes, crates, and most of the upstairs furniture onto the truck. And the insurance adjuster had shown up to take pictures and a video. Bob came across the hall to check on their progress and was impressed.

"You two are pros," he said admiringly. Grace no longer looked like she was in shock or about to keel over, as she had at the shelter or when she first saw the apartment, and Ellen was keeping the workers on track. Grace was full of energy, and had already taken photographs and notes about what she was possibly going to change in the apartment.

"You're really coming back?" Bob asked her, still surprised by that.

"I love this apartment," she said simply.

"What if it happens again? It could," he said practically. Knowing that had made the decision not to return easier for him. He preferred to give up an apartment he loved than to go through it again. He didn't know how Grace could face the thought.

"It won't," she said decisively, but she had said that this time too, and Ellen disagreed with her and hadn't given up yet. "Twice was a fluke. Three times just isn't possible."

"Never trust Mother Nature," Bob said seriously. "She'll trick you every time. I'm going to look at two apartments in Jim's building tomorrow. I like it there, and as much as I love Tribeca, I'm ready to move uptown."

"I used to live uptown—I like it so much better here. It's so staid and boring uptown."

"I'm ready for boredom," he said, glancing at the damage around them. There were watermarks and drying remnants of sewage on the walls. He couldn't face it again, and his apartment looked as bad as hers, if not worse, since it hadn't been as polished as hers to begin with. Most of his furniture had to be thrown out and wasn't worth saving. "I'm going to take a hit when I sell the apartment, but it's worth it. I don't want to be around to pay for the building repairs too." And they would have to. Ellen had pointed that out to Grace, but she insisted she didn't care. She was a stubborn woman.

The movers were almost finished in Grace's apartment by the end of the day, and the place was nearly empty. And without the wet furniture they'd thrown away, it didn't smell as bad and wasn't as awful. The weather had warmed up that day, which made the stench of sewage in the streets worse, and they had all seen rats in the street, escaping from flooded buildings.

The next day, the movers emptied her closets and put her dry clothes in storage, until she found a temporary apartment. The insurance adjuster had already sent boxes of her clothes to a special dry cleaner to see if they could be saved. They had to throw almost all her shoes away. But her insurance company had promised to cover her losses. She was one of the rare hurricane victims who was well insured, but she paid high premiums for it, which most people couldn't afford and didn't want to. It was paying off now, just as it had five years before. But however good her coverage, and their willingness to pay, there were so many things that couldn't be replaced. Fortunately, she had kept all her photo albums of Ellen's childhood and wedding, and her own history and her parents', upstairs, and they hadn't been damaged. Others hadn't been as lucky and had lost all the sentimental and material things they owned. There were thousands of stories of heartbreak and loss in the papers and on the news, and heart-wrenching photographs of people crying. And those who had died in the hurricane were being buried that week. Ben had been one of the first.

By Tuesday afternoon, the apartment was totally empty, and Ellen turned over the keys to her mother when she got back to Central Park West. She felt tired and sad and drained. It was painful to see something once so beautiful damaged beyond recognition, and a whole section of the city a shambles, with people crying on the sidewalk over their losses. It depressed her every time she went downtown. The whole city was affected despite the lack of damage uptown, although people were rallying, and many like Grace swore they would rebuild and return. Ellen still didn't want her to do it, but the human spirit was hard to control or predict or argue with. Most people wouldn't have been as persistent about trying to get pregnant as she had. Everyone had their own blind spots and obsessions, and living in the apartment she owned in Tribeca was her mother's. She loved the building, the apartment, and the location on the river, beyond reason.

Ellen called George that night and missed him again. He sent her a text that he was in a meeting, then at a dinner party and would call her when he got home, but he didn't.

And the next morning, when Grace went to work, Ellen met with the real estate agent she'd been referred to, and began the round of furnished apartments, which was an education in itself. There was a long list to see, and an even longer list of refugees from downtown, especially from the higher-priced areas like her mother's, who were willing to pay any price and were snapping up apartments as soon as they saw them. The realtor had already warned her that they'd have to make a quick decision if they saw something they liked, and Ellen had told her mother that she'd have to run over from her office if a great place, or even a decent one, turned up. It didn't have to be perfect, it was just temporary, until her Tribeca apartment was restored.

The realtor seemed mildly eccentric to Ellen, but if the woman had good listings, Ellen didn't care, and she worked for a well-known, respectable firm. After that, it would be the luck of the draw as to what was available, and it was Grace's decision in the end, since she would have to live there for several months. And of course, they had to be willing to take the dog, which most owners of furnished apartments weren't. They had already ruled out the ones that weren't pet-friendly, since Grace wouldn't have considered them. The realtor had recognized Grace's name and was impressed, which never hurt, and she assured Ellen that they would be able to get her mother approved by any co-op board in the city, also not a given with every tenant. So in theory, if they could find the right apartment, it should be easy. And Ellen had described her mother's needs, and Grace's own list of specifications. She wanted a doorman and fully staffed building, a pleasant view, lots of sunlight, a minimum of two bedrooms, preferably a third so she could use it as an office, ideally downtown in the undamaged parts of SoHo, the West Village, lower Fifth Avenue, or Tribeca, which was a tall order, or the Upper East Side, north of Sixtieth Street and south of Seventy-ninth, or on Central Park West if it was fabulous, but nowhere else on the West Side. Ellen's marching orders were clear, and the realtor knew them all.

They started downtown, since it was the area Grace preferred. Very few buildings had been unaffected by the hurricane, but Ellen saw an apartment in a modern building on a high floor, which her mother had said she didn't want either. She didn't like high floors, in case of a fire in the building. The ceilings were so low that Ellen felt as though they were coming down on her head. The apartment looked flimsy and cheap, and there were sparkles in the paint on the walls and ceilings, which made her cringe and she knew Grace would hate, and the furniture was awful, and was mostly wicker bought in Mexico. The apartment had been lived in by students, and it showed.

The next one was a brownstone townhouse on Washington Square, which was beautiful and exquisitely decorated but had no doorman. The realtor had sneaked it in "just for a look" in case Ellen fell in love with it, and she reminded the agent that she had to stick to their requirements or she'd be wasting their time. She apologized, and they moved on to a loft in SoHo, with a kitchen in the middle of the living room, which Grace wouldn't want. There were three in Tribeca without doormen, so not worth seeing, although the agent swore they were fabulous, and an allegedly incredible one that supposedly had everything they wanted, for forty thousand dollars a month, which was beyond Grace's budget, so they skipped that one too. And a sweet apartment in the West Village that was tiny but very pretty, it had one bedroom and a living room and was claustrophobic. And after that they went uptown. Ellen was starting to get discouraged, as the realtor talked on her cell phone constantly, trading listings with other brokers and negotiating prices. She sounded like a bookie or a drug dealer, and was giving Ellen a headache as they got in a cab and headed north. They had agreed to start at the top of Grace's geographical limit, on Seventy-ninth Street, and work their way down.

The two listings she had on Seventy-ninth Street were well decorated but dreary and dark, with no sunlight at all. And there was a townhouse across from the Frick Collection that had no doorman. Ellen had almost lost hope by then, and wondered if she would find anything. They were at Sixty-eighth and Fifth by then, not far from Grace's office at Fifty-seventh and Park, walking distance on a nice day. And the building on Sixty-eighth was across from Central Park, supposedly with a roof garden, and they didn't mind the dog. Ellen was waiting to see what was wrong with it, as the doorman let them in, as the listing agent was late and had allowed him to do so. And for a moment, Ellen felt as though she had walked into someone's home and didn't belong there. There was a very chic living room, all done in beige, with furniture by a well-known Italian designer Ellen recognized immediately. There was a book-lined den set up as an office, a huge master suite done in pale blue, and a respectable second bedroom in navy and white French fabrics. There was a small dining room and a separate kitchen, with a maid's room behind it. The entrance hall was black and white marble, the view of the park was spectacular, the apartment looked clean and well cared for, and the small roof garden was pleasant and had the same high-quality Brown Jordan furniture that Ellen bought for her clients. She couldn't imagine why anyone would want to give it up. The surface of the apartment wasn't enormous, so it was manageable with one cleaning person, and it was big enough for Grace, even if slightly smaller than the apartment she owned in Tribeca, and it was all on one level, so she didn't need to worry about stairs. And the apartment came with kitchen equipment and linens, if a tenant wanted.

"Why are they renting it?" Ellen asked, mystified by why anyone would want to have strangers in an apartment like it.

"The woman who owns it is trying to decide if she wants to move to Palm Beach, and she didn't want to make a hasty decision before she sees if she likes it. She bought a big house there last year, but she's afraid she'll miss New York if she gives up her apartment here. She can always stay at a hotel, but she's not sure. She's renting this apartment for six months, with an option for another six months, if she doesn't want to come back." It was plenty of time for her mother to get the Tribeca apartment in order, if she remained stubborn on that score. Ellen loved the apartment, and would have been happy living there herself. "If she decides to give it up, the apartment will be put up for sale in six months or a year, and the tenant would have to agree to let us show it."

"How much is the rent?" Ellen asked cautiously, afraid that it was one of the ones over budget. She couldn't remember and was surprised at the price—it was well below anything they'd seen in Tribeca, but the Upper East Side was now noticeably less expensive than the trendier areas downtown that had become so popular and were in such high demand, even after the hurricane. "When is it available?" Ellen asked her—it was the last detail she needed to know.

"Now. She just put it on the market after Labor Day. It's been on the market for just over two weeks, but with the hurricane, no one has seen it for the last ten days. We have two showings tomorrow and another one on Friday." Ellen reached for her cell phone as she said it and called her mother. She walked into the orderly white kitchen so she could speak freely.

"Hi, Mom. Are you busy?"

"I'm in a meeting. Can I call you back? I'll be finished in ten minutes."

"Perfect. Get in a cab as soon as you finish. I think I just hit the jackpot. I found a great place on Sixty-eighth and Fifth. There was nothing decent downtown, and this is a little traditional for you, but I don't think you'll find anything better than this for 'temporary furnished,' unless you like the one I saw with eight-foot ceilings and sparkles in the walls. It'll go quick, so you need to come and see it."

"You're fantastic," her mother said with open admiration. "I'll be there in twenty minutes, less if I can do it. Will they take the dog?"

"The broker said the owner has two French poodles, and doesn't care if you do. Mom, it's perfect. I would live here myself." Grace knew that Ellen's taste was more conservative and less extreme than her own, with a bent for modern design and architectural flourishes, but she had total faith in Ellen's ability to pick something for her. She always knew just what her clients liked. And Grace knew that if there was something right for her out there, her daughter would find it.

"I'll be there as fast as I can," Grace promised.

She was there fifteen minutes later, as the realtor waited with Ellen and returned a slew of calls. And Grace was as impressed as Ellen had been when she saw it, and was delighted with the price.

"I think I'd rather use my own linens," Grace said thoughtfully.

Hers had been drowned and stained with sewage and they had thrown them out, so she had to get new ones anyway, and towels. She kissed Ellen then and smiled broadly. "I'll take it," she said to the realtor and her daughter, and they sat down at the kitchen table to fill out the forms, for the real estate agent, the owner, and the co-op board. It was like signing the Constitution or the Treaty of Versailles, but both mother and daughter were impressed by how easily the process had gone. They had found what she needed in a single day.

"It will take about a week to get board approval," the agent explained to them. They were both familiar with the process, and that it took time, and Grace would need three business references, four personal ones, and two financial, which wasn't a problem either. Her secretary could round them up.

An hour later they left the apartment, after Grace made a few notes and took some pictures. And she said she liked the roof garden too.

"I'll ask them to cancel the other showings," the agent assured them, and they left her outside the building, while Grace thanked her daughter again for doing such a good job. It was a major victory after the miseries of the past week. Grace admitted that she wouldn't want to live there forever, it wasn't her style. She knew she would miss Tribeca and couldn't wait to go back. But certainly for six months, it would be perfect, and even convenient for work. Ellen was relieved to know that she could leave for London, assured that her mother had a place to stay, and she could handle the move-in herself. She could leave her own things in storage and just bring her clothes. The apartment even had walk-in closets. And having accomplished the task at hand, Ellen had two days to shop for clients, and she could go back to London on Saturday, two weeks after she had left. She felt as though she had moved mountains since she'd been gone, but things in New York were on the upswing now, only ten days after the hurricane had decimated her mother's apartment and lower New York.

Grace took a cab back to her office, and Ellen went back to Jim Aldrich's on Central Park West. It was four in the afternoon by then, nine o'clock at night in London, and she wanted to tell George she was coming home. She called him as soon as she got to her bedroom in Jim's apartment, and she was smiling. She was so pleased with the apartment she had found for her mother. It was really perfect for her in every way, certainly for six months.

And this time, when she called George, he answered almost at once. He sounded tired and distracted when he did. But Ellen was so happy over their victory that she paid no attention to it, and thought he'd probably just had a long day at the office.

"I'm coming home," she said happily, excited to see him after the time apart that had seemed endless, and after all she and her mother had been through.

"When?" He didn't sound nearly as enthused as she did.

"I think Saturday makes the most sense. I need to work for a couple of days. I've dealt with nothing but the hurricane till now. I just found a terrific furnished apartment for my mother. She can move in next week, once she gets board approval, so I'm done, and she has a place to live for six months, until she gets her apartment restored."

"She's insane to move back there," he said, sounding annoyed.

"I agree. Even her neighbor is moving uptown, and he's selling. I'm going to work on her, but she's not ready to give up yet. I'm hoping she'll come around." There was a long silence after she said it, and she wondered what he was doing. He sounded like he was thinking of something else, or maybe reading at his desk. There was a pause, and then he finally spoke again.

"We need to talk when you get back," he said seriously.

"About what?" She couldn't imagine and didn't want to guess.

"A lot of things," he sighed. "Four years of futile baby-making have really done me in. I can't do that anymore." She was quiet for a moment, and decided to be honest with him. He had said that before, but he seemed as though he meant it this time.

"I saw a doctor here last week. He wasn't encouraging. He agreed with what they told us in London last time. My eggs are too old. He said we would need a donor egg," which she knew neither of them wanted to do.

"I can't do it anymore," he said bluntly, and for a moment it seemed unfair to her. She was the one taking the hormone shots, going through treatments, having her eggs painfully harvested, and going through IVF, not George. But he had lived through each test, disappointment, and miscarriage with her, which had been hard on him too.

"I'm sorry it hasn't worked." She wanted to ask him if he still felt as strongly negative about adoption and surrogacy, but she didn't dare—he seemed upset, and he had obviously been thinking about it while she was gone. He sounded very definite, which made her sad. The whole process had been sad for both of them for too long.

"So am I," he said, clearly unhappy. "It's taken a terrible toll on us." She didn't agree with him, and thought they had survived it surprisingly well. She'd heard worse stories from others. "Ellen, I'm sorry to say this to you now, but I'm done. I wanted to wait till you came back to tell you, but I don't want to mislead you. I've been thinking about it for months."

"I understand," she said quietly, with tears in her eyes. But he had a right to make that decision, not to pursue infertility treatments anymore. They both had to want to do it, for it to be tolerable and a good plan.

"I don't think you do understand," he said soberly. "I mean really done. With the marriage. It killed it for me. The last year or two were just too much. We should have stopped long before. There's no romance left between us, no excitement, no hope. We've been making love on a military command schedule for nearly half our marriage. I can't bear it anymore. And I'm sure you feel that way too."

"No, I don't," she said, panic rising in her throat, as her heart started to beat faster at what he said. "I still love making love to you, even if it hasn't been spontaneous." Her voice drifted off, thinking back to what it had been like. Maybe worse than she wanted to admit. She had been so goal-oriented that she hadn't thought what it was doing to him.

"I hated giving you shots and hurting you, and going through it every time, your being depressed, crying at every sign, the miscarriages, all the business about your eggs. I feel like I went to medical school. And I never wanted children as much as you do. I would have been fine not having any, but having them like this is just unbearable. It's a wonder it didn't make me impotent. I've been making love to a test tube with a copy of *Playboy* in my hand for four years. I've hated every minute of it." And it sounded like he had come to hate her too. It was the first time he had been that honest with her, and she was suddenly sorry she had pushed him to breaking point. It had obviously been a huge mistake. She had destroyed their marriage without meaning to. And she wasn't sure what to do to win him back.

"We can stop now," she said in a thin voice, sad to give up hope of the baby she wanted so desperately, but she didn't want to lose him either, that was even more important to her.

"I have stopped," he confirmed to her. "I meant what I said. I'm done. There's nothing left in this for me. I want a divorce. It's not fair to you to hang on to something that died for me years ago. We both need to get on with our lives. And I realize now it was never the right match. I know how hard you tried to be everything I wanted and adjust to British life for me, but it's not real. It's all foreign to you, and it always will be. I know that now." The way he said it told her something else, and she felt like her heart stopped beating at his words.

"Is there someone else?" She blurted out the words without meaning to, and there was an interminable pause before he answered. He hadn't wanted to do it on the phone, but he couldn't stand the lies anymore and the pretense that they still had a marriage. He still cared about her, and was concerned about her, like a sister, but he knew now that he wasn't in love with her anymore. The life-and-death pursuit of a baby had killed it for him.

"Yes," he finally answered her. "There is."

"Oh my God, since when?" She nearly choked on the words.

"A while. A year," he said, finally honest with her, which was a relief for him. "I thought it would blow over, and it was just a bit of fun. But it's not, it's serious." He hesitated again for a long moment, and told her the rest. "I love her, and I want to marry her." Ellen thought she was going to faint when he said the words. She felt like a bomb had just gone off in her heart and blown it to smithereens.

"And you haven't told me for a year? She's British, I assume." She sounded bitter when she said it, instead of devastated, which was what she really felt.

"Yes. She's the cousin of an old friend. I've known her all my life. She just got divorced, and I ran into her last year. You were away seeing clients somewhere, Spain or the South of France, I think."

"How nice for you." And then she thought of something else. "Has she been at the house parties with you for the past two weekends?"

He hesitated, but not for long—the truth was easier now that he had started the process with Ellen. "Yes, she was."

"And all our friends thought that was fine? They don't mind? Do they all know her too?"

"Many of them. She's Freddy Harper's cousin."

"How perfect. She's one of you. And none of them felt any loyalty to me, watching you cheat on me and bring your mistress to the parties we go to? I'm sorry, but that's a little too European for me. I would have never done that to you, out of respect for you."

"She's not my mistress. I'm going to marry her."

"She is now. You're still married to me." It also meant that her friend Mireille had known and said nothing to her. She was loyal to the rest of them, not to Ellen. George had played her for a fool. "Just exactly what would you have done if I'd gotten pregnant one of those times in the last year, while you were sleeping with her?"

"It would have been a serious problem," he admitted. "It's been very uncomfortable."

"And incredibly dishonest of you," she said angrily. "You've been lying to me for a year." She felt like an idiot for never suspecting what he was up to, and like her heart had just broken in a million pieces, and she had tried so hard to be everything he wanted, and do it all his way, but she just wasn't "one of them."

"Ellen, it's been pretty obvious for the last year or two that it wasn't going to work. You're the only one who refused to see it. If I thought there was a real chance you'd get pregnant, I wouldn't have let things develop with Annabelle. Our marriage was dead before she came into the picture, for me anyway."

"That didn't make you a free man. And of course I'm the last to know," Ellen said, sounding tragic and feeling like she'd been an idiot not to realize what was going on.

"Maybe you weren't paying attention. You wanted a baby more than you wanted me." She wasn't sure if it was true or not, but recognized that it might be a possibility.

"And will you have children with her?" If he did, it would surely be easier than it had been with Ellen, trying to do everything she could with medical assistance and artificially.

"I have no idea," he said honestly. "We haven't discussed it. She's not as obsessed on the subject as you are, or at all. And she has two children. I'm not sure if she wants more, or if I want any of my own, after what we went through. I would have been perfectly content to have a childless marriage, and a wife who loved me for myself, not just as a sperm donor."

"That's not fair," Ellen said, as tears spilled down her cheeks and dripped off her chin. "I wanted a baby because I love you."

"It got out of hand. It became a medical contest to beat the odds."

"Is there any hope for us?" Ellen asked, desperate, and wanting to know.

He gave her the answer quickly, without an ounce of doubt in his voice. "None. I could never revive what I felt for you ten years ago. It's over. When you come back, I want to put the house on the market. It was absurd to buy it—it's too big for either of us—unless you want to keep it, but it's much too big and always was." She nodded. She was beyond thinking about houses at the moment. All she knew was that she had lost her husband, he was in love with another woman, and her marriage was over. There would be no baby and no George from now on. She couldn't even begin to absorb it. "When are you coming back?" he asked in a businesslike tone.

"I don't have a reservation yet. I just found the apartment for my mother today. But I was planning on Saturday."

"Your mother is lucky to have you there. I'll move out before you get back. We can work out the details when you're home." He hesitated and asked her a question then that hadn't even crossed her mind in the shock of what he had just said to her. "Will you stay in London or go back to New York?" Ellen got the feeling that he wanted her to leave. She had never heard him be as icy before. It was over for him, and he wanted her to disappear. She felt like a business deal that had gone wrong, and not a woman he had loved.

"I have no idea. Why?" She had a decorating business in London, although she could work from anywhere with a computer, as long as she flew in to see her clients in Europe, but she hadn't lived in New York in eleven years. It was all too much to think of right now.

"I just wondered. You might be happier there." It was his way of saying that she had never really fit into his world, and without him, she didn't belong. He had just delivered that message loud and clear, with Annabelle. "I'm sorry, Ellen. I know it's all bad news right now, but it will be better for both of us in the end." For him anyway. She didn't know what was better for her anymore. She couldn't tell. She felt like a hurricane had just hit her with the same devastating effects. In its own way, Hurricane Ophelia had destroyed her life too. Or was it Hurricane Annabelle?

After they hung up, she lay down on her bed in the guest room and sobbed for hours. When her mother came home, she told her she had a migraine and stayed in bed. She didn't tell her about the conversation with George. She couldn't. It was too painful to talk about and too shocking to say. She lay in the dark and cried all night, wanting to hate him, but she didn't. And maybe he was right. Maybe she had wanted a baby more than she wanted him. But whatever it had or hadn't been, it was over now. Ten years of her life had just vanished without a trace. No baby, no husband. She would have to start all over again, making a life for herself, and she wondered if she'd have the strength, or even want to. She felt like she was going to die, or already had. George had killed part of her with his words that afternoon. And she had no idea what was left.

Chapter 10

Grace left for the office before Ellen got up the next day. And when she woke up, Ellen crawled out of bed feeling like she'd been on a two-week bender, remembering everything George had said to her the night before. She didn't hear from him again, he didn't send her a text or email to tell her he was sorry or that he loved her, or had changed his mind, which was what she hoped. It was totally over for him, and all he wanted now was to get out of a marriage that was dead for him. And he obviously expected her to be "stiff upper lip" and businesslike about it.

She wasn't going to make trouble for him, but she felt betrayed by all of them, George, the woman he'd been sleeping with, their friends who had obviously known about the affair for months, even her friend Mireille. And she suddenly wanted to make a clean sweep of it herself. She didn't want to see any of them again, or even George. But they would have to take the house apart together and decide who got what. She dreaded going back to London now, and she had major decisions to make, about where to live, and where to run her business from. It felt overwhelming as she sat in Jim's kitchen drinking a cup of coffee and staring into space.

She had heard Bob's typewriter clacking away from his room down the hall, and didn't notice when it stopped. He came into the kitchen for a cup of coffee, and saw her sitting there. She gave a start when she saw him.

"Sorry, I didn't mean to frighten you. Are you okay? Your mother said you had a migraine last night."

"I'm all right," she said, embarrassed to run into him. She felt awful and knew she looked it. And she didn't know what to say. "My life ended last night"? "It's been a rough couple of weeks" was all she could come up with. Rougher than he knew or she wanted to tell him. She didn't want to tell anyone yet. Not even her mother. She felt abandoned and vulnerable, ashamed and unloved. She didn't even know where she was going to live.

"We all need a break from it, and I'm sure breathing sewage fumes for the last ten days didn't help. I hear you found your mother a great apartment. We'll be sorry when she leaves." He smiled at Ellen, and she returned the smile wanly.

"It's a great place for her. How did you do with the two you saw yesterday in the building?" He smiled broadly when she asked him.

"I got lucky too. One of them is perfect for me. I'm going to make an offer on it. It's bigger than I wanted, and about five hundred square feet bigger than my place in Tribeca, but I like it. It has

the same view as this one. And it'll be nice to be in the same building as Jim. I can run my manuscripts up to him after every chap-
ter." He was joking but was pleased. "The place needs work, the
current owner's mother lived there for forty years, and it needs
some serious help to overhaul it. I was thinking of asking your
mother if she would give me some advice, and maybe hire her on
as the architect. New kitchen, new bathrooms. I think I want to
knock down a wall or two to make bigger bedrooms, and a great
office with a view of the park." He was visibly excited about it, and
Ellen smiled.

"That's right up her alley. She'll love it."

"Your mother said you're leaving at the end of the week. When
are you going back?" He was sorry to see her go, and now she was
too. She was going home to her very own hurricane in London.

"Saturday, I think. I've got a lot to do when I get there." She
didn't say what, and he didn't ask. He could see she was upset.
They sat across the table from each other drinking coffee, and then
she looked at him bleakly. He was a kind person and she liked him,
and she couldn't keep it a secret forever. "I haven't told my mother
yet, but my husband informed me on the phone last night that our
marriage is over, and has been for years in his opinion. He wants a
divorce and is going to marry someone else." Bob stared at her
with a shocked expression, which turned to sympathy rapidly.

"Shit. I'm sorry. That's brutal, and hearing it on the phone makes
it even worse. It's so impersonal." He couldn't believe someone
would do that. But now Ellen could. He had been glacial on the
phone. And she realized now that that was who George really was.

He was heartless, now that it was over for him. And he had lied to her for a long time, a full year, while he cheated on her.

"Maybe it's better. I couldn't scream and lie sobbing at his feet," she said ruefully, but she wasn't the type to do that—she had too much dignity, like her mother.

"What are you going to do? Stay there? Move back here?"

"I have no idea. He asked me that too, five minutes after he told me. I have to figure it all out when I go back. He wants to sell the house, which is probably smart. It was too big for us anyway." She sighed. "I spent the last four years having infertility treatments and IVF, trying to have a baby. He says that ended the marriage for him, which may be true. It became kind of an obsession for me. And I just finally accepted that that's not going to work, so now no husband, no baby, brave new world. It's a lot to figure out. The hurricane was easier to deal with." He nodded, sorry for her. And she was startled at how much she was telling him, and she wasn't even embarrassed.

"Divorce is never pleasant, for anyone. And it's always something of a shock, even if you're the one who wanted it. It's always worse than you expect it to be. I didn't want a divorce either—my wife just fell out of love with me and wanted out. I probably deserved it, but it hurt anyway. Most of us are stupid about relationships, and blind to what the other person is feeling." He was worried about Ellen as they talked. She was destroyed.

"I didn't realize how fed up he was with the baby-making and infertility stuff. He says he hated the last four years, and it's been over for him for the last two."

"He should have told you and not cheated on you," Bob said, and she nodded. She sat staring into her coffee then for a few minutes, and he patted her arm and then went back to work, thinking about her and what lay ahead of her. He felt genuinely sorry for her, and even if she'd made mistakes in her marriage, she was a good person, and he was sure she had done her best. Her husband sounded like a prick to him, but he didn't want to say so and make things worse.

Grace called a few minutes later and asked how her headache was. Ellen still felt rocky but insisted she was fine and was going to shop for her clients that afternoon. After they hung up, she made a reservation for a flight back to London on Saturday night, arriving Sunday morning.

And then she went out to shop for her clients but found nothing. She was too distracted to even see what was in the stores, and all she could think of was what George had told her the night before. She said nothing to her mother that night, and worked on her computer to avoid her, and finally on Friday when she was packing, her mother asked her what was wrong. Ellen was about to lie to her, and then decided there was no point. She sat down on the bed and stared at Grace. Her eyes were as deeply troubled as she felt.

"George wants out, Mom. He wants a divorce. He's in love with someone else." Her mother was as stunned as Ellen had been when he told her. It was the last thing Grace had expected from him. She had thought he was better than that, and a decent man.

"That's it? He told you that while you were here?" Ellen nodded. "Did you suspect it? Have you two been fighting a lot?" George had never seemed like a cheater to her.

"No, I thought everything was fine. He was hard to reach once I got here, but my phone wasn't working most of the time, when we were downtown. He says it's been going on for the last year. He said the infertility treatments and IVF were too much for him."

"Did he warn you of that, and say something?" Ellen shook her head.

"Maybe I should have suspected it. It's been pretty depressing and stressful for both of us. She's related to one of George's friends. I think that's part of it too. He wants to be with his own kind."

Grace looked angry at that. "You did everything his way. Maybe you shouldn't have." It was the only reproach she could have made. "You let him make all the rules. Everything had to be according to his old-school British standards. Was that okay with you?" She had always wondered and didn't want to ask.

"Sometimes it was okay," Ellen said quietly. "It was important to him, so I tried to respect his traditions. It would have been harder if we'd had kids. He wants to put the house on the market when I go back, right away—in fact, he sounds like he's in a hurry. He's decided that it's over, and now he wants out."

"What about you? What do *you* want?" her mother asked her. Ellen never thought enough about that. She was too accommodating, and George had taken full advantage of it. Ellen had trusted him. It had never occurred to her he was cheating on her.

"I don't know what I want. I haven't had time to think about it," Ellen said miserably. It broke Grace's heart to see how shattered her daughter looked.

"Do you want to stay in London?" This was a shock for Grace too, and she felt deeply sorry for her daughter.

"I don't know that either. I thought I had a life there, and friends. But apparently they all knew about this woman and went along with it, and no one told me. She's someone's cousin, and he knew her before. She's one of them. I never was. I realize that now. I'm not sure I belong there or want to stay. Maybe I should try to come back to New York, and run my business from here. I could try it, and go to Europe when I need to see my clients. I could stay with you for a while." Grace looked pensive when she said it, before she answered.

"You could do that. But you can't be a nomad now. You lived by George's rules for all these years and did what he wanted. You can stay with me, but you need your own space, your own life, your own rules. You have to decide what *you* want, not just live in my guest room." Her mother had a point. "Maybe try it here for a while, and commute when you have to." Listening to her, Ellen realized that she no longer had a home in either city. But instead of free, she just felt lost. Her mother was right, she had to figure it out for herself, and what *she* wanted. She no longer knew that, or even who she was.

"I'll figure it out when I go back. Maybe I should open an office here." It was all so confusing and so new, she felt overwhelmed.

"I'm so sorry this happened," Grace said sympathetically as she hugged her. "You'll make the right decisions when you get there." Ellen nodded but wasn't sure—she had clearly been making the wrong ones about George for a long time. She felt betrayed by everyone now, and hated the thought of going to London to take apart her life. But it had to be done, and then wherever she decided to live, she would have to start all over again.

Ellen had lunch with her mother the next day before her flight. And she thanked Jim again for his hospitality before she left the apartment. She had loved staying there. He assured her that he had thoroughly enjoyed having her and her mother as houseguests. The co-op board had approved Grace, who was moving to her temporary apartment the following weekend. Ellen left him a magnum of champagne, and a generous tip for the help, and she ran into Bob as she was leaving for the airport.

"Good luck," he said kindly. He was worried about her. "Take care of yourself in London." They were wise words, and he meant them.

"Good luck to you too, with the offer on the new apartment." She tried to look braver than she felt. It was humiliating to have everyone know that her husband had left her, and she suspected that in London it would be worse. She felt like an utter failure as she hugged her mother with tears in her eyes and left. It had been a strange two weeks that suddenly felt like a lifetime. Everything had come apart, and nothing had been put back together yet. She felt like she'd never have a life again.

*   *   *

The flight to London seemed to take forever. She lay awake for most of it and was exhausted when she arrived at Heathrow. She took a cab from the airport, and let herself into the empty house. As he had told her on the phone he would be, George was gone. She guessed that he was probably away for the weekend with Annabelle, at another house party, with the people who had pretended to be Ellen's friends, and she now knew never were.

She checked the closets in their bedroom, and his dressing room. His clothes were gone. And looking around their bedroom at the small things that were missing, and the photographs of them he had left behind, she sat down on their bed and cried. It was depressing beyond belief to be back. And after what had happened, there was no one she wanted to see or get in touch with.

George called her that night, and she heard the now-familiar icy, businesslike tone when she answered. "You're back?" He sounded in good spirits, as though he'd had a fun weekend. She didn't ask him about it and didn't want to know.

"I am," she confirmed in a dead voice. "I see you took your clothes."

"I think we should get together this week and divide up what's in the house." She had paid for a lot of the furniture, and decorating, and he had paid for the rest. Some of it had been wedding gifts, or from her mother. And he had brought some of his ancestral antiques. The idea of pulling it all apart and splitting it up depressed her even more. And where would she send it? She had absolutely no idea.

"What's your rush?" she asked him in a hollow voice, in order to cover her own confusion.

"I think we need to get this behind us, so we can both go on with our lives. There's no point hanging on," he told her, and he had certainly made that clear since his announcement on the phone four days before. "We should put the house on the market as soon as possible, unless you want to stay there?" But she didn't want to now—it would just be a painful memory for her. It was the house they had bought to have babies in, and they had imagined themselves there for the rest of their lives. She was glad now that they had never bought a country house—it would have just been one more thing they had to get rid of and split up.

"Have you told all our friends?" she asked, curious.

"They know," he said simply, and just as in bad movies and books, she was the last one to know. He had made a fool of her for a year, which made it all even worse. "How was New York when you left?"

"Downtown is a mess. Uptown is untouched." Not that it mattered, given what was happening between them. And she really didn't know what to do now. She felt like a quitter leaving London and going back to New York, but it would be humiliating staying, hearing about it when George and Annabelle got married, and too lonely for Ellen without friends. She had no friends of her own, only George's. And now there was no one left she could trust, since they had all known.

They made an appointment to meet at the house on Tuesday evening after work. She went to her office early Monday morning, answered all her emails, and met with her assistants to catch up on her clients and their news. They all asked about the hurricane, and her assistants saw how devastated she looked, and realized how bad it must have been. None of them knew that the real hurricane for her had happened in London, and was not Ophelia but George.

Phillippa, her senior assistant, stayed in her office to go over some photographs of furniture and fabric samples with her, and when the others left, Ellen told her what had happened.

"We're getting a divorce." Phillippa was shocked at what she said, and thought she'd heard wrong at first.

"You and George?" Ellen nodded. "What happened?" Phillippa was stunned. They were the kind of couple you thought would be together forever.

"A lot of things, I guess," Ellen answered. "Four years of IVF. And he's in love with someone else."

"Christ, I can't believe it. I never would have expected it of him." She had always thought he was a snob and somewhat arrogant. But he was so proper and even tedious at times, she had never suspected he would cheat on his wife. It made Phillippa angry on her behalf to hear about it. Ellen didn't know if she was angry or just sad. Mostly sad for now. Maybe anger would come later.

"Me neither," Ellen said mournfully.

"What can I do to help?" Phillippa offered. She was a beautiful Eurasian girl, and had worked for Ellen for five years.

"Once we divide up our things and I figure out what I'm doing, there will be plenty for us to do." And even more if she moved to New York. "I'm meeting him tomorrow. We're selling the house."

"You sound very calm about it." Phillippa was impressed and worried about her.

"What other choice do I have? He made up his mind. From the sound of it, a year ago, or months anyway. He just wants to get out of the marriage now, so he can marry her."

"He's a fool," Phillippa said loyally, as Ellen wondered if that was true, or if it was in fact the right decision for him. It was hard to know. It didn't feel like the right one for her, and she couldn't imagine it ever would. "Well, let me know if there's anything I can do. I can help you pack up the house when you get to that. Where are you going to go? Will you look for something else to buy?"

"Eventually." And then she decided to be honest with her. "I'm thinking about going back to New York, for a while anyway. I'll keep the office here. I can always move back, and I can fly in to see clients, and work out of my apartment in New York." She'd need at least one assistant there, but it wouldn't be hard to find one, and she knew Phillippa could run her London office and keep her clients happy. And with email and phone, Ellen could stay in close touch with her clients and her London staff.

"I'll miss working with you every day, if you decide to do that," Phillippa said unhappily, but she could see why she wanted to. For the moment Ellen had nothing left in London except work, and Phillippa thought she would have wanted to run away too. "It sounds like you had your own personal hurricane," she said sympathetically, and Ellen nodded.

"Yeah, I did. At least I got my mother organized before I left. I found her a great place. I wish I could get her to sell her Tribeca apartment, but she's determined to move back."

"More fool her after two hurricanes," Phillippa said, sounding very British. "Maybe she'll change her mind." But Ellen didn't think she would. Grace was not one to give up.

They spent the day working together on a stack of projects, and the next day Ellen met with two of her clients, and she left work reluctantly at six o'clock to meet George at the house. He let himself in without ceremony while Ellen was pouring a glass of wine to fortify herself for the meeting, and when she turned to look at him, he already seemed like a different person. He appeared happier, was wearing a brighter tie than she'd ever seen him with before, and had a new haircut and looked younger. But the real change was in his eyes. He looked excited and alive, and totally indifferent to her. It was as though the man she knew had vanished and been replaced by a stranger. In a way it made it easier. There was nothing familiar about him now. And seeing him and talking to him was like a slap in the face. In his mind, she was already out of his life. He had disposed of her in a cruel, heartless way. She had never felt so insignificant in her life. She was history and nothing more. He had given up on their marriage and never said a word to her. He had never given her a chance to change it, or make it work. He gave up in silence with no warning and moved on. Ellen wondered if she would ever trust anyone again. And if she left London, it would be with a lost decade and a clean slate. No man, no kids, no friends. She was leaving their friends to him, and she was deeply hurt by what they'd done. She had been betrayed by everyone they knew.

They went through the house room by room, while they each said what they wanted, and she made a careful list. There were no arguments about it, she wouldn't stoop to do so, and she only wanted to keep what she had paid for or brought to the marriage. And anything he had gotten from his family she was leaving with him, which was most of the art, and some antiques from his grandparents' country house when they died. It was agonizingly sad walking around the house with him. It was just furniture to him, and nothing more. They were relics of a lost life to her. It felt as though someone had died, and they were dividing up the estate, which they were. And what had died had been their marriage, which had been a living entity to her, like a person.

George told her that he wanted to remove his things as soon as possible, since he wanted to get an apartment, and was already looking. She could tell that he'd been busy while she was gone. Her trip to New York had been convenient for him. She wondered if he'd even had the bad taste to have his girlfriend stay at the house with him, and sleep in her bed, but she didn't want to ask.

"So have you decided what you're doing and where you want to live?" he asked, and seemed anxious to know, which seemed cruel to her.

"You only told me six days ago. I need some time to figure it out." But she told him he could put the house on the market. She realized that he wanted to get his money out of it. It seemed like he wanted to divest himself of all signs of the marriage. She had seen other men do things like that, but had never thought him capable of it. It was all a very bad surprise. And she walked around the house with a stomachache after he left, but at least she didn't cry. And she spent the rest of the week trying to figure out what she wanted to do. She remembered what her mother had said, that she had to do what *she* wanted this time, and not live her life for someone else, but she hadn't made her mind up yet.

Grace moved into the furnished apartment over the weekend, and called Ellen to thank her again on Sunday night. She said that Bob and Jim were coming to dinner, and she sounded delighted.

"Say hi from me," Ellen said quietly. It had been a long, arduous week for her, dealing with her clients after two weeks away. She had flown to Nice for a day on Friday, to watch the progress on a house she was decorating in St. Jean Cap Ferrat, and had flown home that night. And like a drumbeat behind all else she was doing, she was trying to figure out what to do with her life, and where she wanted to live.

She didn't expect the house to sell quickly, but once George took his things out, she wanted to move too. It was all happening very fast, and maybe it was just as well. He was being so unkind about it, and so coldblooded that she couldn't harbor any illusions about him and what their marriage meant to him. Clearly, nothing in a long time. Grace said she had lost all respect for him, and Ellen admitted she had too. He was like someone she didn't even know.

She'd been home in London for two weeks when she ran into a couple they knew well, on the street over the weekend. She was shocked by the chilly reception she got from them, as though they scarcely knew her, and she realized that their allegiance had never been to her, and belonged totally to George. She could tell that they were already engaged with his new woman and considered them a couple. Ellen was the openly acknowledged outsider now. It made the decision of what should come next easier for her. She called Phillippa as soon as she got home.

"Okay, I'm done," she said quietly, and her assistant wasn't surprised. She had thought it would come to that in the end. Men like George, and the upper-class circles they came from, were too tight a clique for any of them to stay loyal to her, and Phillippa was glad for her that she had decided to leave, at least for a while.

"I'm going to put all my stuff in storage for now. I can ship it to New York, or you can do it for me, when I find an apartment, unless I find something furnished like my mother's." But she wanted something more permanent than that. She needed a home of her own. She had just been torn out of London by the roots, and she needed to plant them again somewhere. New York for now. "I want to meet with all the active clients in the next couple of weeks, and reassure them that I can be here whenever they need me, while you hold the fort. They can reach me by email, or Skype, or on my cell. I deal with most of them by email now, so it won't be a big change for them." Phillippa agreed with her and set up the appointments for the following week. When Ellen met with them, none of them seemed worried or upset, and they liked the idea of her shopping for their fabrics, furniture, and accessories in New York. And she would fly back for any installations, or problems that they had. No one objected to the change. It wasn't going to be a hard transition for them at all.

It was going to be a lot harder for Ellen, who had lived in London for eleven years. She knew she would miss it, but after what had happened with George so suddenly, not enough to stay. She advised him of the date her belongings would be removed from the house, but didn't tell him where she was going. It was none of his business now. They had no reason to communicate with each other. All the decisions about property had been made relatively quickly, since the only thing they owned jointly was the house. The rest could be handled by lawyers. "You can reach me through my office or attorney," she told him by text.

She and Phillippa watched her furniture, and some of her clothes, being packed and removed to storage, and she stayed at a small hotel near the office for the last few days. And she decided to call Charles Williams before she left. He and Gina had been back in London for a month by then, and she wondered if Gina had stayed. He was thrilled to hear from Ellen when she called.

"When did you get back?" he asked her, and sounded happy and relaxed.

"About three weeks ago. Are Gina and the girls still here?"

"They are. She had another blowout with Nigel. And her landlord in New York told her that she can't move back into her apartment for another three months, so we put the girls in school here. They're happy, the grandparents love it, and it's nice for me to have them here."

"And Gina?" she asked cautiously, not wanting to make him uncomfortable.

"I'm not sure. I haven't asked. I don't want to scare her off, but she seems happy too. Whatever happens, it's been wonderful having her and the girls here. Things seem a lot smoother than they used to be. Maybe we both grew up." He seemed hopeful, and interested in Ellen's news too. "What about you? Everything back to normal?" Ellen laughed in answer. At least she could laugh about it now, and not cry when someone asked.

"Not exactly. My husband told me he wanted a divorce before I left New York. Apparently he's been having an affair for a year. I was an idiot not to see it. They're getting married. I just put my furniture in storage, and our house is on the market. So there's a major change. I'm going back to New York in a few days. I'm going to try living there for a while. It would be too hard here." When she said it, it sounded like she was running away, but she didn't know what else to do. She had lived in George's world for ten years, and she wanted to make a graceful exit. For her, for now, that meant New York, even though she had no set plans there either, and would have to stay with her mother until she found an apartment. She felt stupid that her whole life had unraveled, but it had, and now she had to deal with it and start over.

"I'm so sorry, I had no idea," he said sympathetically.

"Neither did I. It was a hell of a surprise."

"Maybe it will be a blessing in the end," Charles said optimistically.

"Maybe." She wasn't counting on that, but she was doing her best to act as though it was.

"Stay in touch, and let me know if you come back to London for a visit, or to work. I'd love to see you," he said warmly.

"Will do," she said simply. It seemed odd that her only friend in London was someone she had met on an airplane during a hurricane a month before.

Ellen's questions when they spoke on the phone left Charles thoughtful after they hung up. The last few weeks, he and Gina had been getting along and the girls were happy. She was staying with him, and sharing a bedroom with the girls. He had made no romantic advances toward her—he didn't dare. But he would have liked to. She had given him no indication that it would be welcome, although he was almost sure it was over with Nigel. They had had another resounding battle on the phone, where she had accused him of not caring about her or the girls. And Charles never questioned her about it—he thought it best not to, and to let her come to her own conclusions without comment from him.

He told her about his conversation with Ellen that afternoon when she came back from school with the girls, and they went to do their homework in their room.

"How sad for her," she said sympathetically, and he didn't remind her that she had done the same thing to him over Nigel, nearly two years before.

"She's moving to New York, which must be hard for her after so many years here. She must feel like a woman without a country, not just a man. Sometimes it's easier to go home when things go wrong," he said, looking at the woman he had loved for so long, and not just because she was the mother of his children. And after talking to Ellen, he finally got up the courage to ask her what he had been wondering for weeks. He had been afraid to rock the boat till then, but he wanted to know, and not delude himself about something she might not feel. "What about us, Gina?" he asked gently, inching his way along. "Do you ever think about trying again?" She nodded with a smile.

"All the time," she admitted to him. "I didn't know how you'd feel about it . . . after Nigel and everything . . . I didn't want to upset you by asking. . . ." His heart almost flew out of his throat at what she said.

"Are you serious?" She nodded again, and he leaned over and kissed her full on the lips, which he had been aching to do for weeks.

"I thought if you were interested, you'd make a move, but you haven't, so I stayed quiet about it," she said shyly, and she looked more beautiful to him than ever before.

"I was trying to be respectful," he said honestly.

"Me too, after all the mistakes I made before." She leaned over and kissed him again.

"That's new for us," he said, smiling broadly. "Maybe we learned something with everything that happened."

"I think I finally grew up in New York and realized who you are during the hurricane," she said solemnly. "You're a great father, a good husband, and a wonderful man. I think I never realized it before. I was a total fool."

"I might have been too. I never understood how much you might miss your single life and needed to have more fun than just being a wife and mother."

She kissed him again then, and smiled at him. "I'm ready for that now. I wasn't then." He put his arms around her when she said it.

"So you'll stay?" he whispered, and she nodded. "Will you move into my bedroom?" he whispered again.

"Tonight," she whispered back. He could hardly wait while she went to give the girls a bath, and he helped her get dinner started. They had been cooking together every night till then.

He sent Ellen a text when he thought about it, to tell her, like a kid in a schoolroom. "Just asked her. She's staying. Good luck in New York. Charles." And she texted him back a few minutes later, "Bravo! Good move on your part, great decision on hers. Love, Ellen."

And that night Gina kept her promise and moved back into his bedroom, and the good times started all over again, even better than before.

Chapter 11

When Ellen landed in New York, she went straight to her mother's new rented apartment. It had taken her longer than she'd expected to clear customs, and she got there later than she'd anticipated. Her mother looked busy, and was dressing to go out for dinner with friends.

She had settled in nicely, and it was working perfectly for her. She even liked the location more than she thought she would. It was fun being uptown, and seemed more sophisticated and "grown up."

"Don't worry, I won't stay forever, I promise," Ellen teased her, remembering what Grace had said before, about their both needing their own lives, and Ellen needing her own home. She knew that her mother had already started the reconstruction work on the apartment downtown, although the building was still in bad shape. They had installed generators so people could begin repairs, but there was no electricity in her area yet. Downtown New York was not going to be rebuilt in a day. And Grace hadn't changed her mind about moving back when it was ready, even if she was enjoying her temporary apartment uptown. "I have an appointment with the realtor this week. I want to find something unfurnished and bring my things over from London," Ellen told her.

"That sounds like a big decision," Grace complimented her as she watched Ellen unpack, and Blanche danced around their feet.

"It is," Ellen admitted, and hadn't been an easy one for her. "How does Blanche like it here?" she asked to lighten the moment, and her mother laughed.

"She thinks she's an Upper East Side dog now. There are three poodles and another Maltese in the building—she's right at home. I'll never get her down to bohemian Tribeca again." Grace smiled lovingly at her daughter, glad that she was there. She'd missed her during her three weeks away. After all the time they had spent together during the hurricane, she felt even closer to her than before. And it was going to be wonderful having her in New York and seeing her more than a few times a year. Even if they were both busy, it would be nice knowing they were in the same city, and could see each other casually for lunch or a quiet evening.

"Who are you having dinner with tonight?" Ellen asked her. She was happy to see her after the flight. Her mother reeled off the names of two couples she didn't know, and Jim Aldrich at the end. Her daughter looked at her in surprise.

"Jim Aldrich, as in the literary agent we stayed with after the hurricane?"

"Yes," her mother said primly. "I've had dinner with him a few times. He's very nice. And we went to a benefit at the Met a few days ago." She seemed mildly embarrassed about it, and Ellen laughed.

"Go, Mom! That sounds like fun."

"It was. It seems a little silly, at my age, but he keeps asking me out."

"He's not much younger than you. Besides, he's smart and funny, and you can do the *Times* crossword puzzle on Sundays." Ellen loved the idea of her mother having a man in her life again after so many years. She was so busy and vital and interesting, it always seemed sad to Ellen that she was alone. And she was still a beautiful woman.

"He wants me to go to Art Basel in Miami with him in December, but I'm not sure I want to go." She seemed hesitant about it, and Ellen encouraged her immediately.

"Why not? You'd have a fantastic time. It's one of the best art fairs in the world. You should go with him."

She made a face. "I'm too old for romance." But the companionship appealed to her. It was exciting having someone to do things with, and they had many interests in common. Many of her women friends had begun to seem so ancient, and two of them had died recently. Grace was more active in the world than most, since she was still working and very busy, and had friends who were younger, and didn't talk about their ailments and surgeries the way her contemporaries did. She hated that.

"He's sixty-nine, Mom. He's not thirty, for heaven's sake. And you're not too old. You're younger than anyone I know."

"I didn't feel it a month ago. The hurricane really wore me out."

"It wore me out too." And so had George. Her mother asked about it when Ellen followed her to her bedroom while she finished dressing. She had already done her makeup and looked very pretty in a black silk skirt and white satin blouse. And she had done her hair in an elegant French twist. "The move out went all right," Ellen answered her quietly. It had been hard and sad, which she expected.

"Did you see George before you left?"

"No, and I didn't want to. I never heard from him, which is just as well." It stunned her how fast he had exited from her life, and she realized now that in all the ways that mattered, he had been gone long before that, and already belonged to someone else. It was still a shocking blow, but she was glad she had left London and was back in New York. She needed to find an apartment, and an assistant to work for her. She hoped to find both in the coming days.

The doorman rang from downstairs while they were talking about it, and Blanche ran to the front door barking and wagging her tail. It was Jim Aldrich, and Grace told the doorman to send him up. She opened the door to him a minute later, and Ellen came out of her bedroom to say hello. He was pleased to see her and welcomed her to New York. He had heard from Grace what had happened to Ellen's marriage, but didn't mention it to her. He was wearing a good-looking navy blue suit, an Hermès tie the same color, and an exquisitely cut white shirt. He was very elegant, beautifully groomed, and his snow-white hair was perfectly cut.

They made a very handsome couple as Grace put on a black fur jacket and picked up a small black suede evening bag. And she was wearing a new pair of high heels, since she had lost most of hers in the flood.

"You're looking very uptown, Mom," Ellen teased her, and they all laughed. And Grace was happy when she left with Jim, but Blanche was forlorn in the front hall. "It's you and me, kid," Ellen told her, and the little white fur ball followed her into her bedroom and jumped up onto the bed. Ellen had been pleased to see Jim Aldrich with her mother, and hoped she'd continue to accept his invitations, including the one to Miami in six weeks.

Grace came home at midnight, and said she'd had a terrific time with him and his friends. It was a very different life than the one Ellen had seen her mother leading for the past several years. She couldn't remember the last time she'd seen her go out all dressed up on a Saturday night. They had suddenly had a reversal of roles. Ellen was home, feeling like an old lady, and her mother was all dolled up and had a beau.

And the following day Jim was back again to take her to brunch. He had brought the crossword puzzle with him, and they argued over it for half an hour before they went out. Ellen hadn't realized how much her mother was seeing of him. Grace never mentioned it on the phone. But she was happy for her. It added a whole new dimension to her life, instead of just working day and night as she had before. There was clearly a man in her life now, not just an office and a dog. And with Ellen in New York, they could do things together too.

Ellen spent the day unpacking and getting organized, answering emails from Phillippa and her clients, and planning things she had to do, and the following morning, she met the realtor at the first apartment of several they were going to see. Their mission was a déjà vu of her looking for an apartment for her mother, but they had had no luck by the end of the first day, or even by the end of the week. Unfurnished apartments were a lot less charming than the furnished one she had found for her mother. And she was discouraged about it when she heard from Bob Wells on Saturday.

"I just heard from Jim that you're here," he said, sounding pleased. "I'm still working on the new book, and I hadn't talked to him all week. Can I interest you in a walk in the park this afternoon? I've been holed up here all week and I need to get some air."

"I'd love it." And for once she didn't have any apartments to see. She met him outside the Pierre Hotel, and they walked into Central Park, among bicyclists, joggers, people with babies in strollers, couples holding hands, vendors selling ice cream, and all the usual people one saw in the park. They were both wearing running shoes and jeans, and Ellen had worn a big Irish fisherman's sweater in the chill October air. It was a lot cooler than it had been in the city four weeks before, when she left.

"What happened when you were in London?" he asked as they walked along. He had thought about her a lot after what she told him about George wanting a divorce, and how heartbroken and shocked she had seemed.

"Pretty much what I expected. He moved his things out. I moved mine and put them in storage. We called lawyers. It's all done. He acts as if it's been over for years, and I guess for him it was. Once he told me, and about the other woman, he canceled me out of his life totally. It was pretty shocking at first. And a huge change. I left London thinking I was happily married, and two weeks later, discovered I wasn't, and was getting a divorce."

And he suspected it still was shocking for her. It was difficult to accept when one person decided to close the door on the other. It had taken him a long time to recover, when it happened to him. She seemed to be surviving it surprisingly well. "I'm glad I came here. It would have been harder in London, if I'd stayed. He took all our friends with him. They were really his friends, but this made it very clear that they never considered me one of them."

He nodded as he listened, sympathetic to what she said, and how much she seemed to have lost, an entire world.

"How's the apartment search coming?" he asked, to change the subject.

"Nothing so far," she said, looking discouraged. "What about your new apartment? Has my mother worked her magic yet?" Ellen asked with a smile.

"I'm waiting for a proposal from her and some plans. It sounds like she wants to gut it, which is probably what it needs. So I won't be moving in for a while, if Jim can stand me. But it will be convenient living in the building while it's in progress, so I can check on it anytime." It sounded like a good arrangement to her too.

"I gather my mother and Jim have been seeing each other quite a bit," she said cautiously, and he smiled.

"It appears that way. They're sweet together. They're both interesting people. I would never have thought of it, but they're a good match. I should have introduced them before." He didn't say it, but Jim had been given to younger women for a long time. Grace was a departure for him, but the right one, in Jim's eyes.

"She's having a great time with him," Ellen confirmed.

"So is he. He talks about her all the time."

"I don't think that she's convinced that she should be 'dating' anyone, but I don't see why not. And they have so many interests in common. And in the end, maybe good relationships are about companionship, not passion." She had thought she had that with George, but apparently not. They had had nothing together, nothing that had lasted. Not even children. She noticed a stroller rolling by them with twins, and she looked away, as she always did. It was too painful to see, and a reminder of what she would never have. She had to give up on it, but had no idea how to do that yet. The reality still hurt too much.

"Relationships are always a mystery," Bob said thoughtfully. "There is some kind of secret ingredient that makes them work. The ones you think will never make it usually do. And the ones that look like a sure thing wind up on the rocks. I can never predict these things," he commented easily as they walked along. "That's why I write thrillers, not romance." They both laughed at what he said.

"Well, clearly I can't predict it either," she said ruefully, and he smiled at her. "I just watched ten years go up in smoke."

"He wasn't honest with you," Bob reminded her. He had said that before, the day after George asked her for a divorce and she told Bob about it in Jim's kitchen. "He should have told you when it started not to work for him, and given you a chance to fix it, or do things differently. It wasn't fair to you."

"I'm sure you're right, but I think he finally found the right one for him. I tried to be, but I never was. So I'm out of a job, fired," she said, trying to be philosophical about it, but she was still angry at him, and wondered if she always would be.

"He's a damn fool," Bob said softly, and offered her an ice cream cone to cheer her up, which she accepted. And he had one too.

They stopped at the model boat pond, and walked farther into the park, and then back down, and stopped outside her mother's building. She didn't ask him up, because she didn't want to surprise her mother with a guest. It was why she needed her own place. Her mother was right.

"I'll call you when I get a better grip on this book," Bob promised. "I'm still wrestling with it. But maybe we could have dinner sometime." She nodded and thanked him for the ice cream, and a minute later she disappeared into the building with a wave. And Bob walked back across the park to Jim's apartment on Central Park West. He'd had an easy, pleasant time with Ellen. She brought something out in him that no one else did and made him feel comfortable in his own skin. He felt like he could say anything to her. He hoped to see her again soon. She had a lot on her plate at the moment with the shock of her marriage ending, trying to create a new life for herself, and moving back to New York. And he was busy with the book. But after she settled in, he would call her. He wasn't sure what it would lead to, if anything, but at least they could be friends. He liked the idea of that. Writing was so much easier than relationships. It was so much simpler dealing with fictional characters and creating mysteries. But taking a chance on another human being terrified him, and had ever since his divorce. Ellen was the first woman he'd met in years who made it seem worthwhile to take a risk. And being with her felt surprisingly safe. He liked everything about her, except the possibility that one of them might get hurt. He'd been through it, and now so had she. But all he wanted for now, as he walked back to Jim's apartment, was to see her again.

It was a relief when he got home to his typewriter and started to work on the book again. This was the one thing he knew he could do. He was masterful at it. And as he began typing, he pushed her gently from his mind, and reentered the world of fantasy he conjured up so well, where he could control it, and knew exactly how it would turn out. In real life, you just never knew.

Ellen saw eight more apartments the following Monday and Tuesday, all of them in good locations, on the East Side, where she was looking. Downtown held no lure for her, as it did for her mother. She wanted to be on the Upper East Side in a building with a doorman, with enough space for an office. She didn't need a view or a showplace, but a place that felt like home to her was beginning to feel like Mission Impossible, until she walked into an apartment late on Tuesday, and the minute she saw it, she knew that was it. It was big and sunny, in an old building in the East Seventies, facing south. It had big windows on a tree-lined street, and felt more like a house. The maids' rooms in the back would make perfect office space for her and an assistant. And it reminded her a little of the house in London that she had just given up. It had an old-fashioned, European feeling to it, and her furniture would look right in it. There was a fireplace in the living room, and another in the master bedroom. It had a small dining room, with walls that had been painted dark red, and a cozy kitchen. She could see herself living there, listening to music, and reading by the fire on winter nights. She turned to the realtor with a look of relief.

"This is it." She was home, and she knew it instantly. Apartments were like romance, you fell in love or you didn't, and she just had. It wasn't what the realtor had expected her to like, and they'd been looking in modern buildings since she'd arrived. Ellen could already envision the living room with fabrics in warm colors, and a comfortable couch. She needed to buy one, since George had taken theirs for the flat he was going to share with Annabelle. She didn't want to think about it now. She wanted to leave the past behind her and start fresh.

She filled out the application before she left the building, and left a check for the deposit. The rent was even below her budget. No one had had the imagination so far to see what they could do with it. Its main attraction was that it was cozy. And it was available immediately. She could move in as soon as she was approved, and it was in a rental building, so she didn't have to pass muster with a co-op board. All they had to do was check her credit rating.

And she put on the form that she had owned her own home in London for five years. And in the box that referred to marital status on the application, she checked "divorced" with a sinking heart. She could no longer check "married," since she wouldn't be soon. It felt strange when she wrote it, and she looked sad when she handed the application back. But she was excited when she walked back to her mother's apartment, and she told her the good news when she came home.

"You'll be rid of me when my furniture comes," she told her, "if they approve me."

"I don't want to be rid of you. I love having you here," Grace assured her. She was happy Ellen had found something she liked. It was a start for her new life.

They had a quiet dinner together that night and went to bed early. And the realtor called her two days later to say that her application had been approved. She sent an email to Phillippa to arrange to have her furniture shipped. And the day after, she called an agency to hire an assistant. It was all falling into place faster than she had expected. It was dizzying to think about. It felt like mountain climbing at times. All she had to do was get to a safe place so she could relax and catch her breath, but not yet.

And the following week, they gave her the keys to the apartment, and her mother liked it when she came to see it. Her furniture was on its way to New York on a ship, and she started looking at fabric for curtains, and ordered a couch in a warm taupe velvet like the one she'd had in London. Her attorney in London had heard from George's by then, and he was proceeding with the divorce. She wasn't surprised, and didn't expect him to change his mind, but it hurt anyway. It was all happening so quickly. One minute she'd been married, and the next it was all over. It was still hard to understand what had happened, what signs she had missed, and why he had never warned her before he gave up. She tried not to obsess about it, but the questions haunted her late at night. She lay in bed mulling it over, and wondered if he was happy now with Annabelle and her children. She was glad there was no one to tell her about it. She realized she didn't really want to know about his new life.

Ellen had dinner with her mother and Jim one night, and they talked about Bob and the book he was writing. Jim said Bob needed to get out more, he worked too hard, albeit with excellent results. Ellen hadn't heard from him again since their walk in the park weeks before, and assumed he was still working on the book.

And providentially the week before her furniture arrived, Ellen hired an assistant. Alice Maguire had worked for a well-known decorating firm, run by a dragon, and wanted something easier and more agreeable than the pressure she'd been under. Phillippa liked her when she talked to her on Skype, her references were excellent, and Ellen gave her a mountain of files to sort through on her first day, sent her to Ikea for two desks and the file cabinets they needed, and gave her a stack of fabric samples to return that her clients had rejected, and some for herself, and left to see her client in Palm Beach. They were off to a running start. Alice seemed to have everything under control when Ellen came back two days later. She told Ellen that her furniture had cleared customs, was on the dock in New York, and was due to be delivered to the apartment the next day.

"Sounds good." Ellen smiled at her as Alice handed her a cup of tea just the way she had told her she liked it. "We're in business."

And the move went smoothly with Alice's help. By the end of the day, the furniture was in place, the movers had unpacked the china and crystal, and Ellen was unpacking her books. It had been painful at first to see the familiar pieces from her married life, but they looked different enough in the New York apartment that she thought she might get used to it eventually, and they wouldn't remind her quite so much of George. She was trying to do everything she could to excise him from her life. And she realized, as she looked around her, that the decision to move to New York had been the right one for her. As it turned out, it wasn't a step backward, she was moving ahead, with new clients, a new assistant, and a new home.

"Wow!" Grace said when she came by that night. There were flowers on the coffee table, Ellen had arranged the furniture the way she liked it, and it looked inviting and warm, just as she had thought when she first saw the apartment. And the bedroom looked feminine and pretty, with an antique mirrored dressing table she had found the week before. "It looks terrific." Grace smiled at her, proud of how bravely she was embracing her new life. "You should give a dinner party when you get settled," her mother suggested. She needed to get a social life going in New York, although Ellen didn't feel quite ready for that yet.

"I wouldn't know who to invite," Ellen said honestly. She had

lost touch with her friends in New York years before. She had become totally absorbed in George's life in London, and now she had
lost that too. She realized now that giving up her identity for him
had been a huge mistake.

"Blanche and I would love to come to dinner," Grace said gently,
and Ellen smiled, and thought about inviting Bob and Jim. Jim had
just asked them to spend Thanksgiving dinner with him, and Ellen
wasn't sure she wanted to go. She wasn't in the mood to celebrate
this year, and didn't feel festive, and she had told her mother she
might skip it. She had decided to serve Thanksgiving dinner at one
of the hurricane shelters downtown and had just volunteered. Grace
was so touched that she wanted to go too. She had already given
mountains of warm clothes to several shelters when she moved.

When they told Jim about it, he offered to make his dinner later,
so both women could come afterward. When Jim told Bob what
they were planning to do, he called Ellen and said he wanted to go
to the shelter with them. It seemed the right way to spend Thanksgiving that year.

Grace still hadn't decided about the art fair in Miami. Jim was
planning to go anyway, as he did every year. Traveling to Miami
with him still sounded a little bold to Grace, and she had told him
that if she went, she would want separate rooms at the hotel,
which he said was fine with him. He was an easy person and willing to accept whatever terms made her comfortable as long as she
would join him.

"You should do it, Mom," Ellen encouraged her when they
talked about it again, but Grace said she wasn't sure, and had too

much work, although she was interested in seeing the art for some of her clients, several of whom were major art collectors. And the idea of being there with Jim appealed to her, more than she wanted to admit.

After Grace left Ellen's new apartment, Ellen went back to unpacking her books, and found several of George's. She wondered if she should send them back to him, and then decided not to, and put them in her bookcase. To hell with it. He had broken her heart, she didn't need to send him the books. When she finished, she looked around the apartment, and was pleased with the results. Her mother was right, and she wished she could show it to someone. And feeling very brave, she sent Bob a text. It was nearly midnight, but she knew he worked late.

"Still writing? I just moved into my new apartment. It's nice, and I really like it. Come and see it sometime." She signed it "Ellen," and sent it off, and he called her five minutes later. They hadn't spoken since he'd called her a week before about serving Thanksgiving dinner at the shelter.

"I didn't realize you were moving so soon. That was fast work."

"Not really. I've been in New York for nearly a month." She smiled to herself and took a sip of her tea, pleased that he'd called her.

"I lose track of time when I'm writing," he said apologetically. "Did your things come from London?"

"They arrived today. I'm still up to my ears in boxes. How's your apartment coming?"

"They started knocking down walls this week. It's a mess," he said, laughing. "Your mother is merciless. But she's good. She tells me I'm going to love the end result. I believe her."

"You won't be disappointed," Ellen promised.

"I'm sure I won't. I'd love to see your new place," he said cautiously, not wanting to intrude.

"I'll invite you to dinner when I get organized," she said, remembering her mother's suggestion.

"I really want to take you to dinner when I finish the book. I was going to call you, but I'm still trapped here. I'm useless till I finish. I can't keep the story straight if I go out when I'm working. I just hole up till I'm through." Jim had said as much when they had dinner. It was the way Bob worked, but it was hard to argue with success. "I'm in the home stretch. Are you doing all right?" he asked, sounding concerned about her, and she was touched.

"I think so. I have to go to London soon to see some clients, but I'm settling in here. I hired a terrific assistant." But nothing felt familiar yet. It was all new and different, even living in New York again, although she'd grown up there. But after eleven years in London, even her own city felt strange.

"I'm glad you texted me," he said warmly. He liked talking to her. He had liked it particularly when she stayed at Jim's apartment and he knew she was in the next room and he could run into her in the kitchen and talk to her anytime. He thought her husband had been a fool to leave her, but it was hard to know what went wrong between people. "I'll call you soon, I promise." He felt guilty for dropping the ball after their last conversation. He lost track of everyone and everything when he was writing.

"You don't have to promise. I'm not going anywhere," she said. It was nice talking to him late at night.

"Dinner soon," he said again, "I have to kill a couple of people first," he chuckled and she laughed at the idea.

She thanked him for calling and walked around her apartment, feeling good about herself. She had had the guts to contact him, even though he hadn't called her in a while. And she liked the way the apartment was taking shape, and the cozy atmosphere. She could see what she needed now. A bigger desk, a couple of big comfortable chairs, maybe a new coffee table. The end tables were perfect for the new couch. And the lamps were great but needed to be wired for American current. She set her candlesticks on the mantel of the fireplace, and an antique Chinese sculpture she loved. And her English hunting scenes were going to be perfect on the red walls in the dining room. It already felt like her own home, not a compromise she had made to please someone else, neither a client nor a husband. She could already tell it was going to look exactly the way she wanted when it was finished. She went to bed that night with a smile on her face. She wasn't crying for the home she had lost, or for George, or even for the children they'd never managed to have. For the first time since George had told her the devastating news that he was leaving her, she realized that she had the one thing she needed most to get through it, and had missed for so long. Herself.

Chapter 12

Juliette arrived at the ER on schedule for her shift at four in the afternoon. They had power again throughout most of the hospital, but some of their systems still weren't up and running two months after the hurricane, and probably wouldn't be for a while. But the ER was functioning normally again. Juliette had just been off for two days, and she smiled at Will Halter at the nurses' station when she came in.

"How's it going?" she asked him as she checked the board on the wall, to see what her caseload looked like that afternoon. The streets had been icy the night before, and they had a broken hip waiting for surgery, and a broken arm waiting for the orthopedic resident. Other than that, they had three cases of the flu, and a heart attack waiting for angioplasty, and they had just sent a woman in premature labor up to labor and delivery. "Looks like an easy day," she commented to Will. He nodded and walked away to talk to one of the nurses.

"What's with that? Are you two buddies now?" Michaela asked her under her breath.

"He's a nonevent. He's ridiculous. But so what?" Juliette shrugged and smiled at her. Ever since his apology to her the night of the hurricane, the steam had gone out of her anger at him, and she really didn't care how big a narcissist he was.

"You're in a good mood," Michaela said, watching her. She had been for weeks, particularly so after her days off. "New guy in your life, Dr. Dubois?" The two women liked each other, but Juliette kept her private life to herself.

"Maybe." She smiled at her.

"It's written all over you," the head nurse teased her.

"A girl's gotta have some fun on her days off," Juliette said as she grabbed a chart and headed for a room.

"Is that so? That's a new tune for you," Michaela called after her. She had been that way for two months. She and Sean Kelly had been dating since the hurricane, and it seemed to be working, despite their crazy schedules, and what he called their careers based on catastrophic events. He had dealt with a major gas leak that caused an explosion and killed three people, a bomb threat at another hospital that had forced them to evacuate the building in a blizzard, and the endless fallout from the hurricane that wasn't cleaned up yet. Some of the buildings in lower Manhattan were still flooded, and there were pumps on the streets everywhere, trying to empty basements, and one subway line still wasn't running.

And while he handled major emergencies, she was busy with the day-to-day at the ER. And somehow in the midst of it, they were managing to spend time together and have a good time. He'd gotten a promotion after the hurricane, and had a new title, a raise, and a bigger truck. And he tried to stop by to see her when he had time, and they'd have a quick cup of coffee together or even lunch.

When they both had time off, they went to movies, or out to dinner, or he cooked dinner for her at his apartment, which was bigger, tidier, and more pleasant than hers, and he was the better cook.

"Let's hope they never expect you to feed someone your own cooking in the ER—you might kill them," he teased her after the first meal she cooked for him and burned beyond recognition. It had set off all the smoke alarms. He took on cooking duties from then on. But despite her lack of domestic skills, he had never enjoyed any woman as much in his life, and their stressful jobs hadn't impacted their private life so far.

When they were together and both off duty and off call, they turned their cell phones off and concentrated on each other. And when they were working, they were dedicated to their jobs. They were compatible in more ways than either of them had expected. And they loved going bowling, and playing pool at a bar near her apartment. She played pool even better than he cooked, and beat him almost every time. She had taught him some pointers that had made him a star among his friends at the OES on boys' nights out.

"I have brothers—what do you expect?" she said proudly the

first time he saw her play. They had learned a lot about each other in the two months since the hurricane, and liked everything they knew so far.

"You were right," she said to him one day while he made her breakfast before they both went to work.

"About what?"

"One can actually have a private life and do good work. I never thought that was possible," she said as she started to eat the bacon and eggs he had made.

"You just have to want it badly enough," he said as he sat down at the table with her. They stayed at his apartment more often than hers, since hers still looked like a bomb had hit it, and he realized now it always would. She somehow never managed to tidy it up, and it looked like a dump. "That's probably the secret to most of life. If you want something badly enough, you make it work."

"And you want me that badly, huh?" she asked, smiling at him, as she munched on a piece of toast.

"Desperately, but not badly enough to eat your cooking."

"Good. Then you can always do the cooking."

"Sure. You can wash my truck."

"In your dreams," she said as he kissed her. "I'm a doctor. I don't have to wash trucks *or* cook."

"Who says?"

"The Hippocratic oath. It's in there somewhere. No cooking," she said smugly.

"It says 'Do no harm,'" he corrected her and then thought about it. "I guess in your case, that's the same thing." He kissed her again and looked at his watch, wondering if they had time to go back to bed before they went to work.

"No," she said, "I can't. If I'm late for work, Halter will kill me."

"Screw him—he's a jerk."

"Yes, that's true, but he's still my boss and he can tell time."

"Spoilsport." He kissed her longingly, and they cleared the dishes together, rinsed them, and put them in the machine. She made more of an effort at his apartment than she did at her own. "See you tonight?" he asked her, and knew the answer even before she said yes. They were spending all their off-duty hours together, and their schedules were tacked up side by side on his bulletin board so they could coordinate their time off.

They hated to leave each other when they went to work, and then got lost in their jobs all over again. They loved what they did *and* being together. And happiness was written all over her now when she went to the ER for her shifts. Michaela had noticed, and so had everyone else.

He had offered to make Thanksgiving dinner for her, a real one with homemade stuffing and a turkey and sweet potatoes with marshmallows, creamed spinach, and pumpkin pie, but she had to work, so he had promised to have dinner in the cafeteria with her, and cook a real dinner for her on her next days off.

He met her in the cafeteria for turkey sandwiches at midnight on her dinner break, and they were talking quietly at a table in the corner when his cell phone beeped with a 911 code following the ID number. It was his boss. He listened intently, said he'd be there in three minutes, and got up.

"I'm gone," he told Juliette. "Fire at the power plant on Four-teenth Street. Five alarm. They're worried about an explosion." He was halfway across the cafeteria by then while she followed him with her sandwich in her hand.

"Be careful, will you . . . Sean, please . . ." He turned back for only a split second and kissed her.

"I love you—I'll call you later. . . . Happy Thanksgiving." He left the hospital at a dead run, put his siren on, and headed north to Fourteenth Street. There were fire engines everywhere when he got there, OES vehicles, and police. He slipped his heavy coat on as he jumped out of his truck, and threaded his way through the crowd to the other OES workers who were talking to the fire chief on the scene. The fire was still out of control, and an explosion was becoming more likely by the minute.

Juliette went to the waiting room to see if it was on the TV there, and she saw it, a burning ball of fire, and firemen every-where. She hoped Sean was okay, as she felt her heart pound. It was the one miserable thing about his job—she was constantly worried about him, and he was always in the most dangerous places. She didn't like it, but she knew how much he did. And she wandered in and out of the waiting room all night between pa-tients to see what was happening, trying not to panic as she watched the fire get worse. A wide area had been cleared and hun-dreds of buildings evacuated in case of an explosion. She felt dizzy as she saw it on TV.

The fire was continuing to rage at five o'clock in the morning, and at six, the explosion they feared finally happened. The announcer said shortly afterward that several firefighters had been injured in the blast. It said nothing about the OES workers. It never did. They were the unsung heroes at every disaster in the city. She was seized by panic when she saw it on the news, and they both heard and felt the blast of the explosion at the hospital. Tears filled her eyes every time she sneaked into the waiting room to watch the TV. What if he died or got injured? She had never been as happy in her life or loved any man as she did him. Everything about him suited her to perfection, except that he risked his life every day. She felt sick until he finally called her after nine o'clock that morning. Two of the firefighters were in the ER by then, badly burned, waiting to be transferred to a burn unit, and she was breathless when she answered his call.

"Are you okay?" she asked when she heard his voice after hours of agony, praying for him. "I was worried about you all night. I saw it on TV."

"I'm fine. It was nasty, and a lot of guys got hurt. It's under control now. But I'll probably be here all day."

"I'm on until ten o'clock tonight," she told him, feeling calmer than she had in many hours. She didn't want to admit to him how terrified she had been.

"I'll meet you at my place whenever I get home." She had a key to his apartment, and spent all her nights off there. "See you later. I love you," he said, and hung up, but she was relieved to have spoken to him and went back to work with a lighter heart. It was a crazy way to live.

When he came home that night, he was filthy and exhausted,

but not too much to take a shower and make love to her. And then he fell asleep in her arms. She wondered sometimes how long she would be able to stand worrying about him all the time. What if he was one of the ones who got injured, or killed? But she couldn't imagine him doing anything else, at least not for now, and neither could he. He needed to feel useful and know he was saving lives, which was what she did, but she was never at risk, and he always was. But at least he was safe, asleep next to her in his bed, and she couldn't ask for more. The hurricane had blown him into her life, and she had no intention of letting go. He was the best thing that had ever happened to her.

Ellen and Grace put on jeans and old sweaters and were down at the hurricane victims' shelter at noon on Thanksgiving. Bob met them there, and they were assigned to separate tables to serve food to the hundreds of people still living there. Bob was assigned to the crew carving the turkeys that had been donated, while the two women ladled the food onto plates, which the residents accepted gratefully. Bob had finished his book at six o'clock that morning, and looked exhausted but thrilled.

The three of them put in a seven-hour shift, working nonstop, and arrived at Jim's apartment just before eight, filthy and tired, smelling of food, but looking pleased. Jim was filled with admiration for them, as his staff served an exquisitely prepared meal. One of the most famous chefs in the city was in his kitchen.

And over dinner, Jim mentioned a benefit he'd heard about

being organized for hurricane relief. It was a gala event being scheduled in the coming months, and Ellen and Grace both said they'd like to volunteer for one of the organizing committees, and Bob and Jim said they might too.

After that, Grace commented that progress in her apartment was moving slowly—there were so many jobs under way downtown that it was hard to hang on to construction crews for long, and they were spreading themselves too thin. She was beginning to think it might even take a year to complete the work. And Bob said he hadn't sold his apartment yet. No one wanted to live on the river in Zone 1. Except Grace.

The Thanksgiving meal the chef had prepared was delicious, and they toasted Bob for the book he'd finished. His current one was still on the best-seller lists, and this one would be too when it came out. It was always a given with him, despite his modesty about it.

He mentioned then that he was going to L.A. the following week to check on his latest movie deal and work out some details. They were casting and wanted input from him on that and the screenplay. He wasn't writing it, but had approval of the final script, as he always did, thanks to Jim's negotiation of the contract. And Bob was going to see his kids while he was there.

"They're coming here for Christmas," he said quietly. "I'd like you to meet them," he mentioned casually to Ellen, which Grace found interesting. She had never met them when they visited him in Tribeca. Ellen knew that they were in their mid-twenties, building and busy with their careers, and that Bob had had them when he was very young. And he had told her how proud he was of what they were doing and how hard they worked. His son had a good job and was on a career path as an assistant director, and his daughter was an entertainment lawyer at an important law firm, and had been since she graduated from law school at UCLA. "They'll be here for a week," he added, and would be staying at Jim's too.

"I'm going to London this week," Ellen told them. "I have to see some clients, and my attorney." They were filing the papers for the divorce, in response to George, who seemed to be in a rush.

"Will it all be unpleasant on this trip?" Bob asked with concern.

"Some of it, probably. But it'll be nice seeing my clients."

"Will you have to see George?" He was sympathetic.

"I don't think so. I hope not." But it would be strange. It would be her first trip to London staying at a hotel, and not at her home. They had had an offer on the house the week before, but George's attorney had communicated that he didn't think it was enough, and he wanted to hold out for a better offer. Ellen was in no hurry to sell, so she didn't care if they waited, and she had agreed.

"How long will you be gone?" Bob asked her.

"About a week." She smiled at him.

"Let's have dinner when you get back, now that I've finished the book. I'll be back from L.A. by then too. I'm only going out for a few days, since the kids are coming here for Christmas in a few weeks."

"I'd love that." They exchanged a warm look as she said it.

"And what about us?" Jim asked Grace in a moment alone after dinner. "Are we going to Miami?" He was, but Grace hadn't decided yet, and was still on the fence about it.

"Are you sure you wouldn't mind separate rooms?" she asked cautiously. "I'd be happy to pay for mine," she offered, and he smiled at her.

"I invited you. And I don't mind separate rooms if that would make you more comfortable." He had already agreed to it before, and she had told him that she hadn't traveled with a man for a long time, and didn't want to feel pressured into a potentially awkward situation. Jim understood her concerns.

"Then I'll come," she said with a shy glance at him, and he beamed at her, and held her hand for a minute, and then they joined the others again. They all had travel plans in the coming days, and Ellen said she wanted to have them all to dinner when they returned. The two men hadn't seen her apartment yet and said they were looking forward to it. And they'd have a lot to talk about when they returned. Bob's movie, Ellen's trip to London, and Jim and Grace's trip to Art Basel. They were all embarking on adventures and would have much to share. And then they went back to talking about the benefit, and hoped to share working on that too.

Chapter 13

When Ellen got to London, she took a cab from Heathrow to the hotel near her office, where Phillippa had made a reservation for her again. She had stayed there on her last two nights in London, and now it would be her home away from home. It seemed comfortable and the room looked pleasant enough when she dropped off her bag, and then she walked to her office in Knightsbridge, near Sloane Street. It felt very strange to be there and not go home, but she got busy with the projects waiting for her, and she had meetings with clients for the next several days, and an installation to oversee at the end of the week. And as always, Phillippa was a big help.

Ellen met with her attorney too, and she signed some papers they needed. George was offering her a settlement, which she had told her attorney she didn't want. She made a decent living and could support herself. She didn't feel right taking money from him.

The marriage hadn't worked out, there was no amount he could pay her for the disappointment, or the betrayal, for cheating on her and not giving her a chance to do things differently or make it work better for him. How did you pay for that? What price could you put on it? She said as much to her attorney, and he relayed it to George's lawyer. And she was surprised when George called her that night. He called from a blocked number, but she recognized his voice immediately, and she assumed the blocked number was Annabelle's.

"Why won't you at least let me give you some money? No one is as rich as all that, unless you've been holding out on me." She hadn't been the one keeping secrets.

"Because you can't make up for what you did with money, George. Why should I let you buy off your conscience at my expense? There's no price on my heart." He was silent for a minute after she said it. She wasn't letting him off the hook, and felt better about it.

"I'm sorry, Ellen. I know it was wrong."

"I'm sorry I let the IVF go on for so long. You should have said something."

"I wanted to, but I knew how much it meant to you."

"So you cheated on me instead." It was hard to justify that.

"Not for the first few years," he said defensively.

"That's big of you. And you made a fool of me with our friends." She never wanted to see any of them again, and there was no chance of it now anyway, with Annabelle firmly ensconced at his side. She had lost an entire world, and a life, not just him.

"Will you be all right?" he asked her, sounding worried about her for the first time.

"Do I have a choice?" He knew that she had to face her inability to have a child as well as losing him—it was a doubly hard hit that way—but there would never have been a good time, and he wanted to have a life too. "Yes, I'll be all right," she said with a sigh.

"I miss you," he said, which seemed cruel.

"I miss you too," she said sadly. "You should have thought of that before."

"It's different with Annabelle. She's not as bright as you are. I hope we see each other again," he said mournfully. "I miss talking to you."

"Why? You said yourself there's nothing left. It's dead." And he had killed it for her with everything he'd said to her at the end.

"We could be friends," he said hopefully.

"No, we can't. We're not friends." What he had done wasn't friendly or respectful or loving. "We were married, and you cheated on me, for a long time. I loved you, but I'm not your friend." It was the most honest she had ever been with him. She had nothing to lose now. And she had cut him to the quick with what she said.

"Are you seeing anyone?" he wanted to know.

"That's none of your business. But no, I'm not."

"Do you think you will?"

"No, I'm going to become a Carmelite nun." There was silence for an instant, she heard him gasp, and then he laughed.

"You always made me laugh."

"Apparently not enough," she said tartly.

"It got so intense with the baby issue. It took all the joy out of everything we did." She couldn't disagree with him. It had been miserable failing again and again.

"I thought it would be worth it in the end, if we succeeded. I was wrong. It was too high a price to pay, and worse because we didn't win. At least you can have children now." She felt bitter when she thought about it. She never would, since the problem was hers.

"I'm fine as I am. It was never the heartbreak for me it was for you. Maybe you should adopt one day." His not wanting to adopt had been all about his lineage and bloodlines, and she had followed him on that. She didn't want to discuss it with him. It was no longer relevant between them, and it was still painful for her.

"Well, let me know how you are from time to time," he said. She didn't answer, and she had no intention of doing so. It was strange to stop speaking to someone you had loved and been married to for ten years. But the whole concept of divorce seemed strange to her, of just canceling someone out of your life. And since he had done it, she preferred to make a clean break, and wanted to. Why should she satisfy his curiosity, or have him justify what he did? There was nothing left to say.

"Thank you for the settlement offer," she said politely. She wanted to get off the phone—they had talked long enough. And she wasn't going to indulge his maudlin need to cry over what had happened, or tell her how much he missed her, or how she'd made him laugh. He had to live with what he'd done now, without her help or sympathy. She didn't feel sorry for him. She didn't need to. He felt sorry for himself, which seemed pathetic to her.

"I love you, Ellen," he whispered into the phone as they were about to hang up. "I always will." She thought it was disgusting and self-serving of him to say that to her, and she felt a door slam in her heart when he did. She had lost all respect for him in the end. It would make it easier to be free of him.

"Goodbye, George," she said coldly, and hung up. And she wanted to scream when she did. Why tell her he loved her now, when he was divorcing her and marrying someone else? What good would that do any of them? None at all. She tried to put him out of her head and went to bed early that night, and woke up surprisingly refreshed the next morning. She wondered if his appalling performance on the phone the night before would cure her of him forever. She hoped so. She suddenly felt very little for him now when she thought about him, except revulsion. And her lawyer called her again later that morning to tell her that George had withdrawn his settlement offer and was giving her the entire house instead, and relinquishing his share. She thought about it for a minute, and nodded.

"Thank you, I'll take it," she told the attorney. For some reason, having the house seemed just. It had been her house as much as his, and if he wanted to give it to her now, so be it. She would sell it for a decent price, and buy another house with the money one day, but not yet. She still didn't know for sure where she wanted to live long term. Maybe New York, or Europe, or somewhere else. She could do whatever she wanted to. She answered to no one now, except herself. She wondered if he had done her a favor in the end.

She finished all her business in London in five days. She had dinner with Phillippa the night before she left and took her to Harry's Bar for a fancy evening and good meal. They had covered all the business that day at work, and could enjoy each other's company before she left. And she told her about George giving her the house.

"That was generous of him." Phillippa was surprised. But it didn't change what she thought of him as a human being.

"Not when you consider what he did," Ellen answered coldly, and Phillippa nodded in agreement.

Ellen didn't have time to call Charles this time, but hoped he and Gina were doing well. She was planning to call him the next time she was in town, in a month or two, and maybe have lunch with him. She had a warm spot in her heart for him after what they'd been through together in the hurricane, and she wished him well.

The flight back to New York was uneventful, and she called her mother the night she got in. She knew that they were back from Miami, and Grace said it had been fabulous and fascinating and the art had been amazing.

"Did you have a good time, Mom?" Ellen questioned her pointedly, curious about how the separate rooms had worked out.

"Yes, I did," Grace said emphatically, then seemed flustered for a minute.

"Should I be shocked or happy for you?" Ellen asked her, and her mother giggled guiltily.

"You shouldn't ask questions like that. We had separate rooms— that's all you need to know." But she sounded like a happy woman, and whatever had happened in Miami had obviously gone well, and Ellen was pleased for her. She deserved to have a man in her life who loved her and treated her well. No one was too old for that.

"George gave me his share of the house, by the way."

"Good heavens, that's quite a gift." She knew what they had paid for it.

"I turned down his settlement offer, and he sounds like he's feeling guilty, or sentimental or something. I'm sad to say I don't feel that way. But I accepted it."

"Try not to get bitter about it. It will only hurt you in the end. It happened, you have to put it behind you now. If you dwell on it, it will poison you more than him. Let him live with it now. You're free of him, and it might prove to be a blessing in the end, hard as it is to believe now."

"It isn't." The only thing she knew she would regret forever was not having children. Not having George in her life was a different story, given what he had done to her. "I'll see you this weekend, Mom, if you're not busy. I have to organize that dinner I promised to do."

"I'm seeing a client this week who has a proposition to make me," Grace said mysteriously.

"Another one?" Ellen teased, referring to her recent romantic adventure in Miami.

"Stop that. I'm your mother," Grace laughed again.

"I'm not the one who went to Miami with her boyfriend," Ellen reminded her.

"God, what a thought. A boyfriend at my age. We'll have to figure out something else to call him. That's so undignified."

"Just enjoy it, by whatever name," Ellen said, and was smiling when she hung up. She was delighted for her mother, and things had gone well in London. She couldn't ask for more than that. Not now anyway.

Ellen got to work with Alice in the morning, organizing her dinner party. She wanted to find a small caterer who could cook the dinner for them, so she didn't have to spend the whole night in the kitchen. And Alice found one that someone she knew recommended. She got a date from her mother, who cleared it with Jim. And all she had to do now was ask Bob when he was available, and he called her that night when he got back from L.A. He said the movie preparations were going well, and he'd had dinner with his children. And then she asked him about the dinner party date. And the same one worked for him as for Jim and Grace.

"Perfect. It's going to be my first dinner party in the new apartment."

"And I want a date from you too. When can we have dinner?" he asked her.

"My dance card happens to be amazingly free at the moment," she said, laughing. She had no social life in New York yet, and wondered how long it would take to have one. She hadn't had time to get out and meet people. She'd been too busy moving and organizing her New York office with Alice.

"How about Saturday?" he suggested. It was still a few days away, and they both had work to catch up on since they'd been traveling.

"That's perfect. What do I wear?" She was used to asking that question of a husband, not a date, and felt awkward inquiring, but it was better to know than to look ridiculous when he showed up at her door, if she was wearing the wrong thing.

"Whatever you like. I was thinking of a little Thai restaurant, if you like that kind of food."

"I love it." He sounded pleased that she did too. "See you Saturday."

The days flew by until she saw him, and she was wearing gray slacks and a matching sweater when he picked her up. She showed him around the apartment, and he looked impressed. They had just hung the curtains that morning, and they were exactly what she had wanted. She and Alice were both thrilled with them. They gave the living room a warm cozy feeling, but were lush and full and matched the couch perfectly. The living room looked very pretty, and he liked the dining room. She showed him her offices behind the kitchen, and he glanced into her bedroom and guest room. It already looked as though she'd been there for months, not weeks. And she had flowers all over the apartment.

"Would you help me with my place when it's finished?" he asked her when they left for dinner, and she was flattered by the request. "I mean professionally, not as a favor." He liked the atmosphere she had created, and the colors she used, and it wasn't overly feminine, which he liked too. She had created an environment anyone would be at ease in. It made you want to spend time there, alone or with friends.

"I'd love to," she said as they got in a cab and headed for the West Side.

"I still miss Tribeca," he admitted to her. "There are so many good restaurants down there. But a lot of them are still closed. I haven't been downtown in a while, but I hear it's still in pretty bad shape. I'm glad I bought the new apartment. I wish your mother would too. I hate to think of her going back there." He looked worried when he said it.

"So do I," Ellen said. "I don't think we can stop her, although she said the work on her apartment is going at a snail's pace. She can't keep a crew there for more than a few days at a time—they keep getting pulled away to other jobs. There's a ton of reconstruction downtown."

They got to the restaurant a few minutes later, and the food was as good as he had said it would be. And they didn't stop talking all evening, about his movie, his latest book, which he told her about in detail, and his children. He listened to her talk about her clients in Europe and the jobs she was doing, and he asked her if she'd heard from George while she was in London, and she told him about the house. He told her she deserved to have it. And they talked briefly about Jim and Ellen's mother. They both thought whatever was happening was wonderful. He said that Jim couldn't stop talking about what a good time he had had in Miami with her.

They were both startled to realize it was midnight when they left the restaurant. He took her home in a cab, and she thanked him for a wonderful evening, and reminded him of the date of her dinner party.

"I won't forget it," he said, smiling at her. "And don't you forget that I hired you as my decorator tonight. I was serious about that." He looked as though he meant it.

"You'll have to get your architect's permission," she teased him.

"She'd better agree to it, or I'll fire her," he said sternly, and they both laughed. She didn't invite him to come up. The evening had been lovely just as it was, and neither of them expected more. There was no rush. They were just getting to know each other.

He watched her walk into the building, and she turned to wave at him with a smile and then went in, and he went back to Central Park West thinking about how much he liked her and what good company she was.

Chapter 14

The day of Ellen's dinner party, she spent the afternoon looking around the apartment, moving things slightly, fluffing up pillows, unpacking the last box of little objects she loved and photographs she'd brought from London, and arranging flowers. She had hired a woman to clean twice a week, and the apartment was gleaming when she left. Ellen was proud of her new home, and it started snowing that day at noon. She sent her mother a text, reminding her to be careful when she came to dinner, she didn't want her to fall on slippery streets, or ice, and she responded to Ellen while in a meeting not to worry, Jim would be picking her up and bringing her in his car. He was taking good care of her mother, and she was having a ball with him. Ellen was pleased.

She was humming to herself as she got dressed, and there was music playing on the stereo that she and Alice had spent a Saturday afternoon setting up. Alice was proving to be a gem, and was thrilled with her new job. She and Phillippa Skyped every day, exchanging information, shipping samples and floor plans back and forth, and keeping each other informed of details so they could keep Ellen up to date. The arrangement was working well, and miraculously, there was no jealousy between them, which was rare between assistants, and so far Ellen's clients didn't seem to mind that she was in New York. But she was also willing to hop on a plane to London at the drop of a hat, to reassure an anxious client, solve a problem, make a presentation to a new client, or be present at an installation. The transition had come off without a hitch, and she hoped her dinner party would too. She hoped it would be the first of many. She loved entertaining, and once she started meeting new people, and renewing old friendships, which she had promised herself she would do, she wanted to give small dinners frequently. It was good for her business, she loved doing it, and did it well.

She and George had given a big Christmas party every year, for their large circle of friends. She was going to miss it this year, along with their other traditions, and she wondered if he would be having the party with Annabelle. It made her sad to think he probably would. He had moved on very quickly, and with pressure from him, the divorce was advancing at a rapid pace. He might have said he missed her in a melancholy moment, but it didn't seem that way from the avalanche of paperwork passing between their two lawyers, always instigated by him. Once he made his mind up, and told her, he wanted it done.

Ellen was disappointed not to be giving a Christmas party of her own in New York, but it was too soon after she had moved there. She was planning to put up a Christmas tree that weekend. There was a perfect spot for it in the living room. The apartment already had a festive air, with dark red roses in vases and beautiful brown and yellow orchids. She was wearing black velvet slacks and a very pretty gold sweater with black and gold high heels, had brushed her blond hair till it shone, and had just put on small diamond earrings when the doorbell rang right on the dot of eight. She had offered to do it at that hour for her mother, who always stayed at the office late when she was busy. It was late enough by New York standards, where people dined earlier than they did in London. Her first guest had arrived on time—it was Bob—and she told the doorman to send him up. She had added several more touches since he'd seen it the night they'd gone to dinner. And she'd bought a few more pieces of furniture, and he noticed them immediately, after he admired how she looked. He loved both her simplicity and attention to detail, and he could easily see how talented she was at her work, as he glanced around the living room and saw the changes.

"The place looks fantastic, and so do you," he said smiling at her, and handed her a small gift. "It's not a book!" he said disparagingly, remarkably shy about his work. It was a box of chocolates from the Maison du Chocolat, which were her favorites. She thanked him and set them on the coffee table for everyone to share. They were dark chocolates, which he knew she liked best, from observing her at Jim's. Like Ellen, he was a master of detail, and a keen observer of people, which served him well in his writing. He admired the orchids, and everything she'd done since he'd been there. She had added a beautiful chinoiserie cabinet she had found at an antique dealer while walking around her neighborhood. It was a handsome piece.

"I'm so happy you're my decorator." He smiled at her warmly, as she handed him a glass of champagne. "I can't wait to get started." And then he laughed. "After your mother finishes tearing the place apart. She's switching everything around. I can't even remember what the place looked like when I bought it."

"She always does that." Ellen laughed with him. "It's part of her talent. She always has a 'vision,' and amazingly it always works. I don't think she ever misses, and her clients love the results." It had been her success as an architect—she didn't impose her ideas on her clients, but she brought things out of them that they hadn't even realized they wanted and that suited them to perfection. She was sure she would do the same for Bob.

"She's creating the writing room of my dreams," he said to Ellen, which reinforced what she'd said, "with a view of Central Park. I can hardly wait to write a book there. My office in Tribeca was like the black hole of Calcutta, although I loved everything else about the apartment. I just had a decent offer for the place, by the way. Someone with enough guts to live there in spite of the risks. They just moved to New York, and I don't think they had any idea what could happen. They didn't live through Ophelia or Sandy."

"I wish your mother would rethink it," he said soberly.

"So do I. But you know my mother," Ellen said as the caterer she'd hired brought out a tray of elegant hors d'oeuvres, and then Bob looked at her closely.

"What about you? Are you doing all right with all the legal issues in London?" He meant the divorce but didn't want to say the word.

"More or less. It's still kind of shocking. Sometimes I forget and wonder what I'm doing here. It's so strange to spend ten years with someone, and then they suddenly disappear out of your life. And a whole existence, a whole language, a whole way of thinking, and the person you're used to vanishes. It's like learning to walk all over again after an accident."

"Divorces are like serious accidents, or a death." He had experienced both, with the same person, and knew it well. "It makes some of us gun-shy forever, I'm afraid." He looked at her apologetically, and then surprised her with what he said next. "I'd like to see more of you, Ellen. I'm a little erratic. I drop off the face of the earth when I write, which makes me bad company at times. Like most men, I'm not good at multitasking. When I'm working on a book, I can't think about anything else. And when you first found out about your husband, I thought it was too soon to say anything, or even suggest having dinner with you. And I think after that, I panicked a little and got lost in the book, conveniently. I'm not very brave about these things anymore," he admitted with a sheepish look. "My relationship history is pretty dismal, a failed marriage I was in great part responsible for. I spent years feeling guilty and regretting what I lost, and wasting everyone's time trying to get her back, and then mourning her and turning her into a saint when she died, which she wasn't by any means. She was a lot smarter than I was, and she never wanted me back, although I damn near stalked her and hounded her about it. And looking back, I think my obsession with her was more of an excuse to avoid serious relationships after her. The women I went out with were damn tired of hearing me talk about my late, saintly ex-wife and the perfect marriage we'd had, which 'inexplicably' fell apart when she woke up in a bad mood one day and left me. It took me years to take responsibility for my part in it, and once I did, I was too frightened to try again.

"But I'm turning fifty next month, and I realize now that if I don't take a chance once in a while, I'm going to be living alone with my typewriter forever. I thought about it a lot after the hurricane. We sit around waiting, licking our wounds and too afraid to risk getting hurt again, or we delude ourselves that time doesn't move forward and we'll be young forever, and one day you wake up and you're old and life has passed you by. I don't want that to happen to me. I want to live my life before I die one day, and none of us knows when that will be. You have to take risks sometimes, even though relationships can be dangerous business, but if you don't at least try, at the risk of being miserable if it goes wrong, you'll never be really happy either. There is nothing better than sharing your life with the right person, or worse than with the wrong one. I think our friend Jim is discovering that too. He's been alone for a long time. He's great company, and we've had some wonderful times together. I see less of him now, even living in his guest room, but it's a real pleasure to see him and Grace enjoying each other. They both deserve it. And I don't want to be his age when I figure it out. The hurricane made me think, what if we had all died? I've cut myself off from feeling anything for anyone except my children for years. I don't want to do that anymore."

It was a brave speech, particularly for a man who rarely if ever bared his soul, yet he dared to do so with her, and she admired him for it. She understood what he was saying, and she was frightened now too. George leaving her had turned ten years of her life into a total waste, but she realized now that he had been right too. She had stopped seeing him as a person with needs of his own—he had become the vehicle for her to have a baby, which must have felt lonely to him at times.

"I've made my share of mistakes too," she said seriously. "I think I stopped seeing my husband and looked past him to the baby I wanted. I lost that dream anyway, and I lost him in the process. And I lost myself for a while. There were a lot of things wrong with our marriage that I didn't want to acknowledge. I tried to be some-one I wasn't the entire time. He wanted to turn me into one of the girls he grew up with, and I was young and foolish enough to try. I was never going to be one of them, and I forgot who I am while trying to be them. Now he has what he wanted, and I'm not sure he's going to like it as much as he thinks." He was already discover-ing that, judging by their conversation when she was in London. "I lost him, but I got me back, which isn't such a bad thing." It was the most important discovery she'd made, and it felt good sharing it with Bob. It also put him on notice that she wasn't going to give up who she was.

"It's a very good thing, from everything I've seen," Bob said, smiling warmly at her, as she sat on the couch, and he in the big comfortable chair next to her. He wanted to reach for her hand and hold it, but he didn't know if he should, and hadn't had enough champagne yet to dare.

"I don't know if it's good or bad," she said honestly. "But I want to be myself, not someone else's fantasy. Whatever I do next time, I need to be me, and not get lost in the shuffle to satisfy someone else's image of what I should be, or could be, or have to be for them. I'm not sure how that will work, maybe it won't. And I'm a little scared now to get too close to anyone. What if I get lost again?" She was addressing him directly, and he could hear the power of her words and the feelings and fears behind them, which were justified given what she'd just been through. She had made herself over to please a man who had left her in the end anyway for what he thought was the real deal and probably wasn't.

"I don't think you'll let that happen again," he said to her quietly. "If we try hard, we don't make the same mistakes again. We make new ones." He smiled at her. "The pull to repeat old patterns is strong, but you've put a lot of thought into it. And in an odd way, I think that the storm we lived through changed all of us. We all realized how short life can be, and none of us want to waste it or screw it up, if we can help it."

"I think that's true. I haven't seen my mother go out with a man in years, and now she is. I think Hurricane Ophelia woke us all up. Maybe that's not such a bad thing, for those of us who survived it." As though on cue, the doorman rang from downstairs and announced Mr. and Mrs. Aldrich, which made Ellen laugh. Downstairs, Grace looked shocked as he said it, and blushed as she glanced at Jim when they got in the elevator.

"I can't imagine why he said that." She was flustered for a moment.

"That must mean we look good together," he teased her. He hadn't corrected him and was amused. "Maybe someone told him about Miami," he whispered, and she burst out laughing.

"For heaven's sake, Jim! We're having dinner with my daughter. We have to at least pretend to be respectable."

"I think Ellen is a lot smarter than that," he said comfortably, as they got out on Ellen's floor. She was standing in the doorway waiting for them with a broad smile. They were half an hour late, as her mother often was, cutting it too close when she came home from the office and had to get dressed to go out, and Ellen didn't mind at all. It had given her a good chance to talk to Bob, and she liked everything he had said. She wasn't sure she was ready to seriously date yet, but when she was, she agreed with his views about people and life. The hurricane had subtly changed her too. It had made her braver. Having faced terror and looked death in the eye made life that much sweeter. And she could tell it had done that to her mother too. She looked lovely in a black silk skirt, with a gauzy red blouse that was festive and uncharacteristically sexy on her. When Ellen complimented her on it when she took her coat off, she whispered that she had bought it at Chanel in Miami between visits to the art fair. And Jim seemed to like it too. Ellen made no reference to the doorman's faux pas, although she was tempted to tease her mother, but she didn't know how Jim would take it, so she didn't. He actually seemed more relaxed than her mother, and in subtle ways he made it clear that he was "with" her, in the way he spoke to her and about her and smiled at her in an affectionate, private way. Their romance was not the secret Grace wanted to pretend, and it seemed to be thriving, as she was. She had never looked better. They had all recovered from the hurricane better than expected.

They went into the dining room a few minutes later, since Jim and Grace had been late. Ellen had set a beautiful table with the china she'd brought with her, colorful crystal, and small vases of flowers. And the table shone with her antique silver from the silver vaults in London, which had been her passion when she'd first moved there. George had always teased her that they had enough silver to open a shop, and since she had bought it, she had kept it in the division of their respective goods, and he didn't argue about it.

The conversation at dinner was lively, Jim had a great sense of humor and a quick wit, and Grace was an able match for him. Both men were well read and had strong opinions on a variety of subjects—they went from politics to books to history to social commentary. Ellen had more fun than she'd had in years, talking to intelligent people who enjoyed each other's company, would have had much to brag about but didn't, and had an American style that she found refreshing after years of George's snobbish, stuffy friends, who based much of their self-worth on the fact that they'd gone to Eton or on who they were related to, which somehow wasn't enough.

By the time they got to dessert, they were all laughing uncontrollably at some situations Jim described in his early years as an agent, and Bob talked about writing his first novel in a broom closet on a typewriter he had borrowed at Yale. And then he confessed that he hadn't "borrowed" it, he had stolen it, and had been hiding so he didn't get caught. He had been paid $3,000 for the book, and it was his first smashing success, and went right to the number-one position on the *New York Times* best-seller list, but he never gave the typewriter back since he figured it had brought him luck.

"I still have it," he said proudly. "The 't' and 's' keys are broken and always were. My first novel was written without 't's or 's's, and Jim finally convinced me to give it up."

"It was like doing the crossword puzzle reading his early manuscripts, with all the words I had to guess at and couldn't figure out." They all laughed at the image he conjured up, and Ellen was struck again by how modest Bob was. He always made his success sound like a fortuitous accident and not the result of his keen mind and remarkable skill, and he readily attributed his success to Jim and his talents as an agent.

They sat in the living room after dinner, and no one wanted to go home. She served the men brandy, and her mother a small glass of Château d'Yquem Sauterne, which she knew she loved, and had some herself. She entertained beautifully, which Grace readily gave Ellen credit for as due to her own talents and nothing she had learned from her mother.

"When she set the table as a little girl, she would disappear for hours, and pick up things all over the house to make the table pretty. She even sliced colored candles onto my soup once so it would be colorful." Ellen laughed at the memory and admitted it was true. "And I used to build forts out of boxes as a child, for all the boys in my neighborhood," Grace confessed. "I guess our talents show up early."

"Mine didn't," Bob said with a grin. "I wanted to be a fireman until I was fourteen. And then I wanted to be a policeman."

"Well, you sort of are with what you write," Ellen said, and he thought about it for a minute and agreed. And as they sat enjoying each other's company, Grace made a startling announcement, that none of them expected of her, her daughter least of all.

"I concluded a deal two days ago," she said, looking very pleased, "with an old client of mine. I did an apartment for him ten years ago, at the Dakota. It was quite spectacular at the time, on two levels, with overhangs and a balcony. For once, I respected the original architecture, but we made it something very special. I was very proud of it at the time, and he loved it. It might have been my favorite job ever—I think we really got it right. He had some wonderful ideas too, and we were a very creative team working on it together." Ellen remembered it—her mother had been deep in the project when she moved to London, and finished it around the time she married George. The photographs of it had been fabulous. The entire main floor was wood paneled, but it wasn't dark, it was very rich looking, with a remarkable patina on the walls. "He married a Swiss woman and moved to Geneva a few years ago, and he said they never come to New York anymore, so he doesn't use it. He decided to sell it, but wanted to sell it to someone who would love it as much as he did. He really doesn't need the money." She paused for a moment and smiled at all three of them. "He called me before he put it on the market, to see if I knew of a client for it. I bought it, and I'm so happy I could scream." She glanced lovingly at Ellen, knowing how relieved she'd be. "So I won't be going back to Tribeca after all. Life moves in strange ways sometimes. And Jim and I will almost be neighbors a few blocks apart." She smiled at him—it seemed like a good arrangement for them for the moment. "And it's in beautiful condition, so it needs very little work. I can move in when my lease is up where I am, although I'm going to need a lot of new furniture now after the flood." She gazed pointedly at Ellen for that, as they all exploded in excitement at what she said, and toasted her new home.

"That's fantastic news!" Bob said to her, as relieved as Ellen that she wouldn't be moving back downtown at the river's edge. Some risks were just too foolish to take, and they all agreed that that was one.

"I knew I shouldn't go back," she admitted. "I just loved that apartment so much, and the whole area, and being on the river, but I like being uptown now too. And it's a lot easier for me with work." And since she had no intention of retiring anytime soon, or possibly ever, that was an important convenience factor for her that she had chosen to ignore for years. "And I was always in love with that apartment at the Dakota." It was a building full of famous creative people. John Lennon had lived there and a number of other important, well-known people.

"I can't wait to see it," Jim said, beaming at her. It would be so nice having her nearby, and they could go back and forth to each other's apartments, only a few blocks away.

"I can take all of you in this weekend, when he goes back to Geneva. I already have the keys, and it will be mine in thirty days." She could hardly believe it herself. The evening ended on an up note after her announcement, and Bob stayed for a few minutes after they left.

"What a happy surprise that is," Bob said, smiling broadly at Ellen. "I hated the idea of her going back to her old apartment, just sitting there waiting for another hurricane to hit, and you know it will."

"You didn't hate it any more than I did," she said, relieved too. And her mother's surprise news had given her another idea. The woman who owned the apartment where Grace was living for the time being wanted to sell, and if Ellen decided to stay in New York and buy an apartment, it might be ideal for her, if the house in London had sold by then. All their plans were fitting together nicely, and she was thrilled that her mother had found a home she loved. It had fallen right into her lap at the perfect time. Fate had been kind, in so many ways, with Jim, the new apartment, and even with Bob and Ellen and his insisting they stay at Jim's after the flood.

He lingered for a few minutes before he left, and she remembered everything he had said when the evening began, before Grace and Jim had arrived. It gave her much food for thought, and they were getting to know each other well. Living through a disaster together tended to speed things along.

"Why don't we go see your mother's new apartment together this weekend?" he suggested. "I'm dying to see it. It sounds incredible, and maybe it will give me some ideas to steal for mine, if she lets me."

"I need to take a look at it for the furniture she needs," Ellen said practically. "She lost a lot downtown. And I never actually saw the apartment in person, only in photographs and the magazines where it was published at the time. My mother got a lot of praise for that job."

"Of course," Bob said, smiling, "I have the best architect and designer in the city." He gave her a warm hug then, and brushed her lips with his, touched by a lovely evening with a woman he was coming to like and admire more each time they met. She was healing his old wounds, and calming his fears. "See you soon," he said softly, as she smiled at him and gently touched his face with her fingertips.

"Thank you . . . for everything," she said, and quietly closed the door when he left. He smiled all the way down in the elevator, and in the morning, he sent her an enormous bouquet of roses, thanking her for the dinner, with a note that made her smile when Alice handed it to her. "Thank you for a wonderful evening. You are fabulous. Always remember that. See you soon. B." It had been a perfect evening, for all of them, and Ellen smiled broadly as she put his note on her desk where she could read it again, and as she did, she wasn't scared at all. It was a new day, a new man, a new world.

Chapter 15

As Jane and John Holbrook had feared would happen, and had been warned, Peter had started manifesting signs of severe trauma as soon as he got home. And it got worse instead of better for a while. He lost patches of hair all over his head, almost immediately. It came out in clumps and handfuls, and he cried when he saw it in the mirror. It was so embarrassing, he didn't want to go out. He couldn't sleep at night, and would sit in front of the TV, unseeing, until morning, and they would find him asleep and slumped over, looking pale and exhausted. He never wanted to leave the house. He hardly ate, and lost fifteen pounds within a month. He wouldn't speak to his friends, and kept his cell phone turned off. He didn't want to see anyone, and his only friend appeared to be the dog. He isolated himself in his room, and wouldn't eat with his parents. They were worried sick about him, and reported each new frightening development to the therapist they had found with their doctor's help.

Gwen Jones was a very nice woman, trained at Harvard, and specialized in PTSD, post-traumatic stress disorder. The Holbrooks were praying she could help. She assured them that everything Peter was going through was normal, and none of it surprised her. The key was how well he would recover, and how long it would take him to come back from the dark place where he was. She said that he would always have traces of the trauma he'd been through, which might trouble him again during times of great stress or if he encountered triggers from his experience during the hurricane, but with therapy, a loving family to support him, and time, she was confident that he would do well.

The first thing Peter told her was that he wasn't going back to school when NYU reopened. She asked him if he was planning to transfer somewhere else, and he said no, with a sullen expression. His mother had already told Dr. Jones that he was often hostile and irritable now, which was completely unlike him. He had always been even-tempered, and had a happy disposition. And the therapist had noted his flat affect. He was either angry, or had no expression at all. And he had refused to see her at first.

He said that he didn't need her, and Ben was dead, and would be forever, so what difference would therapy make? He claimed he was fine, and he was anything but. And the rapid weight loss and bald patches, and sunken eyes from not sleeping, made him look frightening and strange. He hadn't spoken to Anna since he left New York, and deleted her texts without reading them. Within weeks of his return to Chicago, his parents were gravely alarmed. He was in much worse shape than they had feared. The Holbrooks had called Ben's parents regularly, and they were in awful shape too, and Adam was seeing a therapist now. He was heartbroken over the loss of his brother and cried all the time. And his asthma was the worst it had ever been.

Since Peter refused to go to see the therapist, she came to see him at his parents' home. He said he had nothing to say to her, so she sat and watched TV with him for two hours, without saying a word. And then she thanked him for letting her join him, with a friendly smile, and left. He told his parents she had annoyed him, he hadn't said she could watch with him. But he didn't object when she came back the next day, and he ignored her again.

Out of the blue, after watching TV for a week with the therapist, Peter started talking about school, and not wanting to go back to NYU. He mentioned some of his childhood friends in Chicago, but he never said a word about Ben, Anna, or the hurricane. She asked him about the dog, and he said he had been a gift from a friend. She knew the story of how Peter had saved him, and that he had belonged to Ben, but she said nothing and nodded. Mike seemed to like her when she came to visit, which helped. And she asked Peter what his favorite movies were, and brought DVDs of them on subsequent visits. She brought mostly funny ones, and they laughed together sitting on the couch in the family room, where he preferred to hang out, often sitting in the dark with the lights off for hours, listening to music and staring into space. But laughter formed the first bond between Peter and Gwen. He was actually smiling when she left, after they had spent two hours laughing at a movie he had loved as a kid. He hadn't seen it in years, although he had told Ben about it once.

They'd been watching movies and TV together for two weeks when Peter said something about his hair and how weird it looked.

"It'll grow back," Gwen said, looking confident. "That happens sometimes when people go through something really hard or shocking, like a divorce, or a plane crash, or the loss of a relationship or someone they love." Peter didn't speak again that afternoon, but she could see the firmly closed door opening a crack. And the next day, out of the blue, as they were watching *Star Wars,* he mentioned Ben.

"My friend died in New York in the hurricane." He never took his eyes off the screen as he said it, and didn't look at her. She could see that his body was tense, and a thin veil of perspiration appeared on his forehead.

"I'm sorry," she said quietly. "I know how hard it is to lose a good friend." She had lost her identical twin sister in a fire when they were in medical school together, which was what had led her into specializing in PTSD. Losing her twin had nearly killed her, but Peter had no way of knowing. But the tone of her voice made him sense that she understood.

"Mike was his dog," he admitted for the first time. "His parents let me keep him, because his little brother has asthma. I offered to give him back. We were in the hurricane together." She didn't say anything and waited to see what he would say next. "We didn't evacuate when we should have," Peter confessed, and then the dam suddenly broke and he told her the whole story as he sat on the couch and sobbed like a child.

"You couldn't know it would be the wrong decision," she said gently. She and her twin had gotten separated and had taken different routes out of the building. Her twin couldn't know she'd chosen the wrong one, and Gwen wanted to go back to look for her, and the firemen wouldn't let her. It took her years to forgive herself for getting separated from her at the outset. "A lot of people didn't evacuate when they should have. And on the sixth floor, I guess you figured you'd be okay."

"It sounded like the building was coming down, so I thought we should get out the next morning. We should have stayed, I didn't know how strong the currents would be. It was moving so fast, I don't even remember what happened when I jumped in. I suddenly saw Mike and grabbed him, and then they pulled me into the boat and I told them to look for Ben, but they couldn't find him. I kept waiting for them to bring him to the hospital, but they never did. I couldn't believe it when Anna's mom told me. She was my girlfriend." He explained what the therapist already knew from his parents. "She knew Ben all her life. She probably hates me now for what I did."

"You didn't do anything wrong, Peter. You both made a decision to make a run for it, which would have been the right decision if the building collapsed. A lot of those old buildings did. Ben didn't have to go with you. You both wanted to, and you tried it. You're not responsible for what happened after that."

"I think I talked him into it. And I jumped in first and lost sight of him. We should have held hands or something."

"The water would have pulled you apart in a second, just like it did with the dog—it pulled Mike away from him." Peter hadn't thought about that, or about Ben's free will not to go with him if he didn't want to. It introduced a new element into the equation, although he still blamed himself. "What if you had died and he didn't? What do you think he would say, and feel?"

"He'd feel like shit, like I do. And we were assholes for staying." He smiled at her. "We thought it was kind of funny at first, and like it would be nothing. We bought a lot of junk to eat, and we wanted to watch it. Anna tried to talk us into coming uptown with her, but we didn't want to. We thought they were just girls so they were chicken." He was telling Gwen the truth.

"What's she saying now?"

"I don't know. I delete her texts without reading them. We kind of broke up when I left. I knew we'd remind each other too much of Ben. It changed everything when he died. And she probably hates me for not saving him."

"Do you want to talk to her?" Gwen asked quietly, and he shook his head. "Do you miss her?"

"I miss him," he said sadly, and cried again, for a long time. "I miss him so much. He was the best friend I ever had. And it's my fault he died." She didn't argue with him and let him sit with it for a while.

"Do you think it's possible that it *isn't* your fault? Even if you don't believe it right now, will you accept my word that it really isn't, and it was out of your control?"

"Maybe," he said after he thought about it, "but I'm sure his parents blame me for it, and they're right."

"What if they don't blame you? What if no one blames you, except yourself? Do you think you could be wrong about it?" He shook his head then. "Do you think Ben would blame you?" Peter shook his head again and looked at her.

"He was a great guy. He would never blame me."

"Maybe we ought to start there," she said, latching on to a positive. "Maybe we should let Ben make the decision here. If he wouldn't blame you, he gets my vote. What about you?" He was pensive again, and seemed less tormented when she left a little while later.

It was slow progress after that, as he worked his way through it. She offered him medication to help him sleep, but he declined. He said he wanted to face everything squarely, and he was courageous about it as they talked about all the events in their daily sessions. And three weeks after she had started with him, Peter sat down to dinner with his parents. He didn't say anything or talk to them, but he ate a reasonable meal. He joined them at the dinner table every day after that, and eventually said a few words to them, and he started to gain weight back again. And the hair loss stopped soon after, and he had peach fuzz and then duck down in the bald places. And little by little, his mind followed his body and began to heal. Their toughest battle was his blaming himself for Ben's death.

With Gwen's help, Peter wrote a beautiful letter to Ben's parents, telling them how he felt, how responsible and how wrong he had been, and how guilty he thought he was. Jake Weiss responded almost immediately with a letter of incredible sensitivity and eloquence, explaining that they in no way blamed him for Ben's death, and how grateful they were that he had survived, and he assured Peter that Adam felt that way too. Peter opened their letter in Gwen's presence, as they had agreed he would, and Peter sobbed for hours after he read it, with regret and relief, and some release from the remorse that he'd been feeling. And eventually he read one of Anna's texts and saw how worried she was about him and didn't blame him either. And he spent a tearful night with his parents, telling them every detail of what had happened.

The next day, he went out with his mother to the supermarket, and downtown to dinner with his parents. He wasn't ready to see any of his old friends, but he called Anna one night and they talked on the phone. She said she had applied to Barnard as a special case and was transferring there, and a few days later he told Gwen he might apply to Northwestern, so he could graduate, although he was missing a semester and he didn't know if he'd lose too many credits if he transferred. She told him that she was sure schools were making allowances for the hurricane survivors from schools that were still closed, which was the case for NYU. They weren't even sure if they would be open for the next semester. But he was talking about going back to school, and entering the world again.

Two months after he had come home, Peter looked normal again, and acted it, although he was still deeply troubled and having difficulty sleeping, and he cried when he thought about Ben, or talked about him, but he was no longer so sure he was to blame and could see that he might not be. Gwen told his parents that it would all take time. They couldn't rush the process, he would have to heal in his own time. He still had a nasty scar on his arm from the night of the hurricane, and his mind was certainly just as marked, and needed time to heal. There might always be traces of it, just as there might on his arm, but one day it would no longer trouble him or keep him from leading a normal life.

They went to his uncle's in Chicago for Thanksgiving, as they did every year, and Peter appeared normal at dinner, although everyone had been warned not to mention the hurricane to him, or his friend's death, even to tell him they were sorry. They all followed the instructions to the letter, except his grandfather who had dementia, and somehow remembered hearing about the hurricane, and much to everyone's horror brought it up at dinner.

"I hear you were in a hurricane, Pete," he said from across the table in a booming voice since he was deaf too. "How was it?"

"Pretty bad, Grampa. It was really scary." He offered none of the details.

"Well, I hope you didn't lose your pants in the water and come out naked," his grandfather guffawed, and everyone was so relieved, the entire table broke into nervous laughter, and someone changed the subject after Peter's answer.

"No, I kept my pants on, Grampa," he said, smiling at him, and the moment passed. And his parents realized how much better he was to have been able to handle the awkward moment.

He called Anna a few times, and they enjoyed talking to each other, although it was no longer romantic, and they didn't talk about Ben. But it was nice to hear her voice, and she always asked about Mike. Peter was still seeing Gwen, and he told her three weeks after Thanksgiving that he wanted to go to New York for a day or two, and take Mike with him. She looked startled and asked him why.

"To see Anna," he said quietly.

"To rekindle your romance with her?" From what he'd said so far, that surprised her, although anything was possible, and nothing was forbidden, except self-blame.

"No, it was so weird when I left. We weren't friends, we weren't boyfriend and girlfriend anymore. We were so confused and so messed up over everything that had happened. I just want to see her and leave it in a good place so we can be friends." It sounded like a good plan to her, and she tried to reassure his parents. They were panicked. What if he had a flashback or a freak-out in New York? Or on the plane?

"He's not going to have a flashback, because he remembers everything," she explained to them. "And he may experience some stress, even severe stress, but I think he can handle it now, and I think seeing Anna may give him some closure he needs so he can move on. She was almost like Ben's sister." She asked Peter in their next session if he was going back to see the building, or the street, or make some kind of pilgrimage to the area where Ben had died, and Peter rapidly shook his head with a pained look.

"I don't ever want to see the house again, or the street. I can't," he said in a choked voice.

"You don't have to. I just wanted to know what you had in mind. You don't ever need to go back there." And she hoped he wouldn't.

"All I want to do is see Anna, and then come home again. She said I could stay at her place for the night if I want to. We were friends before we started dating."

"Are you going to see Ben's parents?" Gwen asked him, and he hesitated with a guilty look in his eyes.

"Do you think I should? I wasn't going to. I think it might be too much. I just want to see Anna."

"That's fine. You don't have to visit them. And I think it would be hard too." He looked relieved, and she told him she approved of his plan. And when he mentioned it to her, she gave him a letter on her professional stationery that said he was a victim of Hurricane Ophelia, was currently experiencing PTSD, and as part of his therapy, his black Labrador was to accompany him freely as an emotional support dog, and she signed it. Peter beamed and high-fived her when she handed him the letter, and she laughed.

"Yes!" he said loudly. With her letter he could take Mike in the cabin with him, and not put him in a crate in cargo, which he wouldn't have done. In that case, he would have left him with his parents, but he was thrilled to take him along.

Peter's parents took him to the airport a few days later, with the dog, and they were nervous wrecks the moment his flight took off, and reassured each other all the way home that Peter would be fine. Peter had presented Gwen's letter at the airline desk, they had read it carefully, looked at him, looked at the dog, nodded, and waved him through after giving him back the letter he'd need to get him home too.

And he took a cab from La Guardia to Anna's home. She was expecting him and nervous about seeing him too. Neither of them had any idea what to expect, and Gwen had told him to keep an open mind and just let things flow, and to call her if he felt too stressed. He kept her cell phone number in his phone, and had called her several times when he had a tough time, mostly in the beginning. They both felt he was doing great now.

The moment Anna opened the door to him, she squealed and threw her arms around his neck, and a minute later they were both crying and laughing and so happy to see each other, and Mike was barking frantically, as Anna's mother came out of her room to hug Peter too. For Peter, he had lost two friends. Ben and Anna. And now he had Anna back.

"You look terrific," Elizabeth said, relieved to see him. He was a great boy, and she had always liked him.

"I lost my hair for a while," he said to Anna with a shrug, "but I'm okay now." He felt like he had lost his mind for a while too, but he didn't tell her that. She didn't need to know. And Gwen had assured him that everything he had felt and experienced was normal, given what he'd been through.

"What do you want to do?" Anna asked him, and on the spur of the moment, Peter said he wanted to see the Christmas tree all lit up at Rockefeller Center. He had seen it once as a little kid with his parents and loved it, and now he wanted to go with her.

They took a cab there and left Mike with her mother, and stood in awe of the giant tree with the decorations and lights on it, and then hung over the railing and watched the ice skaters. Anna suggested they go to St. Patrick's and light a candle for Ben, which was the first time they had mentioned him, and Peter agreed. They lit the candle, and both said a prayer and then left, and walked back uptown to Anna's apartment. They ordered sushi takeout, and talked about what they were going to do.

"Do you think you'll go back to school?" Anna asked him. Her parents had left them alone, and they had talked all afternoon. And eventually, he told her about his therapy with Gwen and said he felt better. Anna was seeing a therapist too, for loss in her case, not guilt, although she blamed herself for not "making" the boys come uptown with her. Her therapist had told her that she couldn't "make" them do what they didn't want to do. It had been the same thing Gwen had said to Peter.

"I don't know," Peter said about school. "Maybe. I'm not sure." It felt good to be back in New York, and he loved the city, but he knew he didn't want to go back to NYU. It would be too hard now without Ben, and the location was too close to where everything had happened. And he was afraid that if there was ever another hurricane, he would lose it. "I might come back here to live though one day after school."

"I want to go to L.A. and study acting," Anna said firmly, which she had already been saying for two years, about after she graduated from Tisch. And now she was going to be a straight English major at Barnard. "You can come and visit me when I make my first movie," she said with a grin. There had been no word of their rekindling their romance, and it was obvious that neither of them wanted to. They just wanted to be friends. And in a way, he could step in for Ben now, as her almost brother. It was the role he aspired to in her life, and so did she as his nearly sister. Their dating days seemed to be over, too much had happened, and they had both suffered too shocking a loss of someone they loved. It had ended their romance but strengthened their love for each other.

They talked until after three A.M., and fell asleep in sleeping bags next to each other, holding hands, on the den floor. And the next morning after her mother made them breakfast, Anna took Peter to the airport to go back to Chicago.

"I'm so glad you came," she said as he hugged her goodbye and held her tight for a long moment.

"I'll always love you, Anna," he said with tears in his eyes, "just like he did. I'm not as good a guy as he was, but I'll try."

"I love you too," she said as they both cried. They had something better than a romance now. They were friends. For life.

"Come and visit in Chicago."

"Maybe after Christmas," she promised.

"We can go skiing. I'll show you around." She nodded and they hugged again, and then he presented his emotional support dog letter for Mike, and went through security, frantically waving at her, while they blew each other kisses like little kids.

"I love you!" she screamed loud enough for him to hear her, and she didn't care what anyone thought in the airport.

"I love you too!" he yelled back, and Mike barked. And they could both feel Ben with them, as Peter disappeared through security, and they both knew that they would be the Three Musketeers forever.

Peter's father was waiting for him at the airport in Chicago. Peter hadn't started driving again yet, but now he wanted to and felt ready. He was going to talk to Gwen about it when he saw her.

"How was the flight?" his father asked him, because it was easier to say than ask about the visit to New York. But he could see that Peter was euphoric, and he wondered if he and Anna had rekindled their romance. He didn't understand that the friendship and bond they'd formed was something even better for them.

"It was great," Peter said and meant the visit, not the flight. "We went to see the tree at Rockefeller Center." He didn't mention the candle and prayers at St. Patrick's.

His father smiled at what he said. "We took you there once when you were about five. You probably don't remember. You loved it and didn't want to leave."

"Of course I remember, Dad. That's why we went. I wanted to see it again. And I still love it." He beamed and acted like a carefree child again. The trip to New York had done him good.

And then on the drive home, he told his father he wanted to apply to Northwestern, if he wouldn't lose credits in a transfer. "I want to stay around here to finish school. I might go back to New York for graduate school, like get an MBA at Columbia," he said, looking out the window as his father glanced at him and smiled. His hair had come in thick and full again.

"That sounds like a good plan to me," John Holbrook said quietly, and hugged his wife when he got home. He held her in his arms with tears rolling down his cheeks. "He's going to be okay," he said about their only child, when Peter went upstairs with Mike. He was whole again, and scarred perhaps in subtle ways, but better than ever. It had been a hard road, and a tough journey, but he had found his way back.

Chapter 16

Ellen and Bob managed to have dinner together twice before the pressure of the holidays started, and talked about the benefit for hurricane survivors. They had both volunteered to be on the committee, as had Jim and Grace. It was being held in March.

Ellen wanted to go Christmas shopping, although her list was short this year. Her mother, Phillippa, and Alice, with handsome bonuses for them and all her employees in London. She no longer had to find something special for George or shop for their London friends. And she wanted to find a nice gift for Jim, after housing them during the hurricane. And something small for Bob, if she could find a gift she thought he'd like.

Her mother seemed to be busy in meetings all the time, and out with Jim at holiday parties. Her social life had picked up noticeably, and Grace enjoyed it with him. He was taking her to St. Barth's for New Year's, "like Miami, only better," she told Ellen and her daughter laughed. They were clearly enjoying their romance, and as Bob said, "why not?" Bob had helped Ellen buy a tree and decorated it with her. It suddenly really felt like Christmas, despite the changes of the past year. And they enjoyed spending time together. Aside from dinners, they had gone to the symphony and the theater and loved talking to each other for hours. And when she expressed interest in it, he had invited her to join him at a television show where he was being interviewed. He was blasé about it, but she had found it exciting and watched from the green room at *The Today Show*.

Bob was preparing for his children's visit, and going skiing with them for a few days, but he wanted Ellen to have dinner with them first, and she was looking forward to it. Talking about them led them into a subject that Bob had wondered about but been afraid to ask her. But after a couple of glasses of wine at dinner one night, he did.

"I take it you and your husband decided not to adopt," he said carefully. She had told him the results of her infertility treatments, and that she would never be able to have a child of her own.

"It went against all his ideas about his bloodlines and heritage. He didn't want a child that wasn't entirely his, and I sort of agreed. I don't know if he talked me into it or not, but he was also averse to the risks of adoption, and opposed to surrogacy, so we ruled them out. Adoption seemed like risky business to me too, given drug histories of birth parents and things you don't always know about with adopted kids."

"My son is adopted, you know." He had never mentioned it to

her before. "We wanted a second child, and after five miscarriages we gave up and adopted. He's a terrific boy," he said. "I just thought you should know. It's not always a bad idea. And there are risks with your own biological kids too, health problems you can't anticipate, genetic stuff that turns up from earlier generations you never knew about. Shit happens, as they say. Sometimes adoption is a wonderful idea, if you really want a child and can't have your own." She had never seen it quite that way before, and George had been so violently opposed to it that he had convinced her too. But Bob made it sound almost appealing. "Do you think you'd ever consider it?"

"I don't know. I always ruled it out before. It's hard to say what I'd do. I've been trying to let go of the idea of having kids. We went through so much agony over it."

"Sometimes letting go is the right idea too. Only you can know. And you're young enough to take some time to figure it out. The nice thing about adoption is that there's no clock ticking. You can look into it when you're ready, or not. Children are wonderful, but you don't have to have kids to be happy. I just thought I'd let you know that ours was a real success story. We were always glad we did it." And he smiled at her then. "He's much smarter and better looking than we were. He says he might like to meet his birth mother one day, but he hasn't been compelled to do it so far. He doesn't seem too interested, but he might look into it later. My wife wasn't too crazy about the idea, but we'd have helped him find her if he asked. She was a fifteen-year-old girl in Utah."

"That's everyone's ideal situation but hard to find. I was always scared about some drugged-out kid in the Haight-Ashbury. You never know."

"You can be careful, if you decide to go that route. I just thought I'd mention it as a viable option. I usually don't volunteer that he's adopted, but it seemed worthwhile saying something to you."

"Thank you," she said quietly, as they smiled at each other, and he reached across the table and held her hand. Ellen thought about what Bob had said about his son when he took her home that night. She had never seriously considered adoption, and she still wasn't sure she ever would. But maybe one day she might if she married again. She didn't want to adopt as a single mom. For now, it didn't seem like the pressing issue it had been before. She was alone and had a lot to think about. Her divorce was going to be final in April. And it would be a whole new life after that. It already was.

The night before his children were due to arrive from California, they had dinner again. He looked genuinely excited in anticipation of their visit. His daughter had just announced that she was bringing her boyfriend, which hadn't been part of the plan, but Bob was good humored about it.

Ellen had found a Christmas present for him, and gave it to him at dinner. It was a first edition of a book he had said he had loved as a young man, one of the original Sherlock Holmes books, which had inspired his career. He had lost it in the flood in Tribeca, and had been upset about it. It felt good to replace it for him, and he looked touched when he opened the package.

"I have something for you too," he said, with a tender look. "I was hoping I'd see you again closer to Christmas."

"I didn't know if you'd be too busy with your children, so I brought yours tonight."

"Let's all have dinner together the day after they arrive. I'm taking them to 'Twenty-one.'" It sounded like a good plan.

They went back to her apartment afterward, and he built a fire in the living room, while she told him that she'd had an offer on the house in London. It wasn't fabulous, but it was a good solid offer at a respectable price, on good terms.

"I'm tempted to take it. I'm ready to give up that house. I want to move on. I don't like knowing it's just sitting there, like a relic of the past." It was a past she wanted to put behind her. The more she thought about her life with George, the more she realized that it had been wrong for her, and she had compromised too much. It was what he had expected of her, and she had willingly complied. In retrospect, she hadn't respected herself, only him. Bob had understood that long before she had, and he could see her changing every day. She was more definite, more sure of herself, delicate about it but willing to state her opinions. He was impressed to see how much she had grown in the short time he'd known her.

"What are your plans for New Year's?" he asked her, as they sat next to each other on the couch, looking into the fire. "My kids will be gone by then. They want to go back to California to spend it with their friends. You don't get to hang on to them for long at this age." He said it without regret and had come to accept it—he was

happy they were coming at all. He knew that one day, with partners and children of their own, it would be more difficult. He figured he had a few years left the way things were, but not many.
Otherwise like Ellen, he was alone. Even for people with children,
the holidays could be lonely or hard.

"I don't have any plans," she said, turning to look at him. He
was already keeping her busier than she'd anticipated when she
moved to New York. She hadn't expected to have a man in her life,
or even a male friend to take her out to dinner. And now her
mother was busy with Jim, which was a big change. She no longer
had to keep her mother company—she was out almost every night,
and working harder than ever. "We used to go to friends in the
country on New Year's, typical British house parties, always very
jolly. They love their weekend parties. It's a nice way to see the
new year in." And like everything else in her previous life, they
were now a thing of the past.

"How about dinner at my place?" Bob suggested, and meant
Jim's apartment where he was still living. And Jim would be in St.
Barth's with Grace. "We can cook dinner together and sit by the
fire, and look at floor plans of my new apartment," he teased her.
"Or stand in the plaster dust and dream." She laughed at the
thought.

"I'd like that," she said simply. "I don't like making a big deal of
New Year's Eve. And this year, I think we all have a lot to be thankful for. I was so upset on Thanksgiving about my divorce, but I
realize now that after Ophelia, we're all lucky to be alive. This
could have been a very different New Year's Eve, for any of us."

Her whole life had changed since the hurricane, in a much better way than she could ever have dreamed.

And as he looked at her, Bob pulled her slowly into his arms and held her close to him as he kissed her, and she could feel herself melt into him. It was a new beginning, one neither of them could have expected, and better than anything he could have written.

"You're the best thing that's happened to me in a long time, probably ever," he said with amazement. The mysteries of life were unpredictable and precious, with unexpected blessings where you never thought they would occur.

"It sounds awful to say, given the destruction it caused, and the lives that were lost, but Hurricane Ophelia didn't leave any of us where it found us," Ellen said to him. Ophelia had changed each of them in important ways.

He nodded as he listened to her, and the fire crackled in the grate as he pulled her closer and kissed her again. The future was looking very bright.

Danielle Steel is one of the world's most popular and highly acclaimed authors, with over ninety international bestselling novels in print and more than 600 million copies of her novels sold. She is also the author of *His Bright Light*, the story of her son Nick Traina's life and death; *A Gift of Hope*, a memoir of her work with the homeless; and *Pure Joy*, about the dogs she and her family have loved.

To discover more about Danielle Steel and her books, visit her website at www.daniellesteel.com

You can also connect with Danielle on Facebook at www.facebook.com/DanielleSteelOfficial or on Twitter: @daniellesteel